Ascendance

A Dominion Novel

By Lissa Kasey

Ascendance : A Dominion Novel
2nd Edition
Copyright © 2016 Lissa Kasey
All rights reserved
Cover Art by Simone Hendricks
Published by Lissa Kasey
http://www.lissakasey.com

Please Be Advised

This is a work of fiction. Names, characters, businesses, places, events, and incidents are either the products of the author's imagination or used in a fictitious manner. Any resemblance to actual persons, living or dead, or actual events is purely coincidental.

Warning

This book is licensed to the original purchaser only. Duplication or distribution via any means is illegal and a violation of International Copyright Law, subject to criminal prosecution and upon conviction, fines, and/or imprisonment. This eBook cannot be legally loaned or given to others. No part of this book can be shared or reproduced without the express permission of the Author.

A Note from the Author

If you did not purchase this book from an authorized retailer, you make it difficult for me to write the next book. Stop piracy and purchase the book. For all those who purchased the book legitimately: Thank you!

Chapter 1

I slipped on a pair of heeled calf-high boots and rode the elevator up from my boyfriend Gabe's private apartment to the open lobby. The daylight shone through the main entry as the doors opened. Winter was in full swing, which in Minnesota meant endless cold and snow. The waiting spring crackled through my veins like icicles hanging from a roof waiting to melt. Soon the ground would sprout flowers, trees, and grass. Critters would leave their dens to mate. I'd feel every bit of it, and it couldn't happen too soon for my liking.

The doorman nodded to me as I opened my mailbox and flipped through the junk. A letter-sized manila envelope with my name on it gave me pause. I shoved the rest of the mail back in the box. Gabe would deal with it later.

As I made my way to the car, I opened the letter, wondering who I knew in California. The return address had no name, just a handwritten street and city. Inside, on thick paper with a fancy letterhead, the words looked like legalese. Something about a trust?

I folded it up haphazardly, stuffed the letter in my pocket, and headed to the last class of my college career. The past few years of troubles at the university made the decision not to pursue a master's easy. I was ready to walk away. My professors spoke grandeurs about my graduation, and how I should give a speech.

After all, I was the first male to ever graduate from the magic degree program. The thought of all those eyes staring, judging, just made me shudder.

The class passed as uneventfully as most had in the past few weeks. A survey for the teacher, a few final yawns from the class, and happy hugs for all the girl cliques as I made my way to the door. No one tried to hug me, which I was grateful for. However, waiting outside the classroom, the tall, muscular blond that was my older brother, Jamie, looked like he wanted one.

Someone nudged me. I glanced over to find Kelly, my best friend and Jamie's lover. He winked at me and nodded his head in Jamie's direction. I sighed and walked into Jamie's waiting arms. His hug could probably have crushed a boa constrictor, but it was warm and it was real.

"Congrats, Seiran. It's over. My baby brother—the first male witch to ever graduate with a magic studies degree." Jamie smiled. "No more school, at least until you decide to go for another degree." He could talk, since he had two.

Kelly patted me on the back. "You're so lucky to be done. I'm just starting."

I'd given him as much advice as I could. The years alone at school, alienated, hated, and discriminated against, had taught me a lot. For the spring semester, there would be three male students entering the magic studies program at the university. Dozens had already signed up to test and could be entering in the fall. The idea that I helped others find the courage to step up made me a little less shaky, but I'd never planned to be anyone's leader. If anything, my childhood had taught me to keep my head down and try to go unnoticed. So much for that.

"Wanna go to lunch?" Kelly asked, his hand firmly nestled in Jamie's. He walked proudly beside me, ignoring the glares coming our way. People's opinions didn't bother him much. I wished I was more like him. "I'll drive. I can even drop Jamie off later to pick up your car."

"Sure." I wasn't hungry, but I'd eat because I knew my body needed it. Now that school was finished, I had no idea what I was going to do with my life. Sure, I could work at the Bloody Bar and Grill as long as I wanted, but it wasn't my passion. Not even when Gabe, who was also my boss, allowed me to change the menu, as he often did.

The Dominion, the head of magic in general, had offered me a job as a paper pusher, answering phones and filing. I think they really just wanted to keep me from doing anything important, yet as the first male to be welcomed into their elite female society, it almost felt like a big deal processing papers, delivering things. Had I really gone to school for four years just to become a desk clerk? Sure, it would be an easy job. But after all the pain and suffering I'd put up with, I wanted more. Not that I had to be Regional Director like my mother, but something more important. Something worth giving up all of my previous goals.

I was so lost in thought that we'd gotten all the way to Kelly's new car and I was in the backseat with Jamie sitting next to me before he poked me back to reality.

"Huh?"

"You're sighing. What's up?"

"Nothing." The whole work thing and "what do I want to do with the rest of my life" was an issue for everyone, wasn't it? What *did* I want to do? Kelly worked at the bar now too, but he had great aspirations of creating an equal camp environment for growing witches, female and male. He was majoring in magic, minoring in business and psychology, and was so laser-focused that sometimes I thought he and I lived on different planets. He was super focused until it came to my brother. Then there was the look he got on his face whenever Jamie was around. They both got kind of goofy, which made me smile and feel lonely at the same time. Suddenly I missed my boyfriend.

If it were nighttime, Gabe would be sitting next to me, but even though he was a vampire, he needed to sleep too. I'd snuggle up with him later, so long as I could get Sam, Gabe's newly changed mentee, out of the apartment for a few hours. I knew they had to spend time together; it just bothered me how much time that was.

Jamie nudged me again. "You're sighing again."

I gave him a sideways glare. He could have sat up front with Kelly and left me to my brooding, but lately they both had begun to push. They followed me around and prodded me into speaking when I really just wanted to figure myself out. "Just thinking."

"About?" he asked.

Nothing I was ready to share. Instead, I pulled the letter out of my pocket and handed it to him. "Do you understand this?"

Jamie read it through, seemed surprised for a moment, then flipped it over as though looking for more writing. "It's a letter asking you to attend a meeting in California, just outside LA."

That part I got, but it didn't stop my stomach from clenching up when he said it out loud. "What kind of meeting?"

"Looks like a relative has passed away and he's leaving you part of his estate. So as one of the trustees, you have to attend."

"Who is it?" Kelly asked while he steered us to the restaurant he'd chosen for lunch.

"Charles Merth."

And my dad—our dad—had been Dorien Merth. I knew little about him other than his name and that he'd been executed for supposedly trying to hurt my mom while she was pregnant with me. "Was he related to our dad?" I tugged at Jamie's sleeve, trying to see the letter. How did he get that information out of all that legal jargon?

"His younger brother. I've never met him." The tone of Jamie's voice sounded odd.

"Are you mad 'cause I'm a trustee? What does that even mean? Why would he give *me* something? I've never heard of him." Whatever this stranger was leaving me didn't matter if it came between us. Jamie and I had worked too hard to get this far. Sure, we didn't always get along. He was too touchy-feely for me and I was too reserved for him, but most of the time we fit okay. I liked when he played big brother and took care of me when it came to the small stuff like rides and food, and he liked that I let him. I didn't want that to change.

"Why would I be mad?" Jamie leaned over and gave me a rib-shattering squeeze before stuffing the letter away in his pocket. "The letter says you need to go to California. We'll have Gabe call his lawyer to work out details. Hopefully, they can just read the will over the phone or something. I don't think it'd be wise for you to travel out of state right now. Not with all the press you've had in the past few months."

I'd never been to California. Never been anywhere, really, just Minnesota and Wisconsin in my earlier party days. Funny, since, at twenty-three, I should have had many more party days to go, but that was all behind me now, just like school. Was a life of mindless work all I had ahead of me? And why was some guy I'd never met giving me something when he'd never shown any interest in me while he was alive?

We sat down for lunch and discussed unimportant things like what crazy baby items we had bought for my twins. The babies would be arriving in a few months. They had been conceived through artificial insemination, and Jamie's little sister, Hanna, was carrying them. She and Jamie had the same mother, but different dads, and Jamie and I shared the same dad. I hoped for my babies it would be less confusing. Family was family.

Jamie and Kelly held hands and gave each other occasional kisses. People stared. I drank tea and ate what I could. The earth slept underneath a layer of ice and cold. I couldn't even turn to its ever-pulsing warmth for comfort. All I wanted was for the sun to set so I could be out in the open with Gabe. Sometimes he could chase away the growing melancholy and assure me it was simply the change of the seasons that affected me so badly.

Unfortunately, he spent more time with Sam these days than me. He had an obligation to fulfill as Sam's mentor to the vampire world. Gabe had warned me that it would take up some of his time. I guess I just never thought it would be the time he normally spent with me.

Jamie pushed a piece of cake in front of me. It was red, blue, orange, and yellow, and had white frosting with rainbow sprinkles. "Stop sighing and share some cake with us."

Kelly handed me a fork, as somehow I'd missed the waiter coming to ask us if we wanted anything else. Three forks, a giant piece of cake, and us, hmm. I dug in and shared with my friends, riding the edge of their happiness as if it were my own. Maybe a sunny vacation would be good. I wondered if I could convince Gabe to go. He'd been so wrapped up in Sam and whatever was going on with the Tri-Mega, he always seemed stressed. We hadn't even had a weekend together with just the two of us for months. Well, a few weeks. I missed him.

Kelly dropped Jamie off at school to pick up my car. He left saying something about going to the gym. Kelly declined his invite. He'd rather run or swim than lift or do squats. I was of the same mind, but thought maybe we'd go to the Y for the heated indoor pool over the weekend.

I stopped by Gabe's underground place to grab my forgotten book reader. Sam sat at the counter, glaring at an open bottle of QuickLife. His stillness made him look like the vampire he was. Glazed eyes, waxy skin, pale coloring—was he getting enough to eat? Gabe never looked so inhuman.

Sam flipped through a giant tome of a book, but didn't seem to actually be reading it. I wondered if it was a book on vampires. So much about them was still a mystery. Did I have to be one to learn all the details? Did being the focus of a master like Gabe not win me any brownie points?

I could probably have asked Sam if I could look at the book, or even if it really was about vampires, though it looked ancient and somewhat ominous. But that meant talking to

Sam. I sort of avoided doing that until I had to. His very existence annoyed me. He couldn't help the position he was in. Hadn't asked for it. Gabe was trying to help. And I really didn't wish the guy dead. Or undead, or whatever the hell vampires classified themselves as now. I just wanted more time with my boyfriend.

Sam didn't glance my way as I grabbed my reader and headed back upstairs. The place smelled like him now, not Gabe. I would have taken Gabe's smelly shampoo any day over that musky crap Sam seemed to bathe in. Kelly said he couldn't smell it. Didn't know what I was taking about.

I couldn't even cook in the kitchen down there anymore because everything had been tainted by that smell. Gabe assured me it would pass, saying it was just something new vampires had. I wasn't so sure. But it was his home, so if he could tolerate it, I guess that was all that mattered.

My phone rang with an unfamiliar number. I frowned at it, though it had been nearly a month since anyone had harassed me. Maybe someone I knew had changed his number. "Hello?"

"Hello, Seiran," a smooth voice came across the phone. My brain took a few moments to register where I'd heard it before.

"Tresler." One of the Tri-Mega head vampires was calling me. My heart pounded, and my blood felt like ice water running through my veins. "What can I do for you?"

"I'm interested in how you feel about being Gabriel's focus."

"Is he in trouble?" We'd had a little trouble with the Tri-Mega a few months back. They didn't want Gabe claiming a focus and starting a nest of vampires without notifying them first. I sort of got the impression they would kill us both if we did.

"Of course not. He's filed all the correct paperwork. We've approved his request to form a nest." He sounded amused. "I wonder what interesting vampires will he create, being bound to the most powerful earth witch in the world."

"I wouldn't say I'm the most powerful witch in the world." There were five Pillars. I was only one of them.

Tresler laughed, which sounded creepy and intimidating, even over the phone. But I suppose any guy who could probably melt your brain by just looking at you should have a scary laugh. "So unexpectedly modest."

"Is there something I can help you with?" I finally said after a moment of silently debating how to reply.

"Have you seen any unusual vampires around lately?"

Was this a trick question? Was I supposed to be looking for unusual vampires? I sort of let Gabe handle all of the vampire business. Especially after the death of Andrew Roman, who had been trying to torture Gabe for years.

Vampires were bad news. Except Gabe, of course. "No."

"Good." He hung up.

What the hell? I shoved my phone in my pocket and made a mental note to ask Gabe about Tresler's odd behavior. Last I heard, the Tri-Mega had little to no value for human life, even when that human was the focus of another vampire. We were expendable, easily replaced, nothing but food. Most of the vampires around Gabe didn't act that way, but then I got the feeling he wasn't exactly the norm either.

When I walked into my condo, Kelly sat sprawled out on the couch watching football. I'd never had cable before he moved in with me. Now we had every sports channel the area offered, and the TV was always on with some sort of game. The only one I refused to listen to was basketball. The squeaking of shoes on the floor just made my head hurt.

"You okay?" Kelly asked, glancing my way. "You've been pretty quiet today. Figured you'd be thrilled to be done with school."

"I'm fine," I promised him. Uncertain of what my future held, but I'd manage. "Just sort of—" I had to think for a minute. "—drifting."

Now he looked at me, hazel eyes studying my face so long I had to look away.

"Wanna talk about it?"

I had never been a talk-it-out sort of guy, and maybe that was the problem. But I'd learned that no one wanted you to unload your issues on them. My mother always taught me that when I got emotional, I should be silent. Now that was sort of my normal setting.

"I'm gonna go take a bath," I told him and headed to the bathroom. I turned on the jets in the tub and waited for the steamy water to fill up before stripping down, putting a clear plastic baggy over my reader, and settling into a new book. Surely some hot guy would get his ass pounded by a warrior with a huge rod. That was the kind of escape I needed. Reading wouldn't give me answers, but it'd give me time to not wallow in my own indecision.

My mind wandered a few times to the letter. My uncle had left me stuff. Why hadn't he left anything for Jamie? Was Jamie just not telling me he got a letter too? What had my father been like? I knew he'd been one of the leaders of the Ascendance, but everything I knew of the Ascendance reminded me of Andrew Roman, who had been an evil man. Where had the corruption begun? Had my father known? Had his brother been involved with the Ascendance too?

Kelly popped into the bathroom sometime after 5:00 p.m., probably to be sure I didn't drown. Which was silly, since he was the most powerful water witch in the world; it was unlikely I'd drown while less than twenty feet from him. But he checked on me a lot no matter what I was doing.

The Dominion, the leading body of magic, was still discussing our Pillar ceremony. Since we were already Pillars, I wasn't sure what was up for discussion, but whatever. They did like to blow a lot of hot air around. Kelly was okay just being Kelly for now. And I liked that.

He sat down on the side of the tub, face guarded, but eyes looking me over like he was waiting for me to fall apart. I wasn't that fragile. Not anymore. "Gabe stopped by. He wants to go tree shopping," he said.

I groaned. Was it that time of year already? "I hate how people insist on having a dying tree in their living room, decorating it like it's a fucking clown, and then throwing it away."

Kelly's hoot of laughter almost made me drop my book reader. I carefully set the device aside and turned off the jets in the tub. The bubbles still surrounded me, giving me that sleepy warmth I loved from a bath, but the pruney look of my fingers meant I'd been in the water far too long.

"Don't tell me you actually like Christmas?" I asked, more than a little worried I'd have another red-and-green freak on my hands.

"No. We are strictly Solstice folks in my house." He pulled a giant fluffy blue towel off the shelf and held it out to me. "A clown? For a tree? Really?"

I pushed the buttons to drain the tub and rose carefully, taking the towel and wrapping it around me. The hot, damp air of the bathroom was cold compared to the warmth of the water. "How would you feel if someone put a star on your head and covered you with silly hanging ornaments?"

"Okay, Scrooge. I can expect no presents from you, then?"

Did I need to get him presents? I was new at this friend thing. I opened my mouth to ask, but he held up his hand.

"No worries, Sei. We'll exchange Solstice wishes. Okay? Gifts are not needed." He gestured to the room, even though it was just the bathroom, and said, "This is my gift. I don't have to live with my folks. I don't have to live on campus with those assholes. My best friend doesn't look down on me for being gay or a witch, and I have a guy who likes to wake up with me. What more could I ask for?"

I glanced down at his battered Nikes. "New shoes?" He went through shoes sort of fast.

Kelly's burst of laughter made me smile. Living with him was a breath of fresh air most days. He smiled easily enough, laughed a lot, and didn't let much get to him, even when I was in a pissy mood like I was now. "Sure. Buy me some shoes. I'm a size nine, but get dressed, please. We need to play nice with others, your boyfriend included. Clown tree or not. We don't have to think the same or even like the same things to love them. We just have to be supportive."

I sighed. He was right. Damn, I hated when he was right. Kelly was so much better with people than I was. He knew when to play nice and when to turn on the fake charm. My charm had lost its autopilot button weeks ago and I was still struggling to get it back.

    I trudged to my room to dress for the cold evening coming my way. For Gabe I'd do my best to find holiday cheer when all I wanted to do was sleep.

Chapter 2

Gabe and Sam stood together pointing and discussing things like length, height, and number of branches. If I listened with half an ear, I could probably make jokes that bordered on sexual innuendo from their conversation. If it had been anyone other than Gabe and Sam.

The cold brought a shiver to my legs that wasn't at all related to my normal anxiety tremor. If we stayed out here much longer, I was sure my teeth would be chattering too. Stupid Minnesota winter. Why hadn't I moved to a warmer climate? I was an earth witch, after all. We needed the earth awake and growing to flourish. Only technically the earth was always in a cycle of birth, growth, and death. I sighed and rubbed my hands over my arms to try to warm up.

A heavy weight dropped on my shoulders, but it was warm and smelled of spicy aftershave and Jamie. He tugged my hat down over my ears and smiled at me.

"You'll get cold," I protested, trying to give him his coat back though I had to admit it was nice and toasty.

"Nah. I'm good. Wore my long undies." Jamie pulled me toward the slaughtered trees with him. How could he stand to be here with so much death surrounding us? The ground could take all the trees back, grow more, but they still ached like I imagined an amputee with a ghost limb did. "Breathe, Sei. You're turning blue."

Kelly held his hand but looked out toward the trees, a frown on his face. He turned back and gave me a weak smile. The snow lightly falling on us made him keep glancing toward the sky. Was there a storm coming?

Jamie took a step back from the trees. "Okay, it's kinda bad. Makes you a little nauseous, right?" When I nodded, he continued, "I didn't feel like this last year. So I get it. Maybe we should just stay over here."

"I should make a live tree grow in his house," I said to no one in particular as Gabe turned down the little path toward more piles of trees. The trees could live a little longer, sure, but it wasn't really living any more than a human on life support lived. Without roots, a tree was nothing but flower plucked from its stalk. Roots were life.

"It would die without sunlight. Even a Northern Pine needs some UV rays," Kelly told me absently.

Christmas was so not my holiday. My mom, Tanaka Rou, a leader of the Dominion, had always made a show of having a big party for Solstice, presenting a big tree, cut fresh each year, in the foyer of her mansion, full of decorations. Beneath the tree sat hundreds of multicolored presents for little Dominion girls. The giggling and fluttery sway of dresses always annoyed me. Every girl dressed in shiny layers of flowers, and bright reds and pinks.

In the beginning, my mother had dressed me up and forced me to mingle with the girls. It took only one Solstice to prove to me that, as a male, I had no value to them as anything other than a way to marry into power. I heard a lot of "My mom said I should talk to you because your mom is important." My mom, never me. And even to my own mother, I wasn't important.

I remember sitting on the top of the stairs watching those unknown girls tear into gifts from a mother I'd never received a single present from. She'd always told me it was because Solstice wishes were more important, but as a kid they were just words. Maybe I would have felt differently if she had ever actually said she cared about me. Most of her Solstice wishes to me had been about excellence in school or finding a good match to wed.

I sighed again, trying to brush off the memories. I wasn't that kid anymore. My mother's lack of affection didn't define who I was today. The melancholy would go away. It had to. It was just going to crush me otherwise.

Gabe paused and turned my way. Had he sensed my thoughts? I'd been trying to keep a wall up between us so he wasn't bombarded with my crazy mash of emotions all the time. He patted Sam on the shoulder before skipping back to me, eyes twinkling and smile huge. He was just a big kid and Christmas was his thing. It seemed a little contradictory for a vampire who was two thousand years old. "They aren't very big, but they smell nice."

They smelled like dead tree and cleaner. I smiled at him, but I knew it looked forced. He sighed and pulled me away from Jamie, hugging me tight. "I can get a fake one if you want."

'Cause plastic smelled so much better than cleaner. Right. I shook my head at him, then kissed his nose. I could make compromises too. He wanted a dying tree in his living room, so be it. "Go pick your tree."

"You sure?"

"Yep." The faster he picked the tree, the faster I was in the warm car headed for home and maybe some snuggling. A recipe for cocoa sat on the counter next to the stove, a little smiley face drawn on it by Kelly. Nothing said Solstice more than the smell of melting chocolate, cream, and cinnamon.

Gabe kissed me again, just a fast peck on the lips, then let go to bounce back to Sam's side and the trees that surrounded them like a forest fire waiting to happen. Kelly nudged me. He handed me the silver cap of a thermos filled with some steaming liquid. I expected it to be tea, but when I brought it to my lips, the smell of chocolate broke through all the pine that tainted my nose. I raised a brow in question at him as I took a sip. His rose in return. It was good. Damn good. My recipe, the rich taste of cream, bitter bite of dark chocolate, a spicy kick of cinnamon, and a hint of something else. Chili pepper?

"I did good?" he asked.

"Yum. Very good." I bumped his hip with mine.

Sam and Gabe wandered back through the windy paths of trees, both frowning.

"Find anything?" Jamie asked.

"Nope. We'll look somewhere else. Sam's hungry." Gabe glanced at the new vampire next to him. Sam didn't look at me at all. He and I hadn't talked much since his transformation. I got the feeling he blamed me for a lot of the crap that had happened to him. I guess I was partially to blame, but I had no idea how to even ask for forgiveness since I hadn't actually done the damage. And because Gabe was saying he'd be taking Sam out to hunt instead of going home cuddling with me, I wasn't really all that worried about being forgiven.

"We can drop you off," Jamie said as we headed for the car. "We're going to do some shopping before heading home."

We were? Had I made a grocery list?

"Yeah, I have to find some gifts for my family." Kelly shrugged into the back between me and Sam. The two of them got along just fine. "And Sei promised to buy me shoes for Christmas."

Wait, what? We were going Christmas shopping? Could the night get any more torturous? Maybe some jock to knock me around or a vampire to bite me just to watch me bleed? Shove hot pokers into my eyes? Surely those things would be less painful to me than shopping for presents. Kelly winked at me, then squeezed my hand. Okay, so we weren't going shopping?

Jamie pointed the car toward downtown. Kelly chatted the whole time about some football game he'd watched. Sam stared out the window. Gabe played with his smartphone, and I contemplated what we'd be doing for the evening. The new moon was weeks away yet and I didn't really like the cold, so I had no plans to be outside unless I had to.

We let Sam and Gabe out in uptown. The lights and many bars meant the streets would be filled well into the early hours of the morning. I planned to be sleeping by then. Gabe opened my door and kissed me good-bye before taking off with Sam at his side like some superhero and his sidekick. I guess it bothered me more than I cared to admit.

Jamie smiled in the mirror at me. "Let's go shopping."

"Can you just pull out my fingernails instead and call it a day?" I had to ask.

Jamie's laughter filled the car. "We're going home. Kelly is going to do his shopping on the Internet while you and I bake something tasty. I was thinking peanut butter brownies."

Oh. Okay. "I like that plan."

"Sei is a regular old Scrooge," Kelly commented.

"Am not. I like giving presents. But I can give people presents year-round. Why do we have to have some jolly man in red telling us to cut down trees and give gifts to people or else we don't love them? It makes no sense. It should be about the rebirth of the earth, not about elves and toys."

"Commercial conspiracy," Jamie said. "My family wasn't into the holiday much either. A dinner for Solstice and that's it. No presents, candy, or men in red suits." He glanced back at Kelly with a lecherous smile. "Though it has possibilities."

"Men in red suits? Not a chance."

"Bows are fun."

I laughed at the two. They'd been like honeymooners for the past few weeks. It only annoyed me because Gabe spent so much time with Sam. A sudden flash of pride came through my bond with Gabe. Something Sam had done made him proud? I ground my teeth and shut him out completely. If I had to watch more of the coddling, I was going to hurt someone. Most likely Sam.

"Let's not go home."

Jamie glanced back. "You want to go shopping?"

"Yes. Let's go to one of the department stores." An idea formed in my head. I needed someplace that had luggage.

"Huh?" Kelly asked.

"I just want to pick up some new clothes. Maybe look at some shoes." I smiled at Kelly. He frowned back.

"I feel like I'm not in on a joke here," Jamie said.

"No joke. Let's get the stupid shopping done before all the crazies are let loose from the sanitarium." I didn't even like going to grocery stores this time of year. When some granny smacked you around with her cart just to get to the giant stack of canned pumpkin, you knew *that* time of year had come again. The department stores were even worse. Everyone argued about prices, lines wrapped around the entire store, and the parking lots were always jam-packed with people who had obviously never parked in their lives.

I'd been working like crazy at the Bloody Bar, and lots of people I'd never even met sent me money for graduation. Maybe they thought I'd never find work. And maybe I wouldn't, not in magic, at least. But I could do a lot of other things. If people wanted material things to prove that I cared, so be it.

Money, and now time, were something I had a lot of to use up.

Jamie pulled into the lot of the nearest department store. We parked in the back. The heavy piles of snow made the lanes uneven, and cars jutted out everywhere like a bad accident. The bare trees around the massive building wore lights that danced to overplayed Christmas tunes. Would it be like this in California? Would everything feel so cramped, cold, and dead, decorated like painted corpses while the world moved around at blinding speeds?

I could probably afford a trip to last through the holiday, which was only a week and a half away. Not that anyone would miss me much now that school was over. Jo or Kelly would cover the bar for me, and we had a few temps who were always looking for shifts. The Dominion had gone silent as they prepared for the many holiday parties filled with aristocracies of witches. My boyfriend had a Christmas buddy in Sam, and Jamie and Kelly had each other. That sort of left me as odd man out. A vacation to someplace warm sounded like a great idea to me.

"What are we looking for?" Jamie asked as we hurried through the cold toward the door. Once inside, he went to a shelf filled with colorful stuffed critters set on display near the checkout. Jamie worked part-time as a pediatric RN. He loved the work. I think the only reason he didn't work full-time was because he still worried about me. If I had a full-time day job, he'd probably be working full-time too. Just one more reason for me to find something other than the bar.

He'd buy a couple dozen of those critters just for the kids to take home with them if he thought the clinic wouldn't protest. Plus, they were some kind of charity thing, buy a toy and have a donation sent to XYZ or whatever. To someone with a big heart like Jamie, that made sense. Me, I'd wonder how much actually went to help kids. But I'd been raised cynical that way.

I checked the charge on my phone and waved Kelly toward Jamie. "Take your time. I'm going to shop. I'll text you when I'm done."

"Okay, but don't leave the store without us."

"No problem." I grabbed a cart, using several wipes to clean off the handle before touching it—cold season was in full swing—then steered it toward the back of the store. In less than twenty minutes, I'd grabbed two pairs of new Nikes for Kelly, a smoothie machine for Jamie, some luggage, a couple of cashmere sweaters each for Hanna and Allie, and half a wardrobe's worth of clothing for me. Booking my flight through my phone was easier than waiting for the old ladies in Santa hats to wrap my presents.

Gabe's Solstice gift had already arrived and was hidden away in a drawer back home. The first edition of *The Little Prince* had cost me more than a week of tips, but I knew he'd love it. We both had that story memorized now, having read it together so many times. He still thought of me as his unprotected rose. Sometimes that was cute, the rest of the time just annoying. I had thorns too.

Jamie and Kelly met me at the entrance, each with a cart filled with things. Most of them were wrapped. I wondered what those jolly old ladies had thought of us tonight. Maybe I should have had them wrap some of the underwear I'd bought. Or bought some for Gabe too, just to make them wonder. People didn't stare as much and I didn't get nearly as many "faggot" calls now that my hair was short. But the odd scratchiness of it made me want to grow it long again. I kind of missed people looking at me and missed how I could hide behind my hair. Those days it was easier to get what I wanted with just a smile.

"What's with the luggage?" Jamie asked. I'd chosen a solid case that was bright yellow in color.

"No peeking. There are presents in there."

Kelly laughed and pulled us toward the car. "Let's hope it all fits."

BY THE time we got home, I expected Gabe to be waiting for me in the condo. He wasn't. Everything was dark and cold, or at least it felt that way to me. It was past nine and surely not that late for a vampire, but late for me. Jamie dropped my stuff off. He and Kelly left for his place upstairs, looking like they'd be having some good intimate time together.

I sighed to the empty room. The luggage at my side had seemed like such a good idea at the time. I'd sort of expected Gabe to be here to see it, then talk me out of going. Maybe this trip was really meant to be. We should be vacationing together, not me running off to find out what some dead relative was giving me. But I couldn't get the way he'd been so proud of Sam out of my head. I wanted him to be proud of me. I'd just graduated—though I technically didn't have the degree in hand yet—with a degree in Magic Studies. I was the first male ever to do so. Shouldn't my boyfriend have planned something nice for me in celebration, like a romantic dinner or even a hot bath surrounded by rose petals?

Sure, Gabe was the romantic one. I could screw him without all the brain foreplay, but sometimes it was nice to feel like he loved me enough to do those silly things for me. He had yet to congratulate me for completing college. Maybe he was planning something for after the actual ceremony, which wasn't until February. I sighed again.

I stared at the luggage and realized I wasn't just sad, I was mad. Jealous yes—Gabe was mine, not Sam's—but also mad that Gabe wasn't making an effort. I'd finally agreed to be exclusively his and he rewarded me by pulling away. I couldn't even recall the last time we'd actually talked about something other than a work schedule. And I hadn't had any time alone with him tonight to ask about Tresler's call.

And why would Tresler call me? There was only one reason. And that was because Gabe wasn't doing whatever he was supposed to be. Tresler was a master at head games. He knew it would eat me up with curiosity and worry. Something bad was happening in the vampire world and Gabe wasn't telling me anything.

I dry-washed my face and sighed down at the bags of stuff I'd just bought. Nothing wrong with adventure, right? Space was sometimes a good thing. Room to breathe was what I needed right now. At least if I couldn't have the arms of my lover around me.

I detagged and stuffed my new things into the washer, then called the number on the letter that had been sent to me. Jamie told me to leave it for Gabe, but he had other things to occupy him right now, mainly Sam. The lawyer, a man by the name of Jonathon Odagiri, picked up on the third ring. It really wasn't that late in California yet, but apparently his private office phone rang to his cell after 5:00 p.m.

I introduced myself. "Sorry for calling so late," I told him.

"No, no. It's fine. I'm glad to hear from you. Since your father left you the estate, I thought I'd be hearing from you soon."

"Estate?" Like a house? What would I do with a house in California? Though maybe it would be nice to go there in the winter. Like now when even inside standing next to the dryer, I was freezing.

"Yes, the Merth estate home. There are accounts to help with its upkeep as well. I would love to sit down and discuss all of that with you. There's quite a lot. And of course, Charles Merth's will, which has other additions and provisions."

My head spun trying to make sense of all he was saying. So the house was already mine, but Charles had left me something else? How did that work? "I already scheduled a flight out tonight. I'll just have to find a hotel," I told him.

"You can stay at the estate if you wish. No one has lived there for a few months, but the utilities are still working and I was just inside a few days ago. Other than being a little dusty, the house was in pretty good shape," the lawyer told me.

"So my uncle left me the house?"

"Technically your father left you the house. It should have been yours when you turned twenty-one, but your uncle kept it in trust. Charles left you things in his will as well, but we'll go over that at the reading. There are also funds to help finance taxes and repair of the estate. I can go over that with you tomorrow or in the next few days. It's really not as complicated as it sounds."

Thank the Mother for that. "Okay." My father had left me a house in California and I'd had no idea. I hadn't even been born when he died. How was that possible? "My father lived in the house?" I asked after a minute of silence.

"Born and raised. He traveled a bit after college, but he always returned home to the estate."

In my mind's eye, I pictured a house filled with paintings, photo albums, and memories of a man I'd never had the chance to meet. Would he have wanted me? Would he have loved me where my mother had failed? "I'll be in pretty late tonight," I finally said.

"Give me your flight information and I'll arrange for a car to take you to the estate," he told me. I forwarded the itinerary to him and promised to speak with him in the next day or so. He hung up vowing that someone would be at the airport to guide me to the house and answer basic questions. I worked on laundry, packed, and debated what I would say if someone came back before I left for the airport. There was no way I was not going at this point. It might have started with the chance to run away, but now I saw the trip as an opportunity to learn about my dad and get my head on straight before I did something stupid like broke up with Gabe.

Chapter 3

The doorman told me the taxi arrived just after 11:00 p.m. I thanked him and let him help me to the car with my carry-on. He shut the door of the cab for me, and the driver headed toward the airport. There was still time to go back, to talk to Gabe, Jamie, or Kelly. They would all try to convince me to stay. Or insist on going to guard me from whatever. Not only did I want to escape the holidays bearing down on me, but I also wanted to learn more about my family, specifically my uncle, and my father.

The lines and scanners nearly gave me a breakdown though there were few people this late. The security guards did stare at me, but they also smiled and wished me a good trip like they did all the other travelers. I hurried to my flight and waited close to the gate, reading until they called to begin boarding. I glanced one last time at my phone before turning it off and stepping onto the plane.

No one had called. No one texted. Tears burned my eyes, but I refused to let them go. I couldn't expect them to know if I'd told them nothing. Kelly had been trying to help me communicate better. He said I wasn't the only one with the issue, but if I felt something was hurting me, I just needed to spit it out. I probably should have told him. Even if there was nothing anyone could do about it. I sighed and made my way onto the plane.

After stuffing my bag in the bin, I took the window seat, strapped on the belt, and closed the little flap to the dark outside world. Hopefully I'd get through the four-hour flight without a panic attack. The new book I'd begun earlier in the day was about fallen angels and lifetimes of hard living to find true love. The sex every ten pages or so got old fast, but maybe it could keep my mind off things. Real life was never filled with that much sex, no matter how much I wanted it to be. *Sigh.*

The time passed quickly. I finished the first book and began another before arrival was announced. After flipping up the little shade, I stared out at the bright lights of Los Angeles. From this angle, it looked a lot like the Twin Cities, with the exception of the dark stretch that seemed to be the ocean in the distance. I hoped there would be trees, grass, blooming flowers, and lively critters to make me feel like I was whole again.

The plane landed without incident. I followed the trickle of passengers to the exit, my little yellow bag in tow. There were several taxis hanging around, but I didn't have an address. Maybe I could call the lawyer again? I was beat, more emotionally than physically. I could just go to a hotel for the night.

"Mr. Rou?" a voice asked.

I turned to blink at a young man with brown hair and pale blue eyes. His hair was styled in that messy just-out-of-bed look that was popular, but never reality. He looked like the kid of a movie star, breathtaking in that too-beautiful-to-be-real way. "Yes?"

He held out his hand. "Timothy Merth. Charles was my dad. Jonathon said you were coming, and I told him I'd take you to the house. I'm sure you're tired."

I shook his hand. He felt normal enough. "Okay." Perhaps he'd tell me a little more on the way.

"My car's over here." He motioned us away from the cabs and across to the parking lot and his Chevy Malibu. He put my bag in the backseat and opened the passenger door before I could get there.

"Thanks."

"No problem." He handed me a business card after he got inside and started the car. "Call me if you need anything. My work is sort of sporadic, so I'm usually available."

I took the card and glanced it in the passing lights before putting it in my wallet. I expected it to say he was an actor or something, but it said property management. "Mr. Odagiri said something about the estate?" I prodded. He drove us out of the airport lot, paid the parking fee, and headed toward a highway and the lights of the city.

"Yes. That is where I'm taking you now. It will be yours if you sign the papers. It was your dad's, but he left it in my dad's keeping. He really should have handed it over to you a few years ago, when you turned twenty-one."

Right, his dad had just died, shit. "I'm sorry about your dad."

Timothy shrugged. "We weren't close. I know he cared about me, and I cared about him, but he was never really there, so it's not much different. You know what I mean?"

Sounded like my mom. "Yeah."

"So anyway, the estate is a really big house on about two acres of land. It's probably a mess, so let me know if you need to hire cleaners or something to help you. There's a pretty big trust account to help with the maintenance. You could turn it into a bed-and-breakfast or sell it for a pretty good profit."

"No one lives there?"

"No. My dad lived alone for years, pretty much confined to just a few rooms. In fact, I think your dad's rooms are the way he left them. My dad didn't like others around him much. He had some paranoia issues."

My gut clenched. Maybe my emotional problems came from my dad's side of the family and not just from my fucked-up past. Did that mean it was just going to get worse? "How did your dad pass, if you don't mind me asking?"

"Heart attack."

"I'm sorry." It was never easy to lose people you knew, whether you liked them or not. "Do you know why my dad didn't leave my older brother the house?"

"He gave Jamie money. Your dad was always generous with that. Maybe he just thought you were better suited to the house."

I sighed internally. What would I do with the house? Sell it, probably. I couldn't see needing a home in California. As much as I grumbled, Minnesota was my home, four seasons and all. Maybe I could spend some time learning about my dad before I left it all behind.

At least here the earth pulsed strong and awake. Sure, many trees had lost their leaves, but the grass was still green and bushes bloomed. Maybe that's why my dad had lived out here. The distance made me wonder how he and my mom met.

I already missed Gabe, had been missing him for weeks, in fact. But I didn't dare open the link between the two of us; no telling how he'd react. I didn't want him to be mad. He did this silent stewing kind of anger he'd let build up until he could get away. I never knew where he went and what he did to get out his anger. When he came back, he'd be calmer, sometimes talk about what had been bothering him. Most of the time, he said nothing until I pointed out my own mistake and tried to fix it. Making our relationship work would be so much easier if he'd just talk to me. But I guess I wasn't much on talking to him either.

We pulled up to a gate that had probably been black-painted metal at one time. Now it was overgrown with thick ivy and dark branches. The house beyond towered through the trees in glimpses of windows and pale-beige stucco. The trees loomed as large as the house. The overgrown grass that bent over the path made me cringe and was reminiscent of a dying cornfield before the harvest, sort of creepy even. The smell of fallen leaves and dirt comforted me a little. The earth had really gone wild here. If this was the outside, how bad would the inside be?

Timothy held out a ring of keys for me. "Big one is for the gate. The small one with the red ending is for the main door. The power and water are on, but I don't know how livable it is. I haven't been inside in years. Do you want me to take you to a hotel for now?"

I took the keys from him and stared at the house, wondering what sort of secrets about my family it held. Had my dad known how difficult my life would be? Would he still love me now if he could see how incredibly fucked up I'd become? "I'd like to stay here, I think."

"You'll need food for sure. There's a 24-hour corner-grocery-type store just up a couple of blocks. You want me to drive you there and back?"

"I'll google a pizza place on my phone if I get hungry. Thanks for the ride, Timothy."

He smiled at me, jumped out, and got my bag out of the backseat. "Don't forget to call me if you need anything."

"I won't, thanks." I stepped up to the gate, unlocked it, and pushed it far enough for me to squeeze inside before shutting it again. Timothy waited only a few more seconds before taking off. I turned toward the house, which looked more than a little spooky in the dark. The earth that surrounded it grew up around it in wild patches told me it was free of human life. The power here was strong, beyond anything I'd felt before, but contained, waiting—it almost seemed like—for something to release it. The energy thrummed through me to the very core of my being, filling me, flowing through me, like it was a living, breathing entity. Wow, I'd missed that back home.

I sent a thought out to any critter kinds who might have made the house home, asking them politely to vacate. No need to hire exterminators. Animals gladly moved on when nudged. When I opened the door, the eerie creak reminded me of a horror movie. I paused just inside, waiting for someone to lunge at me from behind the door. Stupid overactive brain. Of course nothing happened.

Using my cellphone as a flashlight, I searched the walls until I found a light switch and flipped it, hoping it worked. When light flooded the main foyer, I stood in awe. This put my mom's house to shame. The wide-open area housed a large oak tree. The leaves had fallen, scattered around the scarred wood-and-tile floor and the staircase that curved around it to the second level. But the trunk was wide enough around to look like one of those ancient trees you could drive a car through. Branches stretched across the room and around corners into other areas.

I touched the base and let the power wash through me. Peace, utter, nondisruptable peace. The tree napped, earth telling me it was time for most trees to rest and renew. My watch beeped 4:00 a.m., and I figured I should probably sleep too.

I carefully made my way upstairs, opening doors, revealing a mass of rooms, one after another. This place wasn't a house, it was a mansion. At the end of the hall to the left, a door made me pause. The faded old sign on it read:

Peace to all who enter, in heart, spirit, and soul.

—Dorien

The black ink was faded, but the scrawl still had an elegant flair. My dad had written this? Was this his bedroom? I opened the door, found the light, and stared at the room. Sadly it didn't look much different than any of the other rooms I'd passed. Empty of all signs of life, it just contained barren furniture and dusty floors. My bright yellow bag was modern and loud compared to the very traditional furniture.

A little red bug that looked like a large ladybug landed on the bag and crawled around a bit. The dust made me sneeze a dozen times. The bug didn't move. I wondered how it had gotten inside, but I opened the window and carefully let it crawl into my hand so I could let it outside. The damn thing bit me before it flew out into the darkness toward an overgrowth of weeds in the back of the house. Obviously not a ladybug, then. Must have been an Asian beetle or something. At least with the window open, the soft breeze eased the musty smell of the house.

The bed was covered with a dust cloth. I carefully peeled it back, found the bed stripped of linens, then had to dig in all the closets until I came across sheets that didn't smell like they'd been put away for years, and made the bed. The bathroom needed dusting too but was otherwise clean.

I stripped out of my clothes and slid into bed, too tired to think about anything else. Sleepiness took over even while I missed Gabe's arms around me. Some adventures just weren't lollipops and rainbows, and that was okay. I closed my eyes and let sleep take the self-doubt away.

Chapter 4

I STROLLED through an unfamiliar garden, not remembering how I'd found my way there to begin with. Flowers bloomed in some Wonderland mystery, towering above my head. The sound of water flowing nearby was relaxing despite my unfamiliar surroundings. Bugs as large as me passed, ignoring me in favor of their work. And they seemed to be working, some carrying things, others digging into the ground, some gnawing on plants. The ground beneath my feet shifted and rolled like freshly turned soil, yet I seemed to float over it without stumbling.

Wandering through the towering flowers, I watched the sky's dark blue light weave between the giant blossoms and leaves. It changed to day gradually, like a slow-moving picture. The world spun as though it were moon-free, the restrictive magnetic waves gone. The change could have taken me at any moment, only I feared I'd trample some of the divine growth, so I fought it, shoving the need back until it just danced along the edges of my power. Everything glowed with energy, life, and strength. I used the light of the blooms above to guide my way, though I had no idea where I was headed.

"Lost?" a masculine voice asked me.

I jumped back a step and looked around until I found a man leaning against the large stalk of an overgrown daisy. He almost seemed to blend in with the stem, though his skin was a pale cinnamon tone and his hair blood red. He wore only a pair of loose-fitting pants of some soft material that clung in places I was sure it had to be cheating to look at. His arms, shoulders, and chest were defined like a man who worked out regularly but not obsessively. His stomach was flat with only the faintest outline of muscles, which led to straight hips, a nicely outlined package, and long legs. He was sort of my ideal man, except he wasn't blond like Gabe.

"Like what you see, Alice?" he teased, forcing my eyes back up. His smile was bright. He shook his head, sending a cascade of his long red hair rippling down his back like some shampoo commercial.

"Alice?" I couldn't help but study his face, triangular in shape. It bordered on beautiful with just the slight edge of handsome that saved him from really looking like a woman. His dark eyes, framed by a soft fringe of lashes, met mine without hesitation. Somehow I'd gotten closer to him, just feet away.

"Like the story. The little girl who got lost in a forest of oversized adventures." He shifted and closed the distance between us. "I don't think my 'drink me' potion is going to make you bigger than the flowers, but I'm sure I can show you a good time." He looked to my crotch. "Maybe it *will* make you a little bigger. Temporarily, at least."

44

His words hit me like a rush of lust. My body tingled and responded, cock hard enough to hurt, nipples taut and sensitive, heart pounding. He wrapped an arm around my waist and yanked me against him. His lips touched my cheek. I should have been pissed that he'd just called me a girl, but none of that seemed to matter when touching him felt like being wrapped up in the earth on a warm summer day. Nothing had ever been so perfect. I'd never had a dream like this that felt so real, with power and lust pulsing through every cell. It was incredible.

His fingers wove through my hair, which was somehow long again, but weightless. He didn't try for more, just stared me in the eyes, breathing my breath, offering his to me as though he wanted me to make the first move. "What is it you long for the most, little Alice?"

"My name's not Alice," I whispered, afraid to break whatever sort of bond we had. "It's Seiran." Would he kiss me? What would he do if I kissed him? Nothing mattered at that moment but how I needed to settle in him. Just like the earth, he was wound completely through my soul. I chanted to myself "I love Gabe," but had a hard time remembering his face at that moment.

"Hmm," the stranger mumbled, nuzzling my cheek with his bow-shaped lips. "Never had one like you. So strong. What do you long for, Seiran?" He repeated his question, my name sounding both foreign and sensual on his lips.

"I don't know what you mean."

He pressed his hips into my stomach letting me feel every hard bit of him. He was only a few inches taller than me, but everything about him seemed larger than the world. My cock ground into his thigh. A sigh escaped my lips as he gripped my ass. For the first time, I realized I wore the same thing he did, just a soft pair of pants with no shirt. My hair was piled on top of my head in some odd updo that left the length of the back to tumble free and loose. I reached out to touch the black curls. They felt like silky darkness, and my hand glowed with a pale inner light. What the hell? This was the weirdest dream I'd ever had, and the thought made me pause and worry for a moment. Was it really a dream?

I looked back to the red-haired man, suddenly not trusting him. "Who are you? What are you?"

His smile was sincere. He spoke, but I couldn't hear him. The night from above turned into brightness so harsh it blocked out everything else.

The sun shining through the window brought me awake like a flower opening for the first time. I stretched, rolled over, and basked in the luminosity of the morning sun for a while. Instead of waking up with a hard-on due to the erotic dream, I felt rested and satisfied. Odd.

The digital clock beside the bed, though ancient, still seemed to work; it read just after 7:00 a.m. Was it all a dream? Never in my life had I dreamt something so real. I could almost still feel his heat, recall the scent of his breath and the power on my skin.

What did it mean for my relationship with Gabe if I was dreaming about some mystery man? Sure, the man had been a personification of most of my fantasies, but he'd felt like the earth. That had been his biggest draw, a moonless night with nothing but carefree adventures to be had. I wanted to dream of him again, but at the same time, I feared it. The idea of not completely letting go of control to the earth had been instilled in me since childhood. The Dominion taught that the element would take you, force out your humanity, and leave you as nothing but a simple-minded creature to be bent to its will. I'd lost myself to the power before, and the earth hadn't harmed me. I couldn't imagine it doing so now, but fear of the unknown remained.

I shook off the groggy memory of the dream, jumped in the shower, and cleaned up. The day was just beginning and I had a house to explore, my father's past to learn, and a mystery of what to do with all I found to solve.

The many windows bathed the house in light. The ceiling above the foyer, all stained glass, bounced rainbows around the entire lower level. I turned my phone on long enough to text Kelly that I was okay, then shut it off again, ignoring all the messages and texts. I plugged it in to charge and headed for the grocery store Timothy had pointed out last night. Cleaning supplies were a must.

The streets were warm and filled with life as I entered the shop. It was more a general store than just a grocery. I bought a small wagon, loaded up my groceries and cleaning supplies, and headed back to my father's house. Something would have to be done with the grass and all the overgrown vegetation. Nature was good, but this was a jungle.

I got through cleaning the bedroom and my bathroom pretty quickly, then found the washer and dryer and put sheets in to be cleaned. The appliances all seemed to have been purchased within the past five years, even the enormous furnace and the outside air conditioning unit. But I'd have someone come out to inspect them all as soon as I spoke to the lawyer about the account set up for house maintenance. The house had a couple of fireplaces, but even in mid-December, the outside temp was in the seventies, so I couldn't see needing them anytime soon. Maybe it got cold in January? Or maybe Californians thought this was cold?

The kitchen needed major cleaning, but it looked like something out of a cooking TV show, with metal counters, stainless steel appliances, a butcher block prep area, endless cupboards, and four massive sinks.

Halfway through my cleaning of the kitchen, the doorbell rang. I didn't even recall seeing a bell last night. I put aside the supplies for a minute and walked to the door, wondering how they'd gotten through the gate.

Two men stood on my doorstep. One was Timothy, the other a well-dressed Asian man in a suit. "Hello, Mr. Rou. I'm Jonathon Odagiri." He held out his hand to me.

Oh, the lawyer. I took his hand and shook it. "Hello. You guys want to come in? I just put a pot of tea on." They both stepped inside as I held the door for them. The crunch of leaves beneath their boots reminded me I needed to get this area cleaned up too. "Kitchen is this way." I led them toward the back of the house and the mostly sparkling kitchen.

"Wow," Timothy said. "I don't think I've ever seen this kitchen so clean."

I motioned them to sit on one of the barstools at the oversized breakfast bar. "I'm just getting started. I hope it's okay that I clean." I looked at the lawyer.

"It is. I brought the paperwork that puts the house and the trust for it officially in your name." Mr. Odagiri put his briefcase on the counter and opened it to pull out papers. "You don't have to sign them right now, but I did bring them for you to have some time to read over."

"Thank you." I took the stack he gave me and glanced through them. "I'm sure I'll have lots of questions about the upkeep. The house is much larger than I expected." By like twenty times. Who knew my dad had been rich enough to own a mansion in California? A document stating a recent appraisal left me blinking wide eyed at the house around me. What was I going to do with a home worth a couple million dollars?

"Do you need help with the cleaning?" Timothy asked, though he didn't appear to like the idea of helping. Or maybe he just didn't like cleaning. "There used to be a caretaker here, but Dad fired him four years ago."

"Thank you for the offer, but I'd rather do it myself." It would take a while, but I had time. "Perhaps you can recommend someone reliable to help with the yard. There is money to cover that cost, right?"

Mr. Odagiri nodded. "I also have an extra key to the gate and the door; once the papers are signed, I'll hand them over to you. Any expenses for the house can be billed to this account." He handed me a slip of paper. "Just have your contractors call me if there are any questions."

"Okay. Thanks." I hoped the account had a lot of money in it because I couldn't imagine how much it would cost to clean up the two acres of land surrounding the house.

"I know a guy who does lawn care that I can have stop by. He's always looking for work and can do what you need without a big crew to bug you all day." Timothy pulled out his phone and appeared to text someone.

"That would be great. Thank you."

The lawyer got up, which made Timothy move too. Mr. Odagiri smiled at me. "I'm sure you want some time to go through your father's things. And while I never served him directly, our firm did, so I'm sure we can find someone to answer any other questions you have about him." He nodded to Timothy, "And Timothy can go through photo albums with you."

"Yep. I may not have met a lot of the people from back when your dad was alive, but I know of them and what they look like. Just let me know," Timothy told me.

"And don't hesitate to call," Mr. Odagiri said.

I agreed as I walked them to the door. Obviously they hadn't planned on staying long. But that was okay since I was already trying to think of where the photo albums they were talking about could be. I'd hadn't seen a study or library yet, though the house was certainly large and prestigious enough to have both.

"You'll be coming to the reading of the will Monday?" Mr. Odagiri asked.

"Sure, if I can catch a ride with someone."

"I'll drive you," Timothy offered.

"Thanks."

They headed out the door. Timothy paused and waited until the lawyer was out of earshot. "Keep the gate locked, doors too."

I frowned at him. "Does someone want the house?"

He shook his head. "Maybe, but I've heard of you, Seiran. Even out here in California, we know of the first male to ever become Pillar. You come from a long line of very powerful male witches. Not everyone likes that, and some like it too much. Be careful."

"Okay." Sounded like life as usual to me. I'd always hated being valued only for my mother's status, and now for my power. Unfortunately, the world was obsessed with power.

Timothy left, throwing occasional glances back my way as he crept through the gate, locking it behind him, and got into the car. I closed and locked the door and had turned to return the kitchen when a tile snapped beneath my feet. I let myself fall to save my ankle from more damage and pain, taking the brunt of my weight with my other knee. The lingering sting left my ankle as a deep, hot pain sprung up in my knee.

I sprawled back, landing on my butt with my back to the tree, sitting in the ring of earth, leaves, and roots. The broken tile hadn't sprained my ankle, thankfully, but the three-inch gash that went through my jeans and into my flesh oozed blood. It hurt too. I clapped my hands over it, wondering if I would need to call for help and get it stitched or if I could just put a Band-Aid on it.

Taking a clean rag out of my hoodie pocket, I blotted at the wound. It wasn't very deep, long and angry, but just a bleeder, nothing serious. I pushed myself up, using the trunk of the tree, and limped to the kitchen to find the first-aid kit I'd bought at the grocery store. The jeans would be ruined. I might have been able to get the blood out, but the long jagged tear in the fabric wasn't going to be something I could pass off as trendy. Later I'd have to go back and clean up any remaining blood in the foyer, but resting until the sting went away wouldn't hurt anything.

Chapter 5

After I finished cleaning the kitchen, my phone beeped that the charge was complete, so I turned it on and listened to my messages. Only two, one from Gabe, one from Jamie. Both fairly calm, which surprised me. My only text was from Kelly, replying to my earlier text with a simple *Glad you're okay*.

Gabe's had been more of a question statement: "You need to talk to me."

And yeah I probably did, but not yet. I needed to learn about my dad. Something about being here made my soul raw and tender, like I was waiting for the hurt when I discovered he hadn't wanted me or something. I sighed, realizing my cynicism wasn't helping me at all. There was lots of cleaning to do and my head worked better when I was busy.

A ladybug, or maybe an Asian beetle, kept showing up in the kitchen with the same coloring as the one in the bedroom: red with cinnamon spots. I finally left the window open, hoping it would find its way out instead of inviting more of its friends in.

I'd cleaned the entire kitchen and was sweeping the leaves in the foyer into piles to bag up when something buzzed. After a few moments of silence, I continued sweeping, then the buzz came again from a box near the door. It looked like the call box our building had back home. I pushed the button and said, "Hello?"

"Hey, is this Mr. Rou? I'm Caleb, a friend of Tim's. He said you needed yard work done."

Oh. That was fast. I put the broom aside and opened the door to head to the gate. I could have buzzed it from the inside of the house, but I wanted to look at the guy from a safe distance first.

My first thought was "wow."

Caleb wore jeans like a man should wear jeans: tight, dirty, torn, but clinging in all the right places. His shirt, a button-up plaid, short-sleeved with a pocket, stretched across his chest and broad shoulders the way they did in cowboy movies. He wore a genuine cowboy hat over what looked like short blond hair and squinted behind dark-tinted sunglasses. Fuzzy blond hair peeked out from the top of his neckline, and his tanned arms were covered in the fluff. He even wore some sort of snakeskin-looking boots. Had I flown to California or Texas? Wow, cowboy, wow.

"Mr. Rou?" he asked.

I blinked a few more times at him before looking behind him to a truck parked in front of the house with a trailer full of yard equipment loaded on it. "Yeah. Sorry." After unlocking the gate, I pulled it open as far as it would go, which wasn't far. He stepped inside.

"I see the problem." He smiled, head swiveling while he surveyed the work to be done. Up close, I could see the scratchiness of a day's worth of growth covering his cheeks, and wondered how good that would feel against my skin. I had to shake it off and remind myself that Gabe and I were still a couple, even if he wasn't here, even if he had been ignoring me the past couple of weeks. Maybe he'd be willing to wear some cowboy-like clothes for a little evening adventure if I could get rid of Sam for a while. *Sigh.*

"I don't want to lose any trees or anything. Just cut the grass to a reasonable length. Vines trimmed so the gate opens. Path cleared of debris. If it's possible to mulch the leavings and put them around the trees or if there are any gardens under this stuff, that would be great." Earth recycled earth. I just wanted it to be more manageable. Hopefully the work would make the outside of the house a little less intimidating.

He nodded. "I've got a mulching machine. It will take more than a day or two to clean all this up, though. It looks like it hasn't been touched in years."

It probably hadn't. "That's fine. If I sweep leaves out of the house, can you take care of those too?"

"Sure. Is there a broken window or something? I can fix it."

"No, but thank you. How soon can you start?"

"Right now, actually. I'm sorta in between jobs. Tim gave me the lawyer's number to call for payment, so I'll work that out with him. The machines can make some noise, so I'll try not to start before eight in the morning."

"Thanks." I would just keep the door locked when I wasn't near it. Mr. Hot Cowboy or not, leaving the door open would only invite trouble. "I will get a copy of the gate key made for you. The gate needs to be locked whenever you're not working within view of it. And once the project is finished, I will need the key back."

"Got it."

I nodded to him and headed back inside while he went to his truck. Instead of bagging up the piles of leaves, I swept them out the door and told the tree I'd bring in some nutrients for it that weren't quite so messy. After the leaves were clear and the door locked, I moved on to the next project.

The day passed into evening without me really noticing. Everything was dusted, swept, vacuumed, washed, scrubbed, and cleaned. The noise of Caleb and his machines had come and gone. A glance outside said he'd worked hard. The gate opened completely, free of the overgrown vines. The path was cleared of debris and wilting grass, and all the leaves I'd pushed out had vanished. A cobblestone walk led around the house toward the back, making me wonder where it went. It must have been covered since I hadn't noticed it at all the day before.

Not bad for a few hours' work. Caleb had even begun trimming one side of the lawn to reveal a garden area that really needed some new life brought to it. Maybe tomorrow I'd explore and play in the dirt I told myself and went back to work. It gave me a lot of time to wonder about my family, the upcoming holiday, my future, and the unusual dream I'd had this morning. Maybe the dream meant I was horny or just needed to plant a garden.

The doorbell rang sometime after 10:00 p.m. I was in the third bedroom on the second floor, so it took me a while to get downstairs to the door. In that time, it rang twice more. Was it the lawyer again? I hadn't given Caleb a key to the gate yet, and I was sure he'd left hours ago since the noise from outside had gone silent. I opened the door a crack, surprised to see Gabe standing there. If Sam hadn't been standing at the bottom of the stairs looking annoyed, I would have thrown myself at him, dragged him to my room, and made love to him all night.

I opened the door wide, but neither of them moved.

"Are you going to invite us in?" Gabe asked. His voice sounded cold and detached. There was a brief flash of red in his eyes that made me take a small step back.

"Are you going to yell at me?" I asked.

"Yes."

I blinked at him, thankful for the honesty, but worried about the fight to come. "I don't want to fight." I didn't handle confrontations well, and while I wanted him to talk to me, yelling wasn't what I had in mind.

"Then you shouldn't have left without telling anyone." It was still that deadly calm voice that said he was seething with anger. I hated when he went cold like this. Before I'd become his focus, I'd never seen this side of him, but since he'd begun mentoring Sam, this dark rage was rearing its head more and more. I wondered how I'd missed seeing this for all those years.

"I'm a grown-up. I don't need babysitters, and I don't need permission." I'd sort of been hoping he'd follow without dragging Sam along. That maybe this trip would have forced him to open up. He never told me vampire stuff, not that I wanted all the gory details, but a relationship was about sharing each other's burdens, right? I really hated feeling like I was the only one in the relationship sharing all the shit of my life most days. I would have loved to sit down with him and tell him all my worries about my dad and explore the house with him, making love to him in every room. But not this Gabe. Not the angry man in front of me. I wanted my calm and patient Gabe, wherever he'd gone. I really wanted him back.

"No, you don't need permission, but you do need to act like an adult. You're like a sulking child. Running away from things you don't want to deal with. Not telling the people who care about you where you're going or why. How should we treat you?"

I folded my arms across my chest, breathing deeply and trying to keep myself from screaming at him, breaking down into tears, and slamming the door shut. This is not what I meant by him sharing with me. Finally, I said, "I'm not running from anything. I wanted a vacation and had an opportunity to learn about my dad. I knew you would have said no. Or at least that you couldn't come." Between his businesses, his fellow vampires, and Sam, Gabe was always swamped with some issue. I'd tried to take evenings off just to spend with him, only to find him doing something else. We both had to make an effort to make this work, right? "Plus you're too busy with *him* to pay attention to me. I'm surprised you even noticed I was gone."

Sam looked up at me sharply, then away, trying to hide his feelings. He could be pissed too, whatever. Fuck him. I was tired of having a shadow dogging my steps. Tired of other people using him to replace me.

"I don't know what else you want, Seiran. I have bent over backward to give you everything and you just smack me in the face. You knew I had to mentor Sam. I told you it takes time."

"I just want you to talk to me! Did you know Tresler called me yesterday? Asked me if any unusual vampires were hanging around? You haven't said one word, but why would he call me first?" Gabe flinched. The answer was that Tresler wouldn't have contacted me first. Even as Gabe's focus, I was human and considered beneath notice for most of their kind. It was all so frustrating. "He didn't call me first. He called you and warned you of trouble, but you told me nothing. There could be some crazy vampire out there to get me and you told me nothing!"

"It's the Tri-Mega's issue, not ours."

"Bullshit! Tresler wouldn't have called me if it wasn't something we should worry about."

"I'm not doing Tresler's job for him. And I'm not discussing this with you. It has nothing to do with us."

Us? I wanted to shout at him. *What us?* He kept pushing me away. Finding other things to do than be with me. "And why aren't you taking time off work to take care of Sam? It's not like you have to worry about money. Instead you use the time that you used to spend with me to take him out and hunt. I'll tell you why, because he makes you proud and happy. If he shares your interests so much, then bond with him." He regretted it, didn't he? Making me his focus.

"You know our bond can't be undone, Seiran. No matter what you may want."

"I'm sorry I disappoint you, Gabe. I'm sorry I'm not what you hoped I'd be." I fought back tears. This was heartbreak, the pain in my chest that clenched and unclenched around my heart. Death would probably hurt less or at least be faster. I took a deep breath and finally responded, "Sun comes up around six here. You probably should find some hunting grounds and a hotel. I don't know how you got through the gate, but I hope you didn't break it. Goodnight." I closed the door on his astonished face and returned to my cleaning. The bell didn't ring again and I didn't dare open the mental link I had to him. Since I was the only one in the house, no one cared when I cried into the mop water.

Chapter 6

CALEB ARRIVED early the next morning, but late enough for me to have been up and gotten him a key to the gate, which was undamaged. There was no sign of Gabe or Sam, for which I was grateful. Maybe coming here without telling anyone was a bad decision, but if Gabe thought he had to work so hard just to be with me, why did he bother? Why had he spent years trying to get me to love him, only to resent me for finally taking that step?

My eyes must still have been red and puffy, 'cause the first thing Caleb said with a slow southern drawl when I handed him the key to the gate was "You all right?"

"I'm fine, thank you. Do you need anything? Coffee?"

He held up a thermos. "Already prepared." He pointed to the garden he'd revealed yesterday. "It looks like it was a vegetable garden, goes all the way around the house from what I can tell. You want it kept that way, or I can get sod to go over it?"

"Keep it, please."

He gave me a salute and walked off to do his thing.

After about an hour of cleaning, I decided to venture outside into the bright warmth and see where the path took me. The uneven cobblestones led around the house and through the back. Caleb must have followed it because the back was still an oversized jungle of grass that was almost as tall as I was, but the stones had been cleared. The path led to a house, smaller than the mansion but still two-story. A carriage house? Did they have those in California? The lower level appeared to be some sort of garage now, only there were no roads or paths for a car to get to it, but the windows in the second level meant there were probably living quarters there. The caretaker's place, maybe? The windows on the lower level were so dirty it was impossible to see inside. If it had been the caretaker's place, the lower level was probably filled with lawn equipment. The garage door looked like an electric type, but I didn't recall seeing a clicker for it anywhere.

The stairs looked secure enough, but obviously needed some work. The paint was peeled and the wood chipped, but for the most part didn't seem to have begun to rot. I supposed down here in California they didn't put salt on everything in the winter to prevent slipping, which also ate away at wood and metal. If the steps were sanded and repainted, they'd be good as new.

I hiked up to the top and tried to peer in the dirty windows before searching through my keyring for something that would open the door. Finally finding it, I pushed the door open and was greeted by the musty smell of mold. The heat inside hit me like opening the door of an oven, and as the door swung wide, a worse smell hit me. Something I wished I didn't recognize.

Unfortunately, I knew death when I smelled it. Was the caretaker still here?

I shook my head. Not possible. He wouldn't still stink like that. Even boxed up with no open windows, the smell would fade in four years. The heat probably would have cremated him. This had to be fresh.

The call to the police took only a few seconds, but I stumbled out, leaving the door open, and sat down on the top step to wait for the parade that would come. Having been through finding a dead body before, I knew better than to go stomping through leaving traces of my DNA or spouting off things to anyone that could be misconstrued later. I had plenty of time to think, though. There was also no need for me to see whoever was dead in that house. Maybe I was overreacting, maybe it was just a bunch of dead animals, though I'd never known animals to smell quite that bad. I also couldn't mistake the buzzing of flies that covered the windows and flew by me now that I sat on the steps. The thought of them and what their greater purpose in life was made me gag. Crap, I was not good around dead people.

No one had lived here for years. So how had someone gotten in? This looked like a nice neighborhood, but maybe all the overgrown weeds made someone think they could hide out for a while and not get caught. That didn't explain the locked door, though, and I'd tested the handle before fiddling with the keys. Of course I'd be explaining that to the police when they came.

I picked at the chipped paint on the stairs. Who would have known the house was back here? It wasn't exactly something you could see from the street. The fence surrounded the main house and the carriage house, and was a good eight feet high with spikes on top—not something the average person would climb just to find a place to crash. The area wasn't exactly a bustling suburb with lots of shops and urban life either. I'd passed hundreds of acres of farmland when Timothy had driven us down from the airport. And the few houses nearby were all just like this one, huge with sprawling land, separated by high fences. The entire area looked old, like it had stepped out of time a hundred years ago and would be perfectly comfortable with carriages and horses wandering the streets.

The sound of Caleb's machines turning off let me know the cops had arrived. He walked them around the house and spotted me on the steps, questions on his face. I stood and waited for the police to come. Thankfully they didn't recognize me, maybe the Californians didn't care about the first male Pillar as much of as the Midwest because they only asked a few things before dismissing Caleb and me.

I returned to the house and continued my cleaning, only stopping to look out the back windows a time or two. The police carried out a body in a black bag but didn't mark the place off with police tape. At least I knew I hadn't overreacted to a bunch of dead animals.

When one of the lead detectives moved toward the house, I knew he was coming to talk to me. Hopefully not to arrest me. That was an experience I hoped to never repeat.

He tipped his hat lightly when I opened the door for him.

"Everything okay? Do you know who it was and how he got there?" I asked, more than a little anxious.

"No identification. But he appeared the homeless sort. Probably picked the lock to get in. We'll know more after the coroner's report comes in. The gardener says you just arrived two days ago?"

"Yes. My dad left me the house in his will, but my uncle was taking care of it until he passed away recently." I gave him Mr. Odagiri's number, just in case he wanted to check my story. "You didn't leave up tape. Will you be dusting for fingerprints and stuff?"

He smiled at me like he thought I was a little silly. "We're a small town, Mr. Rou. It's unlikely that the gentleman who died in your cottage was foul play of any kind. The corner will look at him, and if she finds anything serious, we'll be back out in a jiffy."

Jiffy? "Okay," I told him. A little confused. TV made someone dying look so much more important than this, plus back home every time I encountered a body, someone tried to arrest me. But that was also before Andrew Roman had met his end a few weeks ago. "So there's no evidence or anything you need to gather?"

"We have everything we need, and I'll call you if we don't."

I nodded.

He hesitated, then said, "Did anyone warn you about the house?" He eyed the tree behind me.

"Warn me about what?" Well wasn't that just creepy.

He shook his head. "Nothing. Just rumors. Lights on when no one's home and stuff like that. Legends of a curse." He winked at me. "Kid stuff, really. Could be the squatter. You didn't see anyone in the house when you arrived, did you?"

"In here? No. The house was such a mess it looked like no one had lived here for years. And I didn't know about the place in back until today. Caleb is trying to clear some of the overgrowth for me. The yard apparently went wild and my uncle must have stopped caring for it."

"He your boyfriend?"

"Caleb?" I sighed internally. Was it that obvious I was gay? I didn't have a lisp and my clothes were just jeans and a T-shirt, neither sparkly nor pink. "No. Just someone I hired to do the yard work. I only met him yesterday."

The cop frowned and scanned the interior behind me again. "You might want to invite some friends to stay with you. You never know what might happen. Let us know if you see or hear anything unusual, okay?"

"Sure." What wasn't he telling me?

He left, heading off through the gate. All the flashing lights vanished. I wondered about the house in back. It would need a major cleaning and airing out. I didn't know if I was ready for that yet. The idea that someone died in there made me more than a little nervous. I didn't want to know what was left behind, even if it was just a giant nest of flies. The police's lack of interest worried me. Was it a normal occurrence to find dead people in your garage apartment? I shuddered at the thought and returned to my cleaning. That, at least, was something I could control.

I finished two more rooms before the doorbell rang again. I hurried downstairs, thinking maybe it was Caleb, but when I opened the door, it was Jamie, suitcase at his feet.

"Wow, Sei. This is an amazing house." Jamie stared at the tree in the foyer. "I heard rumors about that tree, but never thought I'd see it."

"Want to come in?" I stepped aside to let him in. "What are you doing here?" More people thinking I couldn't take care of myself. "Where's Kelly?"

He hesitated a moment, then said, "He had some school stuff, so it's just me." Jamie stood just two feet away, looking over me as if for injury. "I was worried," he admitted. "I can't help worrying. You should have said you wanted to come."

"I don't need a babysitter."

He nodded like he agreed. "No. But you do need your family. I know how awful the winter makes me feel. I can only imagine what it was doing to you."

Kelly must have been working on him more than I thought for him to admit I didn't need the protection. I wanted to hug my best friend, but figured I'd give in to the urge later when he showed up too. There was no doubt that if Jamie were here for more than a day or two, Kelly would follow.

"It was awful feeling so detached from the earth. I figured since the opportunity had presented itself, I'd check it out and see what I could learn about Dad."

Jamie looked curious. "Anything so far?" I'd forgotten he had been pretty young when Dad died.

"I've spent more time cleaning than looking for history so far. I'm in his room, though. It's at the back of the house, but it's comfortable."

"I can help clean and look for stuff." Jamie's eyes glowed with unshed tears while he stared at the tree. He was probably remembering Dad. Maybe he'd share some of those memories with me. The good ones, at least. "I expected to see Gabe with you. Where is he?"

I shrugged and turned away, feeling tears suddenly begin to pour down my cheeks. "Not here. I wouldn't invite him in."

Jamie wrapped his arms around me. I cursed myself as I let his warmth take the control from me. He just held me while I sobbed in his arms. "He was worried," Jamie said after a bit. "Probably said things he didn't mean. We all do stupid things when we're afraid."

"He's been sort of off lately. I just needed a break. Hoped he'd come and be romantic again, but he didn't come alone, and then he was angry..." I wiped my nose and eyes and grabbed one of Jamie's bags. "Let me show you to a room. I've got a few clean. Probably another half dozen to go." I gave him a weak smile.

With his help the cleaning was finished just after 8:00 p.m. Even though no one was in most of the rooms, we made all the beds. The mention of window coverings brought up a discussion about blinds and curtains. Curtains fit the house better, but blinds were more practical. Either way, if sleeping past sunrise were to be possible, something was needed.

"We should probably trim the tree back a bit. Before it breaks a window or something," Jamie remarked, still in awe over the tree in the foyer. "I think your mom was trying to duplicate this. She never really succeeded, though."

The earth vibrating through me from that tree gave me a better sense of peace than I'd had back home. My mother's tree at Christmas couldn't give off this sort of energy because it had been cut, roots lopped off like it was an annoying weed. This tree breathed, and the roots dug deep, spanning most of the property. I could probably spend hours tracing the winding length of them through the ground while curled up cradled in the power at the base of the tree. I knew my mom and Jamie didn't get along well, but I never knew he'd actually been inside her mansion at Christmastime. But a lot of my memories from when I was a kid were spotty. Jamie had been a large part of my youth, only I couldn't remember those years. He still didn't speak much of them, but Kelly had told me about a particularly horrible incident that had gotten my brother cast almost completely out of my life. Kelly suspected my mother had wiped my memory of most of the time before that to protect me, but the idea of her protecting me from bad memories made me laugh. *She* was the star of many of my bad memories as it was.

"I'm going to go unpack," Jamie said.

I waved him off and went to the kitchen to find food. Spearing an apple slice from the two I'd cut up, I played a game on my phone.

The doorbell rang.

I sighed again and glared at the darkness. It was probably Gabe, back to yell at me or bully me into inviting him inside. Jamie said he hadn't heard from him. Maybe Gabe really was tired of me. Maybe he finally realized I was too much work.

I opened the door, but the man who stood on my step wasn't Gabe. He was taller, dark hair, chiseled face, broad in the shoulder, and had chocolate-colored eyes that could stare right through a person. He didn't wear a suit, just dress pants and a button-up, but he stood like he should have been wearing one. His hands in his pockets said casual, and he had an almost model-like grace about him. He was also a vampire. The earth that rolled through me told me he was a powerful one too. Not just vampire, maybe even a witch. He smiled, hiding his fangs perfectly like so many of the older ones did.

"Mr. Rou?" He sounded foreign, perhaps Italian.

"How can I help you?" Apprehension slid down my spine like something wet and slimy. If I hadn't just survived the crazy attacks of another vampire, Andrew Roman, a few weeks earlier, and then gotten a call from Tresler to be wary of strange vampires, I probably wouldn't have been so worried.

"I'm Maxwell Hart. You can call me Max. I work in real estate and property management. I heard you might need help with managing the house." He pulled a card from his pocket. "I am also interested in buying the house if you are willing to sell. Otherwise, I can make sure it is taken care of while you're away." His eyes locked on the tree behind us. "Maybe hire a permanent gardener."

I took the card from him, mostly just to be polite. "Thank you, Mr. Hart, but I haven't decided what I'm going to do with the house yet." His interest made me almost instantly decide that selling the house was probably a bad idea. What did a vampire want with the house of an old earth magic family? Most vampires couldn't use magic like witches could. They had their own sort of magic, more spirit based than elemental. Though Andrew Roman had considerable magic. So maybe it wasn't an unusual case as much as something the vampires kept to themselves.

He bowed slightly to me, taking a step back. "Let me know if you wish to sell. I can offer a very fair price."

"I will."

"Have a good evening," he said and headed down the path back through the gate. Caleb waved good-bye and locked the gate behind him. I closed the door and stared at the giant tree. My blood stained the trunk where I'd landed and pushed myself up. The smear was oddly comforting as something that should be there, a connection to the earth. So I left it alone. Once again that odd-colored ladybug crawled around, this time near the blood. I barely resisted the urge to smash the annoying thing. Trees had bugs. That was a fact of life. Even this inside tree probably needed bugs. As long as it didn't bite me again, I would let it live.

Chapter 7

THE NIGHT was young yet, and the ache in my bones from the ever-pulsing earth made me want to have a bit of time away from the human world. Jamie never came back down for dinner. I hadn't wandered to find him either. Maybe he was off love talking to Kelly or something over the phone. Caleb had taken off with his truck of tools. How much of the yard had he finished? Hopefully not all of it.

Jamie came down the stairs, startling me with his sudden presence. He looked pretty dressed up for the evening. Usually he wore just sweats and a tank, but he was wearing pants and a button-up. "Going out?" he asked me.

"I'm going to shift," I told him. Normally I only changed into a lynx on the new moon, when the magnetic waves where farthest from the earth, but something about this land magnified the need. I stared at him, wondering at his clothes. Why would he need to dress up when Kelly wasn't here? Was he cheating on my best friend? He was the one who appeared to be going out. "I won't leave the yard, but please leave the door open a little for me."

"You okay?"

"Yep. Just want to play in the earth a little bit."

"I feel it too. The power here is a lot like the new moon. I could probably put in a cat-sized door. So that way you can come and go without the door being unlocked."

"I don't think I'm staying." No need to make changes like that yet. And just because I was an earth witch didn't mean I wanted raccoons and other creatures in the house. Those things weren't clean.

"Everything okay?"

I nodded to him, headed up to my room, and stripped out of my clothes to shift. Unlike most other non-new-moon shifts, this one went fast and almost painlessly. On four paws, I stretched, letting my brain and body reacquaint themselves to the lynx I became. The house smelled of cleaner, which made me sneeze a few times before I headed downstairs. I could have gone out the back door in the kitchen, but didn't know how far Caleb had gotten in his manicuring of the lawn, so I played it safe by going out the front to avoid getting in his way.

The freshly clipped grass gave off the aroma of home. I jumped around the yard, enjoying the soft grass and heavenly perfume of earth. Following the path around the house led me to the still mostly untouched back and allowed me to revel in life, and I jumped into the overgrowth. I picked up a trail halfway back of something familiar, yet unfamiliar, and followed it to a slew of trees, through the thick brush, and up to the top of a willow tree. Nestled in the crook of the branches above, a black-and-white ringtail twitched.

The creature glanced at me with giant dark purple eyes, wary but unmoving. I could have chased him away, claimed the tree as my own, or even swiped at him with one of my large paws, but he looked so lonely and lost, I let him be. Leaping free of the tree, I bounced in the grass, chased a few mice, and batted at the couple of large spiders who weren't smart enough to seek cover.

The ringtail came down and briefly played with me, pouncing my way before bounding back and climbing a tree. I kept my claws in each time I landed on his tail. His little clicks and grunts made me laugh, which sounded like snorting in my lynx form. We ran in circles for a bit, probably looking, for all intents and purposes, like new puppies chasing their tails.

He raced around the yard at a speed I couldn't match, mostly because of his smaller size. When he popped out of the grass and nipped at my belly, I jumped, landing next to the black fence. On the other side of the fence, a brown wall stood like it could keep the overgrown earth out. I wondered briefly where the walls went and why humans did such things to keep the earth penned in or out.

The ringtail snuck through the metal bars and walked in the space between the fences. For a while we moved together, jumping over or pushing through overgrown areas, avoiding thorns and thistles, batting at smaller creatures. Centipedes were still my favorites, even though they tasted awful. Once we met another metal gate, the ringtail stopped and bounded back as if trying to get me to follow. Instead, I squeezed through the metal slats, feeling a slight magic resistance for a few seconds before it popped me free. Then I followed a little worn path that led into the forest behind the house. Something called me. Some sort of disruption in the earth said it needed me. I was strong. I could help. Save them. I briefly wondered: *Save who?*

Clicks and chirps of protest faded off into the distance while I ventured forward. The path didn't smell of humans, only of animals, rabbits, deer, and a few larger predators like bears, coyotes, and mountain lions. I could outrun most of them, so I kept my ears focused and eyes sharp.

A ladybug landed right in my path. I paused, waited for it to move, and when it didn't, I pounced. Only it flew several feet away, taunting me. A small growl escaped my lips, and I pounced again. It wove away into a briar patch. If I could have frowned as a cat, I probably would have. Instead, I stared into the thorny bush, wondering if it was worth a few scratches to chase the little thing further.

A few minutes passed, and I just waited. Then in a flurry, almost like a bird coming at me, the bug flew up out of the bush, into my face. I swatted at it with both paws, but it buzzed around like I couldn't hit it if I tried. Finally, it landed on my nose. Even in cat form I wasn't lost enough to slap myself in the face.

We stared at each other, cat to bug, bug to cat, a contest of wills. Who would move first? I waited. The night was long enough for me to sit for a while, and I was the predator here. He moved slowly, walking up the short bridge of my nose, making my eyes cross and bringing on a sneeze that shook him off.

Damn. Where'd he go? I peered around, trying to catch a glimpse of the bright colors, a little sad to have the game over so soon. A whir of buzzing flying by had me spinning to the right. The bright spotted wings darted into the distance, and I was off running after it. The bug led me over fallen logs, around sharp bushes, and to the rushing waves of a large stream. The water was warm enough to play in, so I let my new little friend go and chased fish, frogs, and crawfish for a while.

My spotted red friend came back a time or two to dart at me, trying to get me to follow. I finally gave up on the play when he dive-bombed my ear and made it itch. After a good bit of scratching away the tickle with my back paw, I followed the little bug out of the stream, back into the woods, through a maze of trees, and to a clearing. Then he vanished as if he'd never been there into a massive briar bush jutting out from a big rock. Even after waiting a few minutes, the bug didn't return. I blinked a few times and looked around, but still couldn't find him again.

In fact, the entire area seemed to be void of life. Nothing grew other than the briar batches. No trees, weeds, or even grass. The area was brown and cracked in spots like it hadn't had the proper water or nutrients in years.

In the center was a structure of some kind. Circular, with stones on the edges, nothing grew in it. Yet the stones radiated a creepy glow. Stepping closer made my skin tingle as though there were ants crawling all over me. I put my paw on the edge of the ring and immediately saw flashes of human things bloody and dying. Their screams pierced my brain like a stream of bullets, causing pain and fear. I yowled and jumped away, shaking my head until the image cleared, and moved to a safe distance around the space. The earth told me this place was very wrong. It begged me to fix it, but I couldn't fathom how. My cat brain recognized it as broken, but in the back of my mind, I could feel the world *evil.*

A light flicked on, and a man sat in the middle of the circle, a glowing tube in his hand. His hair was dark, face hidden in shadows, but he smelled familiar. He got to his feet, approached the edge of the circle, then stopped when I bounced farther away. He leaned against one of the giant stones, then slowly sat beside it, just outside the ring.

"Didn't take you long at all to find this. We all had bets going. Some said you'd never find it. I knew you would. You're a lot like your father was, Seiran Rou. Such untarnished power. The Dominion is clueless about what power truly is. There aren't five levels of power. There are hundreds. And you are at the very top." He stretched. "It calls to you, doesn't it? Begs for help. The earth is a very vocal element."

I watched the man, wondering how he knew my name, but since he wasn't moving closer, I let him go on. I knew he wasn't my earthman, but he was similar to him somehow.

"Won't you change and speak to me?" He pulled off his coat, tossing it away from him. "For your modesty, perhaps?"

Changing would make me vulnerable. No paws to run on, claws to fight with, or teeth to defend my life. Yet something about him drew me forward. He knew my father. My stunted little brain said that was important. I needed to know. The shift took only a few seconds, and then I pulled the jacket around me, keeping far enough away that I would hopefully have time to change back and run if needed.

The fog cleared away quickly enough. "Max?"

He smiled. "So much like your father. He'd completely forget who he was in his cat form. It's harder to keep the human side of yourself when your power is so high. Tell me, Seiran, do you recognize the ring now?"

My heart skipped a beat while I processed it again, this time as a human and as a witch. A faerie ring. That was the only possible explanation. All the studying I did in college meant nothing in that moment. This very item was supposed to be something of myth. Yet the power pulsed so hard it made my skin crawl in not a good way.

"I can tell from your expression you know what it is."

"It's evil," I told him. The images of death still lingered inside my head, tainting something in me I hadn't known was still pure. I felt like I had taken part in the rituals, killed people, fed on their power. Even at this distance, the pulse of energy made my skin crawl. Darkness. If darkness could have life and movement, this was it. And it wanted to devour everything, including me.

"True. It wasn't always so. Faeries, like humans, are a mixture of good and evil. Creatures of conscience. Though they are more aligned with the earth than most humans could ever hope to be. The ring has been corrupted by those who've used it to gain power."

"Including yourself." He had been sitting in the middle of the awful thing. How could he not feel the ichor clinging to every piece of his being?

"I suppose." He shrugged. "When you're as old as I am, you'll do a lot to feel anything. Love, anger, pain, pleasure, it's all a balance that humans experience so easily. Time, however, wears away the emotions of any creature, dulls us to the very things that once made us feel. This circle has been misused, but the memories make me alive again. It is a nice change from the numbness that has taken over my life."

"Did you lead me here?" I thought briefly of the little ladybug that had been following me around since I'd arrived in California. Was it magic?

"No. The power led you here. Just as it did your father so many years ago. It wants to be used."

That was not happening. I didn't really want to know, but had to ask, "Did he do bad things here?"

"No. Dorien was incorruptible. Which I suppose is why he died in the end. Just like your grandfather Ruffman did."

John Ruffman, leader of the first male revolt against the Dominion, was my grandfather? He created the organization now called the Ascendance. The group of male witches had given me nothing but trouble. First with Brock, then with Andrew Roman. They thought men should have power among the witches, which I supported, only they wanted a man they could control. A puppet. And that was something I'd never be. Not for them and not for the Dominion.

"Ruffman was very close to becoming the GreenMan, Father Earth. The Dominion killed him before he could complete the bond. Your father never aspired that high, but had the power to do it too. *You* have the power to become husband to the earth, living persona of virility and power."

"Not interested."

Max sighed. "This new generation has no ambition."

"I have ambition. I just don't want to hurt people." Which was what anyone involved in the Ascendance seemed to do. "The Ascendance uses this circle." It all made sense now. The reason so many powerful males were popping up now was not because they were born more powerful than their predecessors, but because they used evil magic to boost their abilities. Just like Brock had when he'd killed people to steal their power. How many had died in this very spot? Was the man found in the caretaker's house part of this? A sacrifice, perhaps?

"I see that you understand. The Ascendance was not always as it is now. There are very few males born with power. Not enough to make any sort of movement against a governing body as large as the Dominion. After Ruffman's death, the few remaining members began recruiting. They used their magic to boost the power of the little ones. Corrupt only make for more corrupt."

"What does that say about you?"

"I am not a witch. I am a vampire. I am one of the Ascendance supporters, leaders in fact, if you go just by the amount of money I provide them."

"So you are helping them kill people."

He shrugged again. "It used to mean something to me. I see it means a lot to you. You can change it. You have the power to take control and make it right."

"They want me dead, don't they?" Timothy had warned me that others wanted my power.

They wanted me, and not as a leader of the Ascendance, but as a sacrifice to make more powerful male witches.

He nodded. "Does that frighten you?"

I sighed. Yes, but it didn't really surprise me. "What do *you* want from me?" He could probably move faster than I could shift, and even if I hadn't, he could have easily caught me in lynx form and hurt me to begin with. This man had power seeping from him almost equivalent to a level-five witch. Max could be strong enough to take over the Tri-Mega. The idea made me shiver.

"Destroy the evil and make the Ascendance what it should be. Protect and nurture the young men who have power."

Sounded noble enough, but he was part of the Ascendance. Why hadn't he fixed it already? "The Dominion is accepting males now. I have no need for the Ascendance."

"They are accepting powerful males. What about the little ones who don't have much power? Girls with little power are accepted, treated like princesses, given every opportunity in life. But boys?" He shook his head. "I don't believe you will toss them aside so easily." He rose to his feet but didn't approach me.

"Why do you want to help?"

He appeared thoughtful for a moment. "Your grandfather was a close friend."

"Yet you allowed his creation to become corrupt. You helped them."

He shrugged faintly. "I suppose. Revenge is a powerful thing and a stupid thing. Not only did I fail to get revenge for his unjustified death, but I also failed to keep his dreams alive."

His words sounded genuine, grief-filled, but this vampire had had a long time to study how humans reacted.

My head said, "Be wary," but my heart wanted to believe him. Stupid conflicting emotions.

"The power of the ring is capped. Each time they use it, the earth reabsorbs a lot of the power they seek to distribute. The tree in your house does that. That's why the Ascendance wants control of the house."

"Charles Merth was in the Ascendance—why didn't he just give them the house?" I was pretty sure that's why this ring still existed on his property unchallenged.

"He loved Dorien. I think he believed as long as he kept the house teeming with earth, that Dorien would forgive him for continuing to allow the Ascendance to use other witches."

My heart hurt from the idea of it, but in a twisted way it made sense. The house was the balance that kept the ring's power from overwhelming the area. Hell, maybe even the entire country. That tree pulsing with life in the foyer of my father's home absorbed the wild magic and kept everyone safe even while just a short walk away was the most evil thing I'd never hoped to experience.

"The Merth land sits on the intersection of the two largest ley lines in the country. The power here could be limitless. Charles was nowhere near powerful enough to control it. He feared it. Dorien could control it, and he was the last until you who could. The Ascendance wants it, but releasing the power—by killing the tree and therefore the balance—would cause a catastrophe like the world has never known."

"But it feels so peaceful in the house."

Max shrugged. "Centuries of wards and powerful earth witches, I suppose."

So it would be up to me to maintain that peace. If I let go of the house, someone could abuse that power, let the evil out. Damn.

"It's best if you don't return here. The gate is warded to protect the property from intruders. Mostly other witches. We'll talk again, Seiran Rou. I look forward to it." Max vanished, like *poof* and he was gone. I blinked a few times, wondering how that was possible. Gabe never did anything like that. He didn't have that kind of power rolling off him either.

I shifted back to cat form and ran back to the house as if the devil were chasing me.

Chapter 8

THE HORRIFIC feeling of that ring lingered, making my fur twitch the entire way to the house. Up the stairs and through the tiny opening in the door I ran, not stopping until I was inside and had shut the door with a heavy body slam.

My fur tingled and twitched, feeling heavy, almost like it was covered in blood and evil residue, pulsing from that nasty ring. I stumbled up toward my room, thinking maybe I'd jump in the shower to clean it off before shifting back. Jamie passed me in the hall. I'd almost forgotten he was here. "Back now?"

I ignored him and bolted into my room. The taint of the ring stretched around me like a vise. What an awful feeling, like a barrier between me and the earth of something heavy and with a tar consistency. Thankfully I'd left my door open, and the bathroom as well. I leapt into the shower, wondering how I'd turn the water on with my paws.

The light flicked on and Gabe stood in the doorway. My heart skipped a beat. Something was wrong about him being there, but I couldn't remember why. I was too panicked from the darkness I could feel nibbling away at my power. I curled into the wall as he approached the shower. The evil had to go before I touched anyone. It was ready to leech onto the next person and drain them of all happiness.

Gabe turned on the water, letting it fall in a warm rush around me. I shuddered in the cleansing warmth, begging the earth, the tree that had taken over the house, anything to clear away the evil. The shaking didn't stop, even when the water ran over my skin in a scalding rush. I couldn't stop the tremble. The energy of the house began to pick away at the darkness that clung to me, slowly eating away at it, until the grip finally loosened and the water began to run cold. Gabe stood nearby, still like he rarely was, waiting, it seemed. Normally he'd have joined me in the shower, especially when I trembled as bad as I was. Maybe he was still mad. What if he was just waiting around to tell me it was over when all I really wanted was to work things out between us?

He wrapped a fluffy towel around me, then picked me up and carried me back to the bedroom, cradling me much like he would a scared child. It was the most normal thing he'd done in months. And still it felt wrong. He curled around me, pulled the blankets up to cover us, and held me. I should have been calmed by his presence, welcomed his heat and comfort, but it was like being held by a stranger.

I shook in his arms for a while, silently going through rituals to ease my mind, counting backward, reciting capitals and recipes. This was the first time in a couple of weeks that the panic attack had really been bad. Justified, maybe, but still bad. The light from the bathroom comforted me a little. Gabe softly hummed a tune I didn't recognize—he'd never been particularly musical—fingers combing through my fur in small patterns. It wasn't until that moment that I realized I hadn't changed and had no desire to. The world was too much for my human mind.

Gabe didn't ask me to change back. His touch soothed some of the worst trembles, but my heart still hurt. I wondered where Sam was and how soon it would before he'd pop back in to interrupt my life again.

I shut my eyes, pressing back the tears, the oncoming rejection. Loving someone had never been easy. Somehow I'd hoped that with Gabe it would be just like breathing, since that's how his touch felt most days, like a breeze tickling my skin. The pain in my head spread to my heart. I loved him too much to let go. Why did he let this happen if he was only going to leave? I opened myself to him, willing him to feel me, comfort me. Love me. But my brain kept reminding me he'd left.

You left me, don't you still love me? Tell me how to fix this. His voice in my head was filled with hurt and worry. Jealousy was such a vicious animal. It grew and raged, getting louder and larger until all you could hear was the screaming that ate away at your reasoning. I didn't know how to answer him. Why did he feel so far away?

His lips pressed against my forehead, scratching my ears just so nicely. If I weren't so shaken up from the faerie ring, I might have jumped him right there. Gabe leaned over and flicked the light on beside the bed. I shook out my fur and the chill in the air ran over me, followed by a bit of sadness. Gabe wouldn't be able to stay. We had no curtains yet. This house was like a death trap for vampires. Plus, he'd gone silent in my head again, expression neutral, almost unfamiliar, while I searched for his voice. The silence was more than a little unnerving. He never invaded my mind much when I was in cat form, but I figured he'd feel less distant since he was in the same room with me; only he didn't.

"I found something while you were out. Want to see?" Gabe went to the closet that was filled with my things, shoved the clothes aside, and pressed on the wall in the back. The wall opened, revealing some sort of passage. "It's pretty narrow."

I snuck up close to him and peered inside, looking with my sharp cat eyes but only seeing a tunnel of darkness. Did my father know this was here? Where did it lead to? Stepping inside, the first thing I noticed was that it was clean. Unlike the rest of the house, there seemed to be nothing but the barest of traces of dust. How odd.

"Do you want a light? I can probably find a flashlight." He saw just fine without it, and after my eyes adjusted, I'd be able to as well. Gabe followed me inside. He had to squeeze and duck through some areas. The inner walls were covered with vines like out of some Armageddon movie. They were comforting, a reminder that the earth had control of this house. I could see their pulsing connection to the house and the tree below. Not vines, then. Branches. Amazing.

The cracks in the walls from past settling or maybe even earthquakes seemed to be held together with long, winding green-and-brown limbs. It fascinated me enough that I had to shift back to human. It only took a moment for my eyes to adjust, and though I couldn't see as clearly, I could still see the faint outlines of the walls. They glowed with power. The cold air hit my still-damp skin, forcing me to shiver. Gabe pulled off his shirt and handed it to me. The quickly fading warmth of it reminded me he'd need grave dirt to stay comfortable. Had he brought some? A warm vampire was so much better than a cold one.

I opened the link to him wider inside my head, expecting to feel him at my back, but again it was like he was distant. He wasn't completely closed to me, but he was definitely more reserved like he often was lately. Hesitant maybe to show me all that was in his head. Which, of course, made me worry. Why was he acting normal—like nothing was wrong—when he was obviously so angry?

The tunnel led around, down, and back toward the front of the house. At the end, was a door. Gabe insisted on going first, though I don't know what he expected to be on the other side. Maybe some giant people-eating plant or a deformed relative who'd been locked away, but it was just a room. He flicked on a lamp to reveal more of the odd space.

Like the hall, this room was clean, cluttered, but mostly free of dust. A cot sat off to the side, made up like a bed with blankets and pillows. A laptop computer sat on the desk, closed but plugged in. The walls were lined with books and odd statues. The room curved, shaped sort of like a large slice of a pie. It was then I realized it had to be above the sitting room, near the tree and the staircase. None of the other rooms accounted for that space.

Gabe was already searching through the many books, which surprised me as he was more computer savvy than I. I went to the desk, sat down, and opened the computer. It powered on, not password protected, and came up with a user ID for Charles. So this is where he'd hidden himself away. I wondered if Timothy knew about this space. I already had a lot to speak to him about. There were family secrets I was sure he knew and hadn't shared with me. Things that could be more than a little dangerous to everyone. Like a certain faerie ring.

The computer didn't have much that appeared to be important. Just some information on the house, plumbers and things, nothing that sat on the desktop that said *Ascendance* or *evil faerie ring of power*. Had my uncle been part of the good group or the bad one? Did he know about the circle?

"There are journals here, Seiran. Your dad's and Charles Merth's." Gabe had one in hand and carefully flipped through it. "Only a couple from your dad, and they are in rough shape, but you can still read the writing." He glanced up, looking me over; for what I don't know. Maybe he thought I was going to break down just hearing about my dad.

I peered over the crook of his arm at the pages of the book, seeing my father's writing, which looked just as meticulous as my own. Instead of recipes, he wrote spells, everything from how to do it to how it made him feel, and the results based on the power level of the witch performing the spell. Other pages were just random bits of life, about school, secret meetings with fellow witches, and whispers of hopes for the future. These were the words of a very young Dorien Merth. Before Jamie had been born, before he'd ever met my mother.

I wanted to read every page. Learn every last thought and emotion he had. And I prayed the entire time that somewhere I'd find a mention of myself. An opinion, even in passing, of the child he'd never get to see. A sentiment of love. I blinked back tears.

"Charles has more than fifty of them. A couple per year. Maybe his son will want them?" Gabe scanned through those as well. Had Gabe met Timothy? I frowned at him but didn't ask. "Not much magic in here. It sounds more like raving toward the end."

Was that something I had to look forward to if I lived a long life? Madness? Or had something made Charles Merth very afraid—for example, a faerie ring used to kill people and spread their power to other witches?

"I want to read them all," I whispered, my voice still a little rough from the shift. "Even my uncle's. I want to know my family." I stared at Gabe, trying to read him and think through the swirl of confusing thoughts in my head. It was odd, but being this close to him made my skin itch. Not with the need to touch him, but the need to get away. What the hell was wrong with us? Maybe I wasn't ready to see him yet.

I grabbed the stack of my dad's journals. "I'm sorry. I need some time."

Gabe nodded, his face somber but curious, an unusual expression for him. Another oddity. He was usually okay giving me space, but he always prefaced my retreat with a reminder that he was around if I needed him.

Why wasn't he saying anything? Was he still mad? Why didn't he rave or say sweet things? Anything? Sure, I was still hurt. Still trying to sort out the awful things he hadn't meant to say but had, and my feelings gurgled inside me like a pot of bad all swirled with grim. Something seemed off about him, too, though what, I wasn't quite sure.

"Take your time. You don't have to read them all in one night. I'm going to read through some right now."

That's all we had now, wasn't it? Time. I stared at him a moment longer, confused, then fled through the tunnel back toward my room, pondering Gabe and the words Max had spoken to me. The old have a hard time feeling anything, he had said, so sometimes they created trouble just to feel something. That sounded so crazy. Yet I knew when a cuddle was all I needed to make the world right. Those times, and the times I just wanted to run from the pain, those were moments when the numbness faded. What if I was always numb? What length would I go to just to feel? Without thinking much, the answer was a lot.

Feeling somewhat uncomfortable in the room with the tunnel in it, I dressed, then headed down the hall to Jamie's room. He wasn't there. Had he gone out? Why hadn't he said anything to me? Gabe hadn't followed me out of the tunnel. Was he really going to read when we were still fighting?

Argh! This was all such a mess.

My phone beeped with a new text. Oddly enough, it was from Sam.

Can we talk?

I blinked at it a few times, feeling weirdly mixed about what to do. Talk was the last thing I wanted to do with Sam. Punch him in the face, definitely. Talk, not so much. Maybe we could hash out whatever made me hate him. Or maybe we'd just yell at each other a bit. It had to be better than the silence.

I sent back, *Where?*

He sent me a link to a map to a park that was in walking distance. Was he staying nearby? I loaded up the journals into a backpack I'd found and headed through the night. The air was a little cooler, but still so much better than the cold Minnesota weather I had left behind. There was life here, even if I was still struggling to sort my own out.

Chapter 9

The park was a typical expanse of grass and trees, a playground to one end, benches on the other. It smelled unused, like earth, soil, and pollen, heaven to my nose. It was probably too cold for the natives to use it much this time of year.

Sam sat on one of the benches farthest away from the road. His back to the trees, he gazed out at the street beyond. He looked a little more human than he had a few days ago, but he still stared off into the distance.

I crossed the park, more than a little uncomfortable with such a secluded setting. Was he trying to get me alone so he could kill me without Gabe knowing? No, Gabe would never forgive him, and the world would know I died when the earth rebelled at my loss.

I paused for a minute to reanalyze the setting and calm my thoughts. We were surrounded by earth and no people. He must have gone out of his way to pick something comfortable for me and remote enough for him. The smell of blood made him hungry no matter how much he ate. Gabe told me it was normal, and that Sam would grow used to it. It sounded dangerous to me. I guess here we could both be comfortable.

"Hey," I whispered, afraid of startling him.

He threw me a tight, forced smile. "Sorry, was just thinking. You look okay."

"Yeah. I'm okay. How are you doing?" And boy, wasn't that a loaded question that I really didn't want to know the answer to. I sat on the opposite side of the table from him.

He sighed. "Seiran, you don't have to be nice to me. I know you don't like me, and that's fine. Unlike the rest of the world, I don't need your divine opinion to exist. I just don't like seeing Gabe so torn."

Ouch. Torn. What a word. Would Gabe pick Sam over me? Was that why he wasn't talking to me? I swallowed hard, wondering if I'd survive him saying it was over. Probably not. Plus, we were sort of bound now. With magic. It wasn't something that could be severed. Even if Gabe were to want to.

My eyes betrayed me by tearing up, forcing me to look away from Sam and into the dark shadows of the tree line. "I don't dislike you." The words came out somewhat broken. I didn't exactly like him either. What the hell did he mean, divine opinion? Since when did anyone value my opinion on anything?

Sam touched my hand and the power of earth flared up within me, almost bringing on my change to lynx. I had to yank my hand away from his touch. Shit, that had been unexpected, but he was nodding. The residue of his power remained a stain on my flesh, stinging a little, like an electrical shock.

"This is my curse, Seiran. No one else can mentor me because I will fuck with their power. Gabe is all I have. If he abandons me, the Tri-Mega will kill me. The Dominion already wants to. Who knows what the Ascendance wants. It's National Fuck Up Sam Year. Didn't you know?"

"My year too." Something else we had to share. The Ascendance would love Sam. He could probably make more powerful witches without killing anyone. It was a really bad idea for him to be around them. He'd made Kelly the Pillar of water and turned Jamie into a level-four witch, all without trying. I couldn't imagine what he might do to my power. Sure, he'd sort of been under a curse, but breaking it hadn't changed anyone back to normal, and Sam's power was still pretty wild.

"Look. You know there's nothing between Gabe and me, right?" He looked me over. "I mean, even without the hair, you're breathtaking. You're short and too pretty, but you have a great body. You're smarter than most guys I know and have crazy power. I'm just Sam. I get it. I don't know why you don't."

I narrowed my eyes at him and his half insult, half compliment. "Gabe is spending all his time with you." I probably sounded like a grade-schooler complaining, but Gabe had been hard-won for me, even if I had been battling my own emotions.

"Not really. He's always working, trying to make the bar more efficient so he can take more time off. He's been trying to convince Mike to take a manager role for ages. Every time he clears something up, the Tri-Mega throws him more work. Then he takes shifts when you're working, just so he can watch you. And good God, he can't keep his eyes off you. I'm surprised you don't feel him fucking you with his eyes." He waved his hand in the air like he was dispersing a bad smell. "These super senses really suck, telling me when people are turned on, angry, or whatever. I hate always knowing. It makes me afraid of how people are affected by me. Sometimes it all mixes in my head and I don't know if I'm feeling whatever, or if it's someone else."

My brain moved like molasses to process all he said. Gabe watched me when I worked? Like a lover and not like a boss? And he wanted Mike to be manager? I'd wondered why he had been picking up so many hours. I also had no idea the Tri-Mega had been giving him assignments. Was that normal? Shit, I so didn't know enough about vampires.

Sam's last words made me study him again. "But you still feel things, your own things, not just other people's things?"

"Uh, yeah. Like mad, sad, happy, whatever, yeah. The more pissed you get, the more I feel it and get angry in return. It's a nasty cycle. Why?"

'Cause apparently that's something vampires lose over time. Sam could feel my jealousy and anger, but that didn't stop him

from pissing me off. "So you're not attracted to Gabe?"

He looked uncomfortable, then wouldn't meet my eyes. Damn. The jealousy roared to life in me again, rising up like a monster of the deep. I wanted to break Sam's nose, maybe a limb or two. Instead, I gripped the table to keep from lunging at him.

He sighed. "I know I don't have a chance, so why are you worried?"

Because Gabe was off lately. He was pulling away and spending time with Sam. I was floundering myself. The world was changing around me, expecting me to be a grown-up, and I wasn't ready. Would I ever be? *Dammit.*

"Let's get this over with," he said after a moment of silence stretched between us.

"Huh?"

"You can create a protection bubble, right?" he asked. "I've been doing a lot of reading on magic to try to control this power I have. Shields and protection spells was the first book Jamie found for me. You can create one, right?"

I snorted. "Of course." That was a Spell Casting 101 basic. The protection bubble kept magic from leaking out and harming others while in heavy use, but couldn't stop major damage like earthquakes or floods. They also couldn't be used anyplace that water disrupted the flow. So moving water or rain was a no-no. Thankfully this little park appeared to be dry.

Sam motioned to the open area between the benches and the tree line. "Let's do it, then."

It took me about half a second to realize he meant he was going to fight me. Of course, he said he felt my emotions. My anger made him mad too. I sighed and took a step into the clearing. He didn't wait for me. Sam leapt, picking me up like a doll and tossing me away from the table. I used the training Kelly had been giving me and turned the fall into a roll, but it still knocked the wind out of me. Sam landed on me just as I was stopping. "Create the bubble and let's play. I promise not to kill you." His knee dug into my back. "I'm tired of everyone thinking you're better than me. I'm sick of knowing you're always an inch away from attacking me. Now is your chance. Do it!"

The lunge of his fangs toward my neck had me up and moving. No one got to drink from me but Gabe. That he would dare made me want to break his nose.

I cast the spell with little thought—felt the barrier form around us like a giant soap bubble —giving us enough space to move while I kicked him in the back of the head with my heel. He paused long enough to blink and likely register the pain, but didn't stop, so I awkwardly slammed the palm of my hand into one ear. He howled and rolled away, shaking his head. There was no blood, so his eardrum was probably still intact, but if he got that close again, I'd be sure to cause more damage.

I jumped to my feet, letting myself flex and prepare for the fight. The few weeks sparring and training with Kelly had given me some defense knowledge, but I knew if it came down to hand-to-hand combat, I'd lose.

Sam moved back until he hit the wall of the spell that trapped us in together and protected the rest of the world from our battle. "Good space," he said, then launched himself at me again, speed blinding, but not as fast as Gabe. Gabe could just suddenly appear someplace, and while it wasn't the same poof and gone as I'd experienced with Max, it was almost like magic.

I dodged left, throwing myself out of the way of a flying fist. "What's the point of this, Sam? I beat you up, you beat me up. Who really wins?" That had always been the reason I never started it. No matter how much I wanted to choke him sometimes, nothing would change. But the way he moved meant he took it seriously. He promised not to kill me, but sometimes things happened in a fight. Accidents. Would he kill me? For some reason I didn't think so, and I had no intention of killing him, but he could probably hurt me pretty bad. Kelly could hurt me in the ring. Jamie refused to even spar with me, but I'd nursed a lot of bruises. Could we really work out our differences with our fists? The idea of beating the shit out of him appealed to me.

"Fight back, damn you!" He flew across the grass at me.

I put my hands to the earth, and in a half second, a dirt wall flew up between us. He slammed into it, bounced off, fell backward, but was up and moved around it too fast for me to counter. His fist smashed my face before I could react, snapping my head back, and I toppled to the ground. The pain radiated through my jaw and all the way up through my ears. I shook away stars. Since he was already coming at me again, I didn't have time to be dazed. I pretended to be more hurt, lying in wait, and when he lunged at me, I kicked upward with both feet, crashing into his torso and throwing him backward. He landed with a grunt but didn't stay down long. He jumped up in a rolling hinge like a ninja on an assassination mission to save his country, flipping back upright, shaking off his fall, and running my way again.

He was good. And he was so going to kick my ass. He fought as though he'd been doing it for years, and he probably had. I had used my appearance to keep me out of fights, or used my magic. Magic I had in abundance. But the Dominion didn't exactly have a magic battle tactics class. The ground could give me strength, but it couldn't give me skill. I staggered to my feet, feeling the warm trickle of blood on my face.

He circled, waiting, for what, I didn't want to know. I pulled strength from the earth, let it pour the power into me to make a shield of invisible magic. Before becoming Pillar, I would have never had this kind of control. Now it was as easy as breathing. When Sam struck, the force of the shield rebounded back at him, slashing through him like a lightning bolt.

He trembled with the force of the magic, falling to his knees and sucking in heavy gulps of air, though technically as a vampire, he didn't need to breathe. His hair stood on end, and his skin glowed with a pulse of energy I didn't recognize. A sick feeling hit my gut when I realized that I'd pretty much just supercharged him and he was only staggered by the weight of the power. Shit.

Note to self, don't feed your opponent power.

I released some of the energy back to the earth and sought within the recesses of the soil for strong and willing roots. They writhed, breaking free, jutting from the ground like zombies waking from too long a slumber, and snapped at him. The limbs were thick and grabbing, a dark octopus rising from the ground searching for a meal to nourish the earth.

Several roots grabbed his legs. He took the roots in both hands and ripped them apart, yanking a length of them out of the ground and throwing them at me.

That stung. The earth admonished me with a pulse of pain for being so reckless before raising thicker brown limbs to the surface. Sam fought with them for a few minutes, and the earth even gained a little ground, tugging him a couple of inches into the loose soil. But Sam put his hands to the ground and forced it to a rolling shake beneath me. I struggled to keep my footing. He shouldn't have had the ability to create an earthquake. Not even with my power. Not while the bubble of protection surrounded us.

But the earth wasn't really shaking. Life was dragging itself from the ground. Slowly at first like a corpse dragging itself out of a grave, then with a snap of righteous anger when Sam finally pulled free.

Another root popped up and wrapped around my waist, dragging me toward him and the burbling mass of softened earth. Even with the shield spell, the earth would take back what belonged to it. I squirmed in the grip of the plant, trying to redirect it, frustrated that he was borrowing my power and there wasn't a damn thing I could do about it. I was so not trained to fight other witches. If we survived this, I was going to have to speak to my mother about the lack of training in defensive magic offered in the college programs.

I touched the root, forcing it to curl away, and instead it writhed, shifted, and became a growing sapling, immobile. The others coming at me met the same fate. Changed from root to stalk as easy as breathing. Sometimes I forgot how simple it all was when I just used the power the earth gave me.

And while a forest of new saplings rose up around us, Sam didn't stop. He wove around the trees as though some sort of superhero in a comic book, zig-zagging like he'd taken flight. Vampires couldn't fly. Some could levitate. Gabe could. But I wasn't sure if Sam was or if he was just moving that fast. When he got to my side, we both moved in unison, fists flying—me thrusting the earth into my punch, and him with all his vampire strength and my borrowed power.

The world exploded around us. I felt the bubble pop and the trees in the immediate area flatten as pain coursed through me. I landed on the hard ground, wind knocked from me, every cell in my body spinning with energy and pain. I think I lost consciousness for a few seconds, then blinked my way back to the surface of myself. I hurt, but the earth pulsed energy through me to heal, repairing busted veins, broken bones, and a bruised ego. Something about being in California brought me closer to the earth, gave me more power, or maybe that was just Sam again. His power was fucked up with a capital F. Oddly enough, he seemed to have better control of his power than I had of mine. That wasn't a good thing, was it?

Where was Sam? Was he still moving? Had I lost? I struggled to sit up, finding it hard to breathe even as the pain began to recede.

Sam lay about twenty yards away. He moved slowly, hand to his chest, and shook his head from side to side. The sound of his wheezing and cursing reached me and made me laugh a bitter sound. Wow, we'd really beaten the shit out of each other. And what had we gained?

Did I feel any different? More sure of myself or my relationship with Gabe? No. And I sort of felt bad for messing Sam up. He'd been through a lot and was just trying to find his own way. He might want my boyfriend, but Gabe was bound to me. Even when he was mad at me.

I touched the blood that still trickled from my skull, surprised at the warmth of it. Sam was worse off than me. He had fluid in his lungs, I could smell it. It wouldn't kill him, but it probably hurt pretty bad. I limped to his side. He flinched, but I put a hand to him and to the earth, pouring the healing into both of us. The shock on his face told me he hadn't expected my help. But healing him was super easy since he sort of ate my power most of the time anyway.

"Are you done now?" I asked him. The power I'd been playing with had taken its toll, making me really tired. Even I could handle only so much of the earth at once. The area around us wasn't horribly damaged. It looked like there had been a bad rainstorm with straight-line winds. It could have been worse when the protection bubble broke. We could have leveled cities. This was so stupid.

"You are both done," a voice said from closer to the street. Gabe crouched beside a nearby tree. How long had he been there? He didn't look angry, but he didn't look happy either. He'd changed clothes since I saw him last, now wearing jeans and a T-shirt. When he approached us, I felt him nudge our link and opened for him. This time he was right there:

present, touchable, real. His worry flooded me. "Were you trying to kill each other?"

I flushed, feeling a bit foolish even though I hadn't started the fight. Sam looked away from both of us.

"Come on. Let's get you both bandaged up." Gabe pulled us with him and then dragged us away from the park and toward their hotel, probably. Neither Sam nor I protested. We followed along quietly. Sam limped but no longer wheezed. I couldn't look at either of them. Had I really used my Pillar power to try to mess up a vampire I was jealous of? How stupid was that? I could have hurt Sam just because I was pissed off. I could have really fucked up the planet without trying. *Shit.*

Chapter 10

THE HOTEL was pretty plain, but the windows had coverings specific for vampires. Their room had two beds, one unmade, the other done up military style like Gabe always did. He shoved me to his bed and dropped Sam to the other before disappearing into the bathroom. The water ran for a moment, and then he returned with a first-aid kit and a couple of damp towels.

"That was really stupid. What were you thinking?" He handed a towel to Sam, who wiped off his dirty face. He'd already healed and the blood had begun to dry. Gabe dabbed at the cut on my forehead; apparently it still bled, because it made him frown. It stung a little, but the embarrassment that we had been fighting over him mattered more.

"Seriously?" Gabe asked. He must have finally caught that thought. He glanced at Sam. "Fighting over me?"

"Not just you," Sam protested. "I'm just tired of everyone always thinking Seiran is better than me. Pillar, earth witch, whatever. He's always pissed at me. I thought it would be better to let him get it out of his system."

"Right, because it was all Seiran's fault." Gabe threw sarcasm at Sam. Sam flinched. "Seiran defaults to flight, not fight."

Did Sam think I wanted all this? To be Pillar, to be singled out? To have people want me dead for just existing? I sighed. I wasn't trying to be angry. Really, I wasn't. I knew I was acting like a little kid whose favorite toy had been taken away, but after finally giving myself to Gabe, I didn't want to share him. Not with anyone.

Gabe sighed and said quietly, "There's no one but you. I don't know why you doubt me. I don't deserve that. You know I don't deserve that."

And he didn't. But we both knew I had always been wrong in the head. Whether I was programmed wrong or just different in general, I was needy. And I needed Gabe like I needed air.

He pulled a bottle of some type of glue bandage out of the kit and squeezed the wound together while painting it on. I tried not to move, though it hurt. "Sei?"

He wanted me to admit the truth. But truths were hard. They hurt and sometimes lead to more painful truths. "He started it," I protested weakly. He'd come at me. I wasn't ready to apologize yet.

"And you could have put him in a binding spell and ended it immediately. I know Jamie has been teaching you and Kelly defensive spells. Sam's not a witch. He can't counter your spells, even if he borrows your power. All he can do is enhance and redirect ones others create. You've had years of studying magic. He's had less than a month."

True. I hadn't even thought of a binding spell. I guess I really had wanted the fight. The sad thing was, it hadn't solved anything.

"What is there to solve?" Gabe sounded exasperated. "You fly out here without telling anyone, slam the door in my face, and then decide you need to beat the crap out of Sam. Please tell me what this is doing for you?"

"I came here because I wanted to learn about my dad." *And to get away from the growing gap between us.*

"And you couldn't have said, 'Gabe, let's go to California so I can learn about my dad?' A relationship isn't just about great sex and saying you love someone, Sei. It's about compromise, talking to the other person, and trust. You can love someone and still not have a relationship work out."

"Like you're one to talk! You never tell me anything. I had no idea you were taking on work for the Tri-Mega. And now there's apparently some spooky vampire they are trying to warn you about. And maybe if I knew more about what you need to do to train Sam, I wouldn't be so jealous of all the time you spend with him."

Gabe threw a glare at Sam at the Tri-Mega comment. Probably something he didn't want me to know, which just meant I really *did* need to know. "I don't tell you things that can hurt you, Seiran. You have enough trouble in your life—I know I don't need to burden you with mine."

"You just said a relationship is about compromise and talking to each other. What do you think that means? I don't want your crap any more than you want mine, but I'm here to help you deal with it, whether you like it or not. So stop being an ass and share already. I love you even if you think I'm not strong enough. I'm not weak. You won't break me. You just have to love me and not push me away." I was angry, but tears ran down my face. The truth was that he *was* breaking me, by pulling away. It was killing me slowly.

His expression was shocked, but I didn't try to block him from my thoughts. I totally expected him to throw me out or rage at me again. "I don't think you're weak," he said softly. "You're one of the strongest people I know. And you know I love you. I'm crazy about you. Even when you make me crazy with worry when you leave the state without telling anyone and going to what could be hostile vampire territory."

He hugged me tight for a minute, lips brushing over my hair, chin resting on my head. "You need to talk to me, Sei. Don't let anyone, not even me, kill you slowly." He sucked in a pained breath. "I never mean to hurt you. But I'm always fearful for you."

I'd forgotten about the whole vampires-had-territory thing. Hadn't even thought for a minute that there might be another vampire here who was unhappy with the focus of another master just showing up. Maybe that's why Max had shown up on my doorstep. Was he the master of this area? Maybe looking for Gabe?

"I was stupid to just up and come here. I know that." My cheeks felt hot. The moment that had driven me to go seemed unimportant now. It had been the pride Gabe felt toward Sam. I wanted him to be proud of me, love me, and not some cast-off of my ex-boyfriend. "You were proud of him. I felt it through the bond. I was jealous, and so I made a bad decision. We all fuck up, even you, Gabe."

Gabe released me so he could blot away the rest of the blood from my forehead. He spoke quietly. "I am proud of him. He's learning fast, working hard to hold back the hunger and only take what he needs. The first few months are horrible for a new vampire. More than half have to be put down because they can't handle it." He put away the kit and glared at both of us. We were covered in dirt. "The faster he learns, the faster he can live without constant supervision. I'm not doing this for me, Sei."

He sat back on the bed next to me and swept his fingers through his hair. "Yes. I fuck up too. I will try to share more. It's just hard. Been alone a long time."

"But you need me to be there for you, and I can't do that if you hide the scary stuff from me. I'm your focus, which can't be undone. So when you don't use me as your focus, you're shortchanging your own power, right?" I looked at him, but he wouldn't meet my gaze. "Why do you have to face it alone?" I stared at him, feeling foolish and tired, but no way could I sleep alone tonight. Whatever stupid things we did to each other, I still loved him, and he loved me. I felt it through the bond. He needed me more than anything. He was floundering too, and I didn't really understand how or why, but he needed me to ground him and I needed him too. "All things worth fighting for take work, right? I'm willing to work on this, on *us*, if you are. Just don't give up on me. I'm not a thousand something. I haven't been through all this before. So forgive me for sometimes being young and stupid."

He nodded, grinned, and shook his head a minute, then palmed the back of my neck and pulled me in for a kiss. His lips on mine were sweet water after a drought to my parched earth. "I'm sorry," he whispered between little kisses and flicks of his tongue.

Sam cleared his throat, got up, and threw his dirty towel into the bathroom. "Do I have to be here for this?"

The comment made me want to punch him again. Gabe kissed my forehead and the emotion suddenly vanished into a calm sea of peace inside my mind. All the adrenaline from the fight rushed out of me, and suddenly I was just tired.

The hotel looked iffy, but if Gabe stayed here, I'd have to try. After cleaning for days, I just didn't have the energy in me to fix the hotel room too. And the fatigue ran deep. A tremor began in my hands—brought on by a pending panic attack and exhaustion. Nausea swirled in my gut like it hadn't in weeks. Had I taken my pills? Yes. Religiously. Jamie had been good at drilling that into me. I'd pushed myself pretty hard but hadn't been eating that well. Still, I had no reason to feel this shaken up. Gabe was touching me. He still wanted me. What did I have to fear?

"Do you have your phone on you?" Gabe asked, holding me, breathing life back into me as though he knew I was on the verge of falling apart.

"Yeah." If it hadn't been broken in the fight. I pulled it out of my pocket. The gorilla glass I'd paid extra for was still intact, and the phone seemed to work.

"Call your brother, please."

I frowned at him. Was something wrong with Jamie? I'd just talked to him a few hours ago. After hitting the speed dial, the phone rang in my ear. Hopefully he wasn't asleep yet.

Jamie picked up on the third ring. "Sei?"

"Yeah, what's up?" I glanced at my watch. Three o'clock in the morning.

"You're okay? Kelly said he got a text, but I've been so busy with Hanna...."

Huh? "What's wrong with Hanna?" Is that why he'd disappeared from the house?

"She was bleeding."

My weary brain took another minute or so to process that. Then it clicked that she was girl bleeding and probably shouldn't be since she was pregnant with our babies. Now the panic was really eating at me. "Are the babies okay? Is Hanna okay?"

"They're all fine. Resting. Hanna is on bed rest for now. It happens sometimes, but we're keeping an eye on her."

My stomach flipped over. "Where are you?"

"At home right now. I left Hanna's after midnight once she was tucked in. Allie said she'd call me if anything went wrong. Kelly's got his phone on too, just in case."

He was at home, like Minnesota home? With Kelly? How was that possible? "When did all this happen? Why didn't anyone tell me?"

"I got the call after we dropped you off with your gifts. Your phone kept going to voice mail, and I'd already left a message. I figured you'd call. Kelly said he got your text but hadn't heard from you since. I didn't want to worry you."

So he'd never left home. The room suddenly seemed to spin. Who had I let into my house? Who had hugged me when I cried? Gabe's arm snaked around my waist. He had my phone now. He spoke to Jamie. I just let the last few days replay in my head, heart pounding like crazy. "Come home with me," I begged Gabe.

"Are you going to let us in this time?"

He'd already been inside. But my heart thumped in a crazy beat while my head replayed those moments. Something had been off about him. That "something" was that it hadn't been him. Oh blessed Mother Earth. Someone was pretending to be Gabe and Jamie; at least, I hoped it was the same person both times. I'd let them in the house, past the wards that had been built up for decades, and hadn't even felt the difference? What was wrong with me?

My world dissolved into black and white stars spinning about my head. The room lost all its air. Gabe was saying something, his arms wrapped around me, but I couldn't understand the words. His voice broke through in my head first. *Sei?*

I grabbed his shirt and pulled him down to me, not for a kiss, but to sniff his hair, which smelled like that awful fake cucumber-mint shampoo he always used. The other Gabe, the one in the bathroom, had smelled like nothing. His touch had made my skin twitch. Oh sweet goddess, I'd let him touch me...

"I invited someone in. Another vampire, I think." I had invited Jamie in. Only it obviously wasn't Jamie. Was there a way to undo it? Who was it? Max? But then why introduce himself to me if he was already pretending to be Jamie? And then at the faerie ring, only to meet me back at the house as Gabe? Who else could it be? Caleb? Timothy? Mr. Odagiri? My heart seemed to be beating too fast for me to catch my breath, and my sight was spotted with black dots.

Gabe and Sam led me out to a rental car. Sam got behind the wheel while Gabe and I sat in the back. I couldn't focus my mind enough to even care where we went. Maybe they would just take me home to Minnesota. We could drive the whole way for all I cared. But what if whoever was in my dad's house destroyed something? Maybe took something that would have led me to more information on my father? I blindly reached for the bag with the journals in it and found it in Gabe's lap. The tremble in my limbs shook me like a seizure. I couldn't breathe.

"Sei, you need to focus on my voice, okay? Your mind is retreating to your cat form. Don't let the panic force the change. We can fix this, but I need you functioning as a human, not a lynx."

"Are there vampires who can change shape?" Sam asked from his seat behind the wheel.

"No. Whoever is doing this is good at illusions. To fool an earth witch of Sei's level, he'd have to be really damn powerful too."

The earth welled up around me, offering comfort and peace, rest. The earth could fix everything, protect me, all I had to do was let it. A sharp pain pierced my arm. I blinked away the stars and looked at Gabe, who'd pinched me really hard. That would bruise.

"Stay with me, Sei." He kissed one cheek, then the other, his lips like soft caresses. My right hand gripped his blond curls so hard it probably hurt, but he didn't pull away or reprimand me. He tried to hold me still, keep the shaking down, but my teeth chattered. I was losing focus again. "Seiran Rou, you will stay with me," he commanded. "Breathe, calm and slow. I'm here."

The fire of our mingled blood kicked at me, telling me to obey. He didn't often use that power. Having become his focus had faded most of the ability. Yet I wanted to give myself over to his control. The tears that blurred my sight and the feelings of helplessness would pass eventually. If I could give him the reins, he would take away the fear, steer me back to a sound mind. "He could have killed me," I whispered.

I'd let a stranger hold me. How easy would it have been for them to kill me? Or even knock me unconscious and drag me back to that awful faerie ring? How many thousands of witches could they create by redistributing my power? What sort of catastrophe awaited the world?

Gabe rocked me and whispered soft words into my hair, his lips dancing across my skin in gentle touches reminding he was real. I was safe with Gabe. He wouldn't let anyone hurt me. The world would be safe because with him I was invincible. Right?

How did I even know this was really Gabe? I sniffed his hair again, sneezing at the heavy cucumber-mint smell. Could an illusion get a smell right?

"We'll have to put up new wards. I can't do that. Even with his power," Sam was saying. "The books all say it's a bond with the home. His ancestors will help his bond, but not mine. I'm not even sure if it would work at all for me since

I'm a vampire. Magic works a little different when you throw death into the mix."

"He can do a total revoke of all invites and recharge the wards pretty easily. I just need to get him calm and focused."

"Jamie could do it." Sam parked the car in front of the house. The lights were on upstairs, though I hadn't left them that way. Was someone still in the house? The gate was closed and locked. Gabe took the key from me since my hands were shaking too hard to steady it.

Was the strange vampire still in the house? Was it even a vampire? Or a witch? A witch could have crossed the portal without an invite, but they'd leave most of their power at the door. Maybe it was a witch so powerful it didn't matter if they left most of their power behind.

"Jamie's not here," I heard myself say. "He hugged me and let me cry, but he's not here. He said things. I really thought he was understanding me finally. That maybe I wasn't such a freak." I clung to Gabe as we headed through the manicured path toward the door. What a dumb idea to come here. Had I gotten complacent these past few weeks? Forgetting about the safety and necessity of wards and how other people always wanted to hurt me was stupid. Just because I'd graduated college didn't mean the attacks would end. This was proof of it. No matter what job I took, they'd still come for me. Pretending to be my family was unforgivable.

"He does understand you. And you're not a freak." Gabe unlocked the front door but didn't try to open it. He stood for a moment, listening. Neither Sam nor I moved. "I don't sense anyone, but I need you to go inside, Sei. Stand in the threshold and revoke the invite. Recharge the wards. Then you can invite us in."

I nodded, raising one shaky foot after another to mount the stairs and shove the door open. My mind kept flashing images of someone waiting on the other side of the door with a gun or some other horror movie image, but no one was there. I flicked on the light and stood in the doorway, tuning myself into the earth. The tree welcomed me home, told me the house was empty, and appreciated my strength renewing the wards. I whispered, "None but myself shall be welcome within this dwelling. Let the earth reclaim that which doesn't belong, and clear the thresholds of any taint."

The magic coursed through the halls almost like a living being. I could feel it racing from door to door, window to window, removing all trace of anyone else from the house. A glow of power raced through every inch of the space and rang like a bell when it was all clear and clean. The power whooshed through the open doorway like the house was expelling bad energy.

I'd always excelled at wards. Even now I could feel layers of them, dozens, maybe even hundreds set one over another. Different castors, but all with the same intent. Intricate spells woven together like an expensive rug to make one grander piece. The house was to be protected at all costs. The wards were masterful. I'd have to study them while I was here as I couldn't recall ever experiencing anything quite as detailed before. Not even in the many Dominion books I'd "borrowed" from my mother's private library.

After the tingling of the cleansing spell subsided—despite my exhaustion—I poured power into the threshold, pulling it up from the earth, through the tree and expanding it around the house, bonding with the wards and adding my will to them. The old magic recognized me, giving me a bit of a welcoming surge of warmth. Wards, unlike spells, were tied to objects, so if the castor passed, the ward remained instead of dying. I wondered if any of this power was my father's, then sought out the feel of his magic for a moment and could trace a caress of it like a brightly burning candle of energy. His warmth held me for a moment in a soft, almost ghost-like, embrace before racing to the edges of the property to renew the fences and thick overgrowth of trees. Dorien Merth's power was alive and well even if he was not. I sighed as his presence faded. This, this was what I'd come here for. Even as my heart chased after the fading sensation, I knew I'd be searching every corner of the mansion for any lingering trace of him.

I turned back to Gabe and Sam. "Gabriel Santini, I invite in you and your spirit, all you are, and all you may become. May you come and go in peace." I watched his face while he recognized the invite for what it was. Anyone pretending to be him would not be able to pass, but he would have total power to come and go. He stepped through the threshold, set his bag down, and kissed me.

After a moment, I let him go and turned to Sam. "Sam Mueller, I invite in you and your spirit, all you are, and all you may become. May you come and go in peace."

Sam looked shell-shocked but entered the house too. We shut the door. I locked it and wondered what was next to come. The night had already given me several unwelcome adventures, and I was now wary of everyone. I'd be smart to just pack it all up and take the history home with me, sell the house, and forget about the faerie ring of evil.

Sadly, Max's words were true. I couldn't leave knowing that thing was still in use. I couldn't let young witches continue to be abused. And I couldn't let more people die for power. It just wasn't right. And my dad was here. Not physically. But part of him. And I badly wanted to learn about him, yet feared it all at once. What if he hadn't wanted me? But why leave me a home with so much lingering magic that trailed back to him if he didn't want me?

I sighed. Sleep. I so needed sleep. My anxiety always got worse when I didn't sleep well, and I hadn't been sleeping much since I'd arrived. Never slept well when not with Gabe.

I showed Gabe and Sam the closet in my bedroom, still more than worried about whoever had been in the house and if they might still be there. They'd known about this space, yet the earth magic had obviously taken over this part of the house. It reassured me we were alone, but couldn't tell me if anything was missing.

The real Gabe looked around the study but didn't touch the journals. He opened the laptop and began searching through files, just like I thought he should have earlier. He'd also make better sense of any financial documents and property management info that might be stored on the computer. I'd been a condo owner only a few weeks and was only beginning to comprehend what that meant.

The office space was small and cramped. "The room we came through was my dad's," I told them both absently. "But it's empty of his stuff. Maybe his brother got rid of it all?" I really didn't want to return to the large, lifeless room alone and sleep in a cold bed. This room was light safe at least, but two vampires and me? There was totally not enough room for the three of us. Maybe there was a stash of hidden blankets somewhere I could hang over the windows. Only none of them even had curtain rods. I frowned at the thought. Who didn't have curtain rods or blinds in this day and age?

Someone afraid of the dark, perhaps. I hadn't seen anything yet to make me afraid of the dark in the house so long as strangers weren't inside the wards. So maybe it wasn't the first time someone had used an illusion to get inside. Or maybe Charles Merth really was as mad as the world thought he'd become in the end.

"Does that look like a ladder to anyone else? Or just me?" Sam asked, pointing toward a wall of vines.

"Ladder to where?" Gabe approached the area of wall Sam pointed to. He touched the wall, which just looked like a mash of branches. "Real vines," he said and climbed halfway, then stopped. "This part is painted, not real." He pressed his hand to the wall.

"Looks real from here," Sam said.

Gabe felt around the wall a bit and then there was a soft *snick* sound. A panel shifted, opening to a passageway. Gabe glanced back at us but climbed inside.

"Shit, Gabe! Don't go by yourself," I called after him. He'd already vanished into the dark beyond. I worried at my lower lip every second I didn't see him. Maybe there was a psycho relative hidden away up there or even a man-eating plant.

"I don't smell, hear, or sense anyone in the house but us," Sam assured me. "You know my senses are better than yours. Even if the house wasn't coursing with earth magic."

I stared at him, barely breathing, but hopeful.

Then Gabe popped his head out of the opening above. "Do you have some clean sheets somewhere, Sei? There's a bed up here, and the windows are covered." He glanced back in the room. "King-size, it looks like. Maybe even a

California king. Sort of takes up one whole area."

I blinked at him for a moment, wondering just why there was a hidden room. Did it matter if it was someplace I could stay with Gabe? I raced back through the main tunnel, grabbed a sheet set and a couple of pillows, and then handed them to Gabe. He vanished again. Sam looked at the cot, then around the room.

"I'll stay down here. Looks secure enough. You go on up." He didn't look at me at all while he spoke.

I stared at him a minute, wondering if I should apologize for the fight.

"Don't worry," Sam finally said. "He's all yours. I've had enough vampire lovers in my life. I think I'm going to try humans for a while."

"Even if you are tempted to eat them?" I had to ask.

He shrugged. "Better them than me."

At least he wasn't sulking. I followed Gabe up into the space. An old lamp encased the room in a soft glow, casting shadows on the walls, which were covered in vines. The bed took up one entire end of the space, below a window and the peaked ceiling, but looked comfortable enough. Gabe patted the sheets and covers down, then threw the pillows toward the head of the bed.

"The room will need some cleaning, but there's a private bath and it's secure from sunlight." He pointed to a small door on the other end of the room.

The bathroom was pretty small, but it had a toilet, a tiny sink, and a huge wooden bathtub. I tested the water. It ran clear and, after a moment, warm. This would do. The little door to the hidden space had a steel-gauge lock and made another sort of mini threshold. The entire room seemed to be carved from earth. The perfect hidey-hole for an earth witch and his vampire boyfriend.

I sent a quick text to Timothy and set my phone to wake me up at noon. Tomorrow more obstacles could be conquered. For tonight I just needed sleep, hopefully in Gabe's arms. Sam handed us some towels and a jar of dirt and said goodnight. While Gabe opened the jar, I stripped out of everything except my briefs and waited for Gabe, who did the same, then grabbed up the blankets and pulled us both down onto the bed. He wrapped his arms around me but didn't bother turning off the lamp. I fell asleep within minutes of listening to his heartbeat.

Chapter 11

I DREAMT again of being in Wonderland. This time, instead of exploring, I found a comfortable spot in the bloom of a giant dandelion. The feathery petals cradled me like a super soft mattress. The powder-blue bright sky stretched clear and calming. Like a plant, I seemed to be soaking up the nutrients from the sun, and it made me sleepy.

Was it possible to sleep in a dream? My soul rested wrapped in the warmth of the earth, safe and protected. The heat of a body pressed against me awoke me slowly. I expected to awake in the hidden room, sleeping beside Gabe, but I opened my eyes to a darkened sky, glowing flowers, and the red-haired man curled up beside me.

His dark eyes stared into the distance, unblinking. I turned in his arms to face him, confused at why it didn't scare me to be so close to him. Was he the vampire who'd invaded my father's home? Had he invaded my dreams as well? And why did it feel so amazing to be entwined with him? Was I guilty of cheating on Gabe if I let him hold me, even if it was all in my head? I'd have to tell Gabe about the handsome fantasy man. He would brush off my idea that it was cheating. He wasn't even bothered by my flirting with others. Never really was, until I took someone else home. He said it was because I'd always come back to him. But now I had no plans to leave him. This was all just a dream. It had to be.

A ghost of a smile touched the man's lips. He ran soft fingertips over my face as though memorizing how I felt.

"Will you tell me your name this time?" I asked him.

"Wouldn't matter. Wouldn't make any sense to you. You're too human." He didn't sound bitter about it, just matter-of-fact. "Usually we take the name we are given by your kind. I haven't yet been given one."

Human. What did that make him? "Are you a vampire?" But vampires had names. Often they changed their names as the years passed to better blend in, but they still had names. What else could he be if he wasn't human or vampire?

"Not vampire," he assured me.

"Do you want me to give you a name?"

"Only if you want to." He said it like it didn't matter.

I frowned at him, wishing he were more direct. A name would help me identify him, even if it were just to myself. I couldn't keep saying the mysterious red-haired sexy man from Wonderland. It was silly. "Are you the earth? Like the spirit of the GreenMan?"

He laughed, his voice rolling over me in a feathery caress, turning me on faster than it had a right to. "Do I look green to you?" He shifted to press himself against me, hips grinding into my stomach, and ran his hands through my hair—which was long again just like the last time I'd dreamt of him—holding it in front of my face. "You look more like the GreenMan to me."

The length just looked dark to me; only then I touched it and the light glowing beneath my skin illuminated everything from my flesh to my hair. And I was green. Glowing fucking green. How was that possible? It didn't hurt; in fact, I couldn't remember feeling more rested or in tune with the earth. Was that a bad thing? The color rolled through my skin like a wave cresting and retreating, over and over. I could feel the pulse of the earth moving through me. It took no energy; it just flowed with the continuous revolution of power.

"Are you doing this to me?" I asked him. "Changing me?"

He shook his head but settled me against his chest. His heart beat slow and gentle, flesh warm against my face. Alive. He implied he wasn't human, but he was something living. He breathed and had a heartbeat. His skin was warm and I could feel him attached to the earth. He was something. Not human. Not vampire. Not witch. "You've been changing for years."

"Not like this." I stared at my glowing hand, turning it to and fro to study the light as it moved. "What am I?"

"That is always the question, isn't it? The better question is, what do you want?"

"You keep asking me that, but I don't know what you mean." I wound his red curls around my fingers, marveling at the brightness of the color. It didn't look dyed, and it felt like the softest silk or the petal of a rose. No one's hair felt like flowers. Nor had I ever met a redhead with hair so dark it looked like cinnamon or maybe even dried blood. Under the glow of my skin, it was bright rose red. "Are you a sprite? Like a tree sprite?" They were legends, but maybe...

He snorted out a laugh. "No."

I frowned at him, but he pulled me close. His lips hovered just inches over mine. "Tell me. What do you want? Money, power, love, lust, whatever. What makes you tick, Seiran of the green skin and hair?"

I blinked at him, studying his face and breathing in the scent of him, which seemed to be the smell of freshly cut grass. "None of those things *make me tick.* I have money. I'm one of the most powerful earth witches in the world, so I don't need that. And I'm in love with Gabe, and pretty much madly in lust with him too, so I think I'm good. I just am what I am. Why do I need to want something?"

He tilted my head up to look at him. "You have to want something."

"Like world peace or something?"

He shrugged. "I was thinking more for yourself."

"Nah. The only thing I want for me is happiness, and I'm pretty much there so long as I have Gabe. I've got a brother now, and he's pretty cool. And a best friend. Oh, and babies on the way. Twins. And my mom is sort of mellowing in her old age. So while I'm not always happy and life isn't always perfect, I've got it pretty good." And I realized I did. Especially now that Gabe promised me he wanted to work on us too. He wasn't casting me aside for Sam, and I just needed to be patient with him. "I'm good. Are you some sort of wish-granting genie?"

"Would that change your answer?"

I shook my head. "Nope. I've read those stories. That sort of thing always backfires. What about you? What do you want?"

He looked shocked that I asked, then thoughtful. "Freedom."

"From what? To do what? Don't we all have freedom? I guess it's different for everyone. Like, I never really got to decide what I majored in, but it was my choice how to approach it. Waste it or make the most of it. We're all sort of slave to the grind. Working for the man and all that bullshit. Though I sort of work for my man right now. And I wouldn't have to work if I didn't want to. He's got lots of money. I just don't like him to buy me stuff. My mom raised me to earn what I made, not just take from others. Even though I come from a very wealthy family." I knew there were people out there who were taken advantage of, enslaved, maybe even young male witches. He could be a witch with strong spirit powers to enter my mind. I looked him over for signs of neglect and abuse. "Is someone hurting you?"

"Free will," he whispered into the cool night air. "That's a nice dream. Even for a human."

I pulled away from him, sitting up to stare at him curiously. Was this really some sort of forbidden wonderland? Was he stuck here? Who stole his free will? "Am I really dreaming? Are you a witch? Making me dream to help you? Can I help you?"

He laughed so hard he shook and rolled onto his side, holding his stomach. It went on so long, I turned away and folded my arms across my chest, feeling a little humiliated like he was laughing because he'd fooled me. Why *was* he laughing at me?

Finally, he sucked in a deep breath and then sprawled out, hands beneath his head, staring back up at the sky. "You are too beautiful to be real. And so young. How can you be so untainted when you have so much power?"

"Look who's talking." I tugged lightly on his red hair and slid close enough to touch him again. The overwhelming peace made me close my eyes and breathe slowly in through the nose, out through the mouth.

"Are you the spirit Pillar?" The fifth and final Pillar would feel like this, right? A complete collection of energy, alignment of the soul. There was a rumor that the spirit Pillar was almost a millennia old, but even witches didn't live that long. Though if the world always felt like this, I'd be okay with staying here a long while. So long as I could have conjugal visits with Gabe.

"You ask a lot of questions, but you're still tired. You should rest. Recharge. The earth needs you," he told me. Sleep overtook me again, pulling me away from my mysterious red-haired friend and back into normal rest.

My phone alarm broke me out of a deep sleep in which I dreamed of my father reminding me how to reawaken the slumbering earth. The two different dreams felt so disjointed, I began to wonder if the first was really a dream or just the earth's way of communicating with me. Both were vivid, but the Wonderland more confusing. Especially since I didn't have any clue who or what the mysterious redhead was.

The light from the lamp stung my eyes. Gabe must have forgotten to douse it or left it simply because I hated waking in pitch blackness in an unfamiliar place.

Timothy had returned my text, telling me he'd be here after two. That gave me just over two hours to be ready. I slipped out of bed, careful not to wake Gabe—he needed his sleep too—and dragged all my things up to the hidden upstairs room. I cleaned before I hopped in the tub to wash away the previous day's hardship and grime. The wards on the house were strong. I could feel them pulsing with life and stretching all the way to the edge of the property. Less outside the house, and a complete blank where the ring was, but still enough to know Caleb was out working on the lawn. The noise of his equipment would have clued me in even if the magic had not. Every tree, flower, and blade of grass seemed to be connected to the energy and life of the tree in the foyer. And through it, me. No wonder Charles had let this place grow wild. I could only imagine how much energy all the overgrowth had thrown at him. Hopefully he hadn't used it to fuel evil faerie-ring spells.

I added my father's journals to the shelves of other journals, most of them nicely worn but still readable. Here were dozens of books filled with my father's words, all neatly arranged by date. His handwriting was a lot like mine. I traced the words in one volume, awed by how, though time separated us, I still almost felt a connection to him.

The dresser contained his clothing, some of which was wonderfully vintage. Most didn't have tags, and only a few looked really worn and unusable. They made me wonder at his style. These clothes would have certainly made him stand out, even twenty-five years ago. He'd been well-dressed, but not in a flashy way. I tried on a handful of things, marveling at how cool they looked on me. My dad must have been taller than me by several inches, but he had the same build. Maybe a good tailor could hem up the pants for me. I modeled it all for myself and a still-sleeping Gabe in the full-length mirror beside the dresser. I could almost see my dad looking back at me, grinning, maybe even laughing at how silly I looked his old things.

This had been his space. His private sanctuary. The cot below proved either his brother hadn't known about this space or had left it undisturbed. I closed my eyes and just breathed, imagining I could see my father, maybe even smell his aftershave or favorite soap.

The buzzer from the main door rang, making me nearly jump out of my skin. Gabe even twitched in his sleep, but I soothed him with a few words and made my way downstairs. It was just after two, and though it took me a few minutes to get to the door, the buzzer didn't ring again. I hoped Timothy stuck around. When I hit the stairwell, I heard the sound of yard equipment coming from the back of the house, which meant Caleb was finally cleaning up the back. I couldn't wait to see it when it was finished.

Sprinting the last few feet, I opened the door and smiled at my cousin. Wow, I had a brother and a cousin now. My family was growing exponentially. Just how much did Timothy know about his father? I narrowed my eyes at him.

He looked nervous. "You wanted me to stop by?" He looked at the doorway. "Pretty strong threshold. Going to invite me in?"

I shook my head, keeping a fake smile plastered on my face. He didn't need an invite if he left most of his power at the door. The wards would effectively bind his powers until he left. I'd spent months studying legal wards and training others on their use; there wasn't much I couldn't do with them now. The stuff I'd learned in school barely breached the surface of what could be done with magic. Maybe I'd convince my mom that the education of witches really needed to be overhauled.

Timothy could decide to stay outside, not step through the wards. That was his choice to make. I did, however, step aside to give him space to come in. He passed slowly through the doorway, paused just inside, and shook himself like he was trying to brush away the feeling of cobwebs or ice rain. "Harsh, Rou."

"You've heard of me," I repeated his words back to him. "I've found living cautiously when around other witches is best."

He just frowned.

"Let me make you some tea." I headed for the kitchen without waiting for him to follow, but he stayed only a few steps behind me. He sat down at the breakfast bar, feet hanging and kicking like a little kid. After the kettle heated up on the burner, I sat down across from him and decided to be blunt. "So were you born with the power or did you get it from some tainted faerie circle?"

His jaw dropped, and he gaped a few times like a goldfish. Maybe he hadn't expected me to catch on quite so fast.

"It takes a powerful witch to change on a non–new moon night." He'd been the ringtail I'd played with last night. It felt like days ago, but was less than twenty-four hours. "Why are you sleeping in the trees here? Don't you have a home? Or are you spying on me?"

His face flushed with color. "I'm not spying on you. I just don't have anywhere to sleep other than my car. It's safer here with all the wards. I work in construction, but work is hard to find, so money is really tight. Housing isn't exactly cheap in California."

"So why didn't you ask to stay? I'm surprised your dad didn't leave you the house." There must have been some way to buck the paperwork that said it was mine, else he wouldn't have remained in possession of it for so long.

"I don't want the house. It was never meant to be mine anyway." Timothy jumped up from his seat and began pacing. "My dad wouldn't give me anything. He hated me. After I went into rehab four years ago, he pretended I didn't exist."

Rehab? "Drugs or magic?" The second was as impossible to cure as the first. It was all about self-denial. But the second was much more dangerous to the public at large as those who were addicted to magic often ended up executed by the Dominion after some pretty horrific mass killings.

"Drugs. I try not to use magic." He glared at his hands. "They did this to me when I was a kid. I never asked for it."

"Your dad?"

"Yeah. It's part of why I turned to coke and heroin. I just couldn't handle it all. I'm a level-four witch that was born a level-one. The nightmares of the ritual..." He shook his head and gulped air. "They never end. The faces... If I could undo this, I would."

"How much was your dad involved in the Ascendance?" Did Timothy know how deeply his father was involved in the corrupt organization?

"A lot. He was a leader, which really just meant he got to decide who lived and who died for the good of the whole. It was a bunch of crap. Just like any other religion, they think they are right when all they do is hurt others." He crammed his hands through his hair, making it stand up in crazy ways, tugging on it. "The meetings, the chanting, the memories of people screaming..." Timothy paused and looked at me. "You have no idea how awful it was. When he threw me out, I'd never been so happy in my life."

"You were the caretaker." That made sense. His father had given him the responsibility, but when Timothy turned to drugs and away from the Ascendance, he was cast out. "The house in the back was yours."

"Yep. The bastard didn't care that I had nowhere else to go. After I left, he just got worse and worse, paranoid of everyone and everything. Refused to talk to anyone, answer the door, or even leave that office of his in the wall. He complained of noises and strange lights. The police were out dozens of times searching for people he claimed were in the house. They never found anyone."

The hidden room. So Timothy knew about that too. "How did he really die?"

"Heart attack. Or at least that's what they told me. I got a call from someone at the hospital. I don't even know how he got there. He never left the house. They never did let me see him. Said he wanted to be cremated."

"Why did he leave me the house?"

"It wasn't his to leave. Your father left you the house years ago. My father claimed he was just caring for it until you were old enough to take over. He really just wanted the power, but he couldn't control it. The wards, the tree, none of it responded to him. They were Dorien's power, fueled by the earth at each turn. When I was a kid, I'd hide up in the top branches of that tree. After they changed me, the tree no longer welcomed me and I had no place to hide."

Was there a way to change him back? To release the power he'd wrongfully been given? None of my training in school spoke of something like that, but stealing another's power was so dark, it would never have made it into the curriculum anyway. Maybe my father's journals said something or Jamie could find out something. I'd have to call him later.

"You can stay here, but your power stays outside." I poured him a cup of tea. "I've seen that ring and I want it nowhere near me."

He sat down and glared into the pale brown water. "It feels odd but quiet in my head. Maybe I can have my powers bound permanently. I've heard the Dominion does that sometimes. Never thought of it before. They would ask questions, though. About how I got so powerful and no one knew." His voice grew a little panicked. "Maybe they'd kill me."

I shook my head. "Not because of what was done to you." Binding spells were fairly simple but rarely used. My mother probably had more information on that. The Dominion had entire archives of spells and information. Even working as a paper pusher, I'd have access to it. Maybe that alone would make the job worth it. "I'll do what I can to help. Go get your things. You can stay in the caretaker's cottage." The wards extended that far, but were weaker outside the house. It would need its own wards since it was a structured dwelling anyway. I wondered if he knew anything about the body that had been left there, but the police thought it might have been a squatter. I'd have to call the police station to make sure it was clear, but since they hadn't been back or left up tape, it was unlikely they planned to return.

Timothy got up to leave.

"And Timothy?"

He turned back. "Yes?"

"You don't want to see what I do to people who wrong me."

He nodded his head and practically ran for the door. I dumped his cup, washed it out, and poured one for myself before making a few calls. If Timothy proved to be genuine, he could take care of the house in my absence. However, I'd have to deal with the faerie ring first. No more would die if I could help it. If all that was left to the Ascendance was evil, then it was time to put that demon to rest.

Chapter 12

The phone rang several times before a female voice answered, "Hello?"

"Hi, Hanna." I felt like crap for just calling her now. Was she mad? I should have been there when there was an issue with the babies. I wasn't just a sperm donor. I wanted to be their daddy.

"Hey, Seiran. How are you? We were all a little worried." Her voice was warm and soft as always, no hints of hidden anger.

"I'm fine. It's nice and warm here in California. How are you? How are the babies? Is everything okay?"

"We're all fine." I could almost hear the smile in her voice. "It happens sometimes in the early stages of pregnancy. It's more troublesome if it's later. Allie and I think the stress got to me. But I'm rested now, and the babies seem back to normal."

I laughed, trying to imagine what that would be like. "Should I come home? Do you need me there?"

"Oh, sweetie, no. I know you're searching for stuff about your dad. I'm fine. I promise. The babies are fine. We just needed some rest. The new house will have to come together a little slower is all. There's time. The twins won't be here until May at least."

"House?" As far as I knew, Allie and Hanna lived in a condo much like mine.

"I didn't tell you? We bought a house. Well, it's a very large house, lots of land. We closed on Wednesday. Your mom helped us find it and get a great deal on it. Jamie helped us with the down payment. Allie and I figured we'd need the space for the twins. And she's been talking about having a baby too, once the twins are a few years old. I know she's always wanted a big family."

Her comment made me realize how little I knew about Hanna's mate, Allie. Was she a witch? If so, what kind of witch? How did she feel about Hanna having my babies? "I can't wait to see it. I can help clean and move stuff when I get home. Don't push yourself."

"I won't. Jamie's been following me around and making me sit and rest all the time. I'd forgotten how overprotective he can get."

No kidding. I was glad he had someone else to be protective of for a while. We talked a little longer about the babies and the house. When I finally let her go, I felt better, but still a little sad I wasn't home to see more ultrasound pictures and help get the nursery ready. Maybe coming here for the holidays hadn't been such a great idea.

The call to Jamie was much the same. The sound of his deep voice was soothing, even when he went off on some medical tangent about the babies. Jamie would take care of everyone at home. It's what he lived to do. Hanna was in good hands, and Kelly would make sure Jamie didn't get too bossy.

"Kelly wants to talk to you. He's been worried."

I smiled since I knew the one who was worried likely wasn't Kelly, but I let it go. "So put him on."

Just as Kelly got on the line and started talking away about some football game the Vikings had lost, I felt a prickle of pain down my spine, much like the first twinge from my previous back injury when I strained it.

"Hold on, Kelly."

"Huh? Okay."

I waited another moment, waiting for the sensation to return, and even stretched my magic to the edges of the property. Was it the ring?

When the pain didn't come again, I turned back to the conversation. "What about the football players?"

"The tight end left the quarterback wide open. It was like a nightmare in professional football—"

Pain sliced through me so hard I fell from the stool to the kitchen floor. My gut convulsed, my spine spasmed, bowing my back and stealing my breath away. My head filled with piercing white light. I lay there blinking and trying to suck in air for a moment, then it happened again. It was like someone was cutting off one of my legs. The pain was excruciating, and I had to blink through tears of panic. I wasn't bleeding, and all my limbs were attached. It made no sense.

Kelly's voice shouted through the phone, which lay inches from my fingertips. I couldn't function through the pain. Another searing cut tore through me, pulling a scream from my lips.

Then I heard it—the sound of a chainsaw. Each spurt of noise was followed by a burst of agony slicing through my limbs. I dragged myself to the back door, finally pried it open, and stared into the mostly trimmed backyard. The chainsaw whirred again. I lost my lunch this time, though at least it was in the grass instead of on the kitchen floor. When the sound paused, I screamed, "Stop!"

The noise didn't come again. A few seconds later Caleb appeared, covered with sweat and leaves. I pulled myself upright, told Kelly quickly that I'd call him back, and turned to my lawn guy, feeling enough rage at that moment to level a city. The earth was angry and with it so was I. My soul still pulsed with raw pain and the memory of being cut apart.

"Everything okay?" Caleb asked.

The lower rungs of some of the largest trees had been cut—trees hundreds of years older than I would ever be—branches left where they were fallen, like a forest of severed limbs. The earth cried, and I had to fight back a pained sob myself. "I told you not to cut any trees."

He glanced back at the shaded backyard, then wiped his brow with the bottom of his shirt. "I just trimmed them so you can walk under them. Didn't cut any down."

"No more trimming trees. Don't *touch* the trees." I'm sure he heard the anger in my voice because he paled beneath his California tan. I probably looked like a crazy man to him, face red from anger and eyes puffy from tears, telling him not to cut the trees.

"Okay. Sorry." He didn't really sound sorry, but he turned back toward the area he was working, walking away as fast as he could without running. I closed the door, then leaned against it to catch my breath. That had never happened to me at home. Sure, the trees shared things with me, but never that kind of pain. Here, the house was the tree, the yard, the earth. Maybe that's why the connection was so strong.

Gabe's voice inside my head nudged our link open. He'd felt my pain, heard my scream, but was trapped by the light of the sun. I realized he was sitting in the bathroom of the little room, nursing a nasty burn on his arm from trying to step out of the closet and into the bedroom.

You okay?

I'm fine, I told him. *Stupid gardener not following orders. You?*

I'll heal.

Sleep, I told him. After he rested, I'd stop up and give him some blood, which would speed the healing. His thoughts mingling with mine dispersed some of the anger.

When the sound of the equipment didn't begin again, I wondered if I'd scared Caleb off the property. The yard wasn't finished, but I hadn't meant to make the guy run away.

I dialed Kelly back to assure him all was okay. I really hoped Timothy worked out as a caretaker, because I was pretty sure I couldn't stay here much longer without losing myself to the earth. There was just too much life here to ever truly disconnect from it. I hadn't realized I'd been standing in the doorway to the backyard staring at the trees and swaying in the soft breeze until Kelly's voice jerked me out of the trance.

"I'm losing it," I confided to him.

"You're stronger than you think," he reminded me. "Survived a couple attempts on your life and a lifetime of crazy people doing shit you don't even see in HBO movies. You got this. It's just power. You and power are drinking buddies and you can drink him under the table."

"You're so weird," I sighed, thankful for my best friend, and for my boyfriend. Sometimes it was all about the little things.

Timothy returned with his car full of things, and I decided it was a good time for a nap. The sun would be setting soon, which meant Gabe would be up in just a few hours. Maybe we'd go out and do something tonight, just the two of us. After all, we were in California; was that likely to happen again anytime soon?

I hadn't been dancing in forever, but I didn't want anyone else to touch me. Gabe was pretty good at dancing. He could also put off this vampire-type vibe that kept others away. We'd have to find a vampire club, though, since the normal clubs frowned on using vampire stuff on the plebs.

Timothy had begun hauling his things back into the caretaker's house when I passed the windows upstairs to the secret room. He told me he'd clean it up. The stink of death probably still lingered inside. I wondered if Timothy knew anything about it, but didn't ask. His secrets would come out eventually. Everyone's did.

Sam dozed on the cot curled around a blanket, looking very human and young for once. Was the jealousy fading or was Gabe still eating the waves of it? I looked Sam over for a minute, trying to decide what I felt, really felt. Honestly, I felt nothing. Not angry or jealous. It made sense. Sam wasn't a friend. Not yet. I'd never let him that close. But if he couldn't be my enemy, he had to be something else, right? I could work on putting him in the friend box. Maybe.

Neither of them had left to feed. Maybe the house and my power fueled them better than blood could. Vampires were creatures of the earth. Another thought to ponder.

Up in the attic room, Gabe lay sprawled on the bed, chest down, face buried in my pillow. His bandaged arm sprawled across my side of the bed. I brushed my teeth, washed my face, and glared at my short hair in the mirror before returning to the bed. Gabe had flung off the blankets as he usually did, and took up a good part of the huge mattress. Books and movies said vampires slept like the dead, stiff and unmovable. But I'd always found Gabe particularly pliable when sleeping. Which was good, because he was kind of heavy if he settled against my back or wrapped me up too tight. He might be hard to wake sometimes, but he was easy enough to shove over if he was hogging the bed.

Taking the discarded blankets, I swung them over myself and lay beside him, staring at the ceiling. The pain from the tree. I wondered if it was the sort of sensation an amputee experienced. That sort of ghost-limb tingling just this side of hurt. Was it because of the tree in the foyer? Or the ring? As Pillar, technically I could feel every blade of grass in the whole world. Except it took a lot of effort to break down the power that far. Well, normally it took effort. Here every strand of life connected to me as easy as drawing breath. Had my mother known my father came from such a powerful family? She had to have known. Probably planned it. Hoped she'd have some superpowered girl child, only to be stuck with me.

And then there was the ring. All I could think about was how to destroy that awful ring.

What if there wasn't a way to break the magic? What if there were millions of rings all over the world being used this terrible way? How did I fix something I knew nothing about?

Gabe inched closer, like he was trying to be sneaky, making me smile. I threw the link wide open between us and let him have all the jumbled thoughts. His trickled back warmth, hope, and desire. He sorted the thoughts easily, putting things we couldn't solve right this second into a later bucket, which left me smiling. He wanted to snuggle. Snuggles couldn't solve the troubles of the world, but they sure did make us both feel better. I let him throw his arm over me and pull me into a tight embrace. He adjusted the pillow beneath my head, breath soft and warm on my face.

We stayed that way for a while, holding each other. Soaking in human touch, life, and love. If I could have wrapped myself up in his sky and lived there, I'd have been thrilled. He peppered my face with soft kisses. With the link wide open, I could feel his excitement, but knew he'd only push for sex if I wanted it.

"I'm sorry for being a hypocrite," Gabe whispered against my hair. "I shouldn't tell you to compromise and talk to me when I'm not doing the same. If I'd told you about the bar, we probably wouldn't have had this fight."

"You love the bar." *I* loved the bar. It was a second home to me. No one judged me. I got to make up some cool menus and spend time with the guy I loved while still earning a living.

"But you aren't going to be able to work at the bar forever. You're meant for better things."

I snorted. "Like paper pushing for the Dominion."

"There's an opening in the Magic Investigations department. Entry-level research and analysis. Your mother sent it to me, her not-so-subtle way of saying it would be a good fit for you." He kissed the tip of my nose. "The description sounds nice. Exciting like a mystery novel, and safe, since you're mostly working behind a desk and not in the field."

I frowned at him. He smiled back.

"I need you safe. I exist for you."

And of course I melted.

"You should apply."

"MI," I said, thinking it over. MI researched anything unusual in magic, Sam being the most recent subject to pique their interest. Their methods were a lot like the FBI or any other investigative body—lots of research, questioning, observation, and analysis. At entry-level, I'd be doing mostly book research while training for other things. It sounded interesting and intimidating all at once. "But I'm a guy, and that's a pretty important job. It would be my research that the field agents would take with them into dangerous situations."

Gabe kissed me again, then wrapped his leg around mine to pull me closer. "You're Pillar, which makes you crazy powerful. And you're kind of nosy—smart, but nosy. Perfect for that job."

I slapped his fine ass for the "nosy" comment. "I'll think about it."

"You have to submit your résumé by next Wednesday. Your résumé looks good, by the way. I snuck a peek at it before you left home. Was a little surprised when you didn't send it out anywhere. Why didn't you?"

I shrugged. I hadn't known where to start. Or what I wanted to do with the rest of my life. God, what an awful phrase. The rest of my life. With my whole life ahead of me, I had options, right?

"Did you want to go back to school for something else? Cooking? Nutrition, maybe?" Gabe prompted.

No. I was about as done with school as a person could be. Plus, I was pretty sure my mom would veto anything that wasn't magic related.

"She doesn't control you anymore."

"Not true," I told him. "The Dominion controls me. She's part of the Dominion."

"Your magic isn't all you are. Not even as Pillar. You're still Seiran Rou, Pillar, college grad, junior chef, and maybe Magic Investigator."

I kind of liked the idea of that. "Sounds important. Like *I'm* important."

"You are."

I studied his face. "You're too perfect."

He snorted but gifted me another kiss. "If anyone knows that's not true, it's you. Now, will you apply?"

"Maybe."

"Do you have your résumé saved to your phone?"

Yeah, it was on my phone. I was pretty sure it was backed up to his Cloud since that's all we used at home. The idea of applying for such a lofty position made me both nauseous and excited at once. Sure, not everything about the job would be interesting. In fact, it would probably be a lot of tedious work, not much different than the paper pushing of a desk clerk. Yet it had so many more opportunities. And total access to all Dominion information, libraries, and computer systems. Shit, I so needed that job. "Help me fix my résumé so it's perfect, please."

"My own private dick," Gabe teased, hips grinding into mine.

"That was awful!" I pushed him over onto his back, straddling his hips. Just the little bit of friction made me hard. It'd been far too long since I played with him.

"You don't love me for my dry sense of humor. You love me because I'm beautiful and rich."

I laughed. That was so not why I loved him. I ground my hips into his, letting his emotions and mine mingle. Gabe's humor was a dry wit not many got. Still, he made me smile, and he, unlike Max, seemed to have no problem feeling emotions. Right now he was happy and filled with lusty ideas. One of them had me raising a brow at him while I straddled his waist. "Really?"

He flushed, pale pink touching his cheeks so sweetly I was more than willing to make the vision come true to keep that image in my head. "We don't do that often. I was thinking maybe...."

Yeah, I was definitely all for keeping that shy smile on his face until he dissolved into a mass of pleasure-filled jelly. Gabe's hard cock ground into my balls, and precum wetted his boxers. I stripped out of my shirt, pants, and socks, wanting to feel him against me. Through my bikini briefs, I rubbed my ass over the length of him, driving a groan from his lips. He fisted my hair and dragged me down for a kiss. We shared the flavor of my mint toothpaste and his copper taste.

We dueled tongues, and our bodies rubbing together lasted for a while, both of us panting and devouring each other in endless moments of peace and pleasure. This was what I'd missed these past few weeks. Not just the sex, but the closeness. His body pressed to mine, our lips connected, minds open to one another. His pleasure heightened mine to feverish levels. We didn't need hours of foreplay, just kisses and bodies pressed together. He was already everything I could ever hope for.

He let go of my hair to run a hand down my spine and dip into my undies. The vision in his head was so different than what he was doing. He hesitated to ask for what he wanted. Had I made him this way? Afraid to request something for fear I'd turn him away? I kissed his lips one last time before trailing more little nibbles down his chest and to his bulging boxers below.

Gabe's breath hitched in a sexy way that made me grab my cock a little harder than usual to keep from coming right away. He'd expected me to swallow the whole of him, bury my nose in his golden pubes, and suck like I always did. The image replayed strongly in his mind. I smiled while I delivered soft, teasing licks instead. The saltiness of his balls made me want to roll them around in my mouth. The desire was so strong I gave in to it, taking them in my mouth and watching Gabe writhe and grip the bed to try to keep from coming. His eyes were closed, head thrown back, shoulders and arms straining, knees spread wide, but I was nowhere near finished.

After torturing both of his wonderfully tasty but sensitive balls, I dipped below to his taint, lapping at it and digging my face into the soft flesh. This time he did come off the bed, fighting not to rip himself away from me, throw me down, and slide into me, his thoughts inside mine almost as seamless as our bodies could be.

Gabe cried out, "Christ, Seiran."

His cock was so hard it pulsed darker than usual, begging. I reached up to give him a rough squeeze. "No coming yet. I want to be in you first."

He flopped back on the bed, struggling to breathe and keep himself from letting go. I gave him a moment's reprieve to calm his body before following that lovely darkened flesh down to his tight, puckered hole. The sweet little hole clenched and unclenched in anticipation. I tickled him with my tongue, using my hands to hold his cheeks open. Not all vampires were as clean as Gabe. I liked to think he just came that way, but he'd probably learned the habit from me over the years. He tasted salty-sweet, and his rim was so sensitive he couldn't keep from squirming beneath me.

The grunts, sighs, and moans coming from him had me leaking too. A little trail had already spilled against his belly from his weeping cock, warning of things to come. My own undies were wet and beyond uncomfortable. I wiggled out of them, not pausing in my assault on Gabe's hole. Once I was free of them, I repositioned myself for a better angle, wetted a finger, and gently pressed it inside, teasing at first.

Again Gabe came off the bed, back arching, hips thrusting down onto my finger and lips. "Please, Sei. Oh God!"

I smacked his ass lightly. "Not yet." Pressing another spit-slicked finger in, I purposely avoided his prostate, enjoying watching his hips move as he tried to force me to touch it. If he didn't stop looking so incredibly fuckable, I was going to come without even touching myself.

A small bottle of lube appeared next to me. Gabe's eyes were wide, almost glowing green. The earth flowed through him just like those giant flowers in my sleepy Wonderland. Power lit his skin in a way I'd never seen before. It was my power flowing through him. I wondered if I glowed too.

He had one hand on the headboard, the other two inches from the bottle. "Fuck me, Sei. Please."

I spread some of the lube on my cock, slowly stroking myself while he watched every move. His eyes followed my hand while I rubbed the slick down my length. I was nowhere near as big as him. He had width as well as length. My cock was thinner but still reasonably sized. Since he rarely bottomed, I'd have to move slowly.

He kept muttering, "Please, please, please," which was so incredibly hot. The link between us spoke of nothing but desire and lust; where one left off and the other began, I didn't know. Our thoughts and emotions were one. It was time to complete the connection. I positioned the head of my cock against him, keeping the pressure constant until his ring loosened to let me inside. I didn't top much, so I waited to let his body adjust before slowly moving forward.

The process probably only took a few minutes but felt like years of torture. I just wanted to adjust his hips so I bumped his nub each time and then slam into him, pounding him until stars filled my sight. Instead I breathed and waited, letting him feel my love through our bond, as well as how tight he was around me. When he put his other hand on the headboard, I knew he was ready, and pulled back, leaving just my tip inside before ramming back to meet flesh to flesh.

The sounds of our cries, the flesh slapping, and the bed quaking had me fighting to keep from tumbling over the edge. Gabe lost all coherent thought to the pleasure and just let his body feel. My skin radiated light against his pale brightness. Only my light was pale green. His eyes were shining, boring into me with nothing but need. This is why groupies flocked to vampires to feed them, though very few ever experienced this total assault on the senses. Vampires were predators with seduction as a primal instinct. Humans were easily attracted to beautiful things, therefore prey.

Gabe was filled with earth, power, and peace, because those were the things I craved most. What he became to others, I had no idea and didn't really care. Maybe I glowed because that's how he saw me, but I felt like the sun filled my skin.

We moved in a rhythm that almost seemed to force us off the planet and into the cosmos.

His power combined with my magic sent us to heights neither of us had ever experienced. By the time the end neared, all I could see were those beautiful eyes of his. The earth pulsed through both of us, each small movement another powerful thrust. I clung to him, felt his body jerk as he came, then slammed home twice more before letting go my own release deep inside him.

The house seemed to shudder with the strength of the energy. My body shook with uncontrollable pleasure, and my scalp burned, every strand of hair aching like I was on fire. I collapsed on top of him, still inside, though I could feel my come leaking out around me. If I'd had any energy left, I would have dipped my head to his stomach and licked his mess from him.

He sucked down air in thick gulps, skin and eyes still filled with magic. Finally, he said, "I think you killed me." His hands were threaded through my hair. "But I've never felt more alive."

I laughed, knowing what he meant. Through our link Gabe felt boneless, weak, and yet he had power racing through every nerve. Sometimes being an earth witch in love with a vampire really had some perks.

"No kidding," he mumbled in response to my thoughts. He tugged me up before putting his arms around me and hugging me tightly. He brushed my hair out of his face. "We so need to do that more often." Whether he was referring to the magic, my topping him, or the complete release of control, I wasn't sure. Not that it mattered; I was willing to do it all again, and soon. "Although if your hair grows like that every time we have sex, you might be Rapunzel before the end of the week."

I yanked a hank of dark hair around to see it. Sure enough, my hair was long again, like it had never been cut. Gabe kissed me, combing through my hair in reverie. I couldn't help but stare at it and compare it to the dream I'd had.

"Does it look green to you?"

Chapter 13

The embarrassed flush on Sam's face told me he must have heard or even felt the time I spent with Gabe. The fact that I could make Gabe go that wild made me proud and possessive rather than ashamed. Sam couldn't meet my eyes and didn't try looking at Gabe. He disappeared into the other part of the house as soon as the sun set, which was just past five. I showered downstairs, dressed, and stared out the window of my father's old bedroom at the place where I knew the ring was hidden behind the trees and overgrowth.

Gabe's gentle hand on my shoulder nearly made me jump out of my skin. "Sorry," he whispered. He peered out into the darkness too. "You should probably stay away from that ring. I can go look at it, see if there is a physical way to destroy it."

"You are not going there alone. That place is awful." I met his gaze and held it. "Death magic, Gabe. Kelly described how the tower felt when he rescued Sam, and this is a thousand times that." I shivered in remembrance. "It's evil." That was the only way to describe the darkness, death, and hunger for power.

He frowned. "Okay, we'll go together, have a quick look, then come back behind the wards. It'll be okay." He laced his fingers through mine, and we headed toward the back door. Sam sat in the kitchen glaring at another bottle of

QuickLife. I didn't know what he had against the synthetic blood but was pretty sure it wouldn't taste better with age. "We'll be back in a few, Sam."

I didn't want to go at all, but I let Gabe lead me through the backyard, around the caretaker's house, and into the woods beyond. The lights from the cottage faded quickly into the darkness along with the sounds of Timothy moving around. I tried to let the soft tinkle of the stream push out all sense of fear in my head. The earth surrounded us, but I'd have felt better if I could have wrapped us in a blanket of wards. Gabe's presence in my mind and at my side was the only thing that kept me from running when the eerie arrangement of stones came into sight. My skin buzzed and crawled with the sensation of biting ants swarming me. It brought a catch to my breath, and we still stood ten feet outside the circle. Gabe didn't attempt to move closer either. His side of our bond closed. One second he was there, and the next I was alone in my head like a door had slammed in my face. That hurt.

"Gabe?" I asked. His eyes were shut, and he was still as death. Then he took a sudden step back. I gulped, heart thudding in my throat. Did it feel as terrible to him? Another step back, this time dragging me with him. He pulled me into the yard, under the thick growth of trees, and swept me into his arms. He didn't breathe or move for several minutes, and I couldn't see his face. Everything I sensed about him spoke of danger, little flares of warning at the edge of my brain, like a warning a new vampire would give me. Only the oldest of vampires could hide that odd Spidey sense. Gabe could rip out my throat or tear off my head, but I wouldn't let him go, even when he finally pulled away, revealing eyes that were glowing red with no whites around the edges instead of his normal green. I sucked in a deep breath, scared for the first time. I'd read about it in books. Even seen a little of it from Matthew after he'd kidnapped me, but never in Gabe. I'd sort of forgotten there was this side of him. Primal. Deadly.

He pushed me away. "Go inside, Seiran," his voice grinding out like wheels on gravel. "Sam."

Sam appeared beside him. He couldn't pop in and out of locations like Max could, but he could move fast enough to make it seem like he could. I'd been too focused on Gabe to notice him until that moment anyway. They both turned away and headed around the front of the house to the car. They'd hunt. I prayed for the Mother to watch over them so neither of them would get hurt or harm anyone else.

"Everything okay?" Caleb's voice startled me out of my daze. Why was I so jumpy?

"I thought you'd be finished up for the day," I told him, trying to shake off the lingering taint of the ring.

"Just packing up. I've pretty much finished, unless you've changed your mind about me trimming the trees. The lilacs could use some control. Everything up to the fence line is finished." He pointed to the other side of the lawn, the wall of tall bushes, and the fence behind it. I bet the lilacs smelled nice when they bloomed.

"I could probably use some help replanting the gardens if you're willing." There were large chunks of the garden that was down to bare earth. Any plants left in those areas had long since withered, and Caleb had turned the soil so it would be ready for planting, even if it was just to seed it for grass.

"Sure. I'll bring some catalogs of plants tomorrow for you to pick from, since we don't get a lot of rain here."

"Thanks." I waved good-bye to him and headed inside, pausing again because the lights were on in rooms I hadn't been in. Was the place haunted? I didn't believe in ghosts any more than I believed in faeries. Maybe I'd have to rethink that, having found a faerie ring. I sighed. Alone again.

Making my way to my room, I shut down the unnecessary lights and headed up to the hidden space. Perhaps my father's journals would shed some light on the history of the house and how to destroy evil faerie rings.

Several hours of reading didn't reveal much more than the fact that my father was as in tune with the earth as I was. He met Jamie's mother in college, and they had a brief affair. When their trysts produced Jamie, my father fought for partial custody. He lost but was allowed visitation rights. I scanned through a lot of those journals, putting them aside for Jamie, who would love to read about how much Dad had missed him in between visits.

The bits of magic scattered throughout the journals all related to the earth, but none of them were finished spells. Many of the spells related to the house, which he'd inherited from his father. I began reading the account of Dorien Merth watching his father burn to death, but had to stop. The entire thing brought back memories of those pictures Sam had sent me of my father's death. There was nothing beautiful or peaceful about dying by flame. It haunted the living and made an awful death. My heart broke just thinking about it.

I searched through the journals until I found a mention of my mother. Dorien thought she was an exotic beauty, and at the time, "she was disenchanted with her family." She'd run away from home to escape an arranged marriage. My father wrote that Tanaka "seemed haunted by a horrible childhood, like most Dominion girls." Having never met my grandparents, I suppose it was likely they had treated my mom badly, too, since she was an only child. The pressure to carry on the Rou line must have been terrible.

The lamp flickered on the other side of the room, like the bulb was dying. I set the book aside. There were bulbs under the kitchen sink. The light in the bedroom downstairs was on again. I sighed, left it on. Every light was on as I passed, the hall, each room and bathroom, the living room, the main entry, everything. It took almost twenty minutes to shut them all off and get back to the hidden bedroom with a light bulb. The lamp had completely gone out.

I fumbled through the dark, flicked the light off, unscrewed the bulb, put in the new one, and turned it on. The soft glow of the energy fluorescent in the earth protected room made me sleepy. Maybe I could nap a bit.

After wrapping myself in the warmth of the blankets, I closed my eyes and reached out for Gabe. His walls were solid against my probing. Something had scared him about that ring.

The house hummed softly of life and peace, putting me to sleep before the ideas began to form in my mind. I dreamt again of my father. He walked through the house with me, explaining some spells I'd never heard of before. The one that made the house and tree was so complicated my dream brain turned it into a mush of sounds. My red-haired friend seemed to have vanished, and I missed him more than I cared to admit.

My dad smiled indulgently at me. I felt younger in these dreams, a small child following his footsteps. He'd touch my head, running his hands over my hair, eyes shining bright with pride. Would he have ever looked at me that way in real life?

The sound of growling edged into the dream. My father didn't seem to hear it, but I stopped following him, searching for the source of the sound. Nothing looked out of place, but my father had gotten so far ahead I couldn't see him anymore. I turned again, only to see a dark shape lunge toward me.

I woke up screaming, heart pounding, to a darkened room. Hadn't I left the light on? Then the growling began again, only this time in reality. The low rumble sounded like a large cat or ridiculously huge dog, and it was inches from the bed. My sleep-fuzzy brain took a few seconds to catch up, but when I stretched my magic through the house, there was nothing. No animals, no people. What the hell?

Ghosts didn't exist. This I knew because the earth recognized no such thing. After death, the human body decomposed and returned to the earth. The power that made up our spirit fled back to the element from which it came, creating a balance. Objects could hold memories, but not people. And whatever was growling was not human, dead or alive.

Silently I cast a spell and closed my eyes for a second as the light brightened the room. No animal, ghost or otherwise. I blinked again, seeing something out of the corner of my eye. A bug? Then it flew at me, like a dive-bombing bee determined to sting. I rolled back, landing on my back on the bed, sprawled out, blinking at the tiny colorful bug that hovered above me.

A voice boomed in my head. *Usurper! Thief!*

"Seriously?" I asked, then cast a binding spell. Was this for real or was I still dreaming?

The small creature thunked to the bed, rolling around, struggling against the invisible bonds. It cursed and shouted at me with a voice that only I could hear. Unusual, since I'd put my personal walls back up.

I picked it up and moved it a few inches away so I could study it. What sort of bug could talk to people and make growling noises? I smiled. It probably could turn on lights too. "What an interesting little bug."

Bug? Not a bug!

"Well, what are you, then?" My dad's journals so far hadn't spoken of any unusual creatures in the house. And nothing I learned about at school resembled this little thing.

Looking closer at him, he looked sort of like a small man. His hair was blue, long, styled almost to look like the head of a thistle. He appeared wrapped in green, but whether that was clothing or just the color of his skin, I couldn't tell. He weighed nothing more than a fly would and had almost invisible iridescent wings. Overall he was smaller than my thumb, but had a fierce-looking face, with a large mouth and extreme expressions. His little eyes glistened a dark black, angry and flashing.

Holy Mother Earth! This had to be a faerie!

Release me, Usurper!

"Why do you keep calling me that? I haven't taken anything from anyone."

This dwelling, man-thing! It belongs to the earth!

"I have no intention of taking it from the earth. My father left me this house. I don't know what I'm going to do with it yet, but I'd like to keep the earth intact. The peace here is comforting, but this is not my home."

Liar, blasphemer! Release me! You cut the trees!

"Could you stop shouting? You're giving me a headache. The gardener cut the trees, and I yelled at him for it." I wondered if my father knew about faeries. Maybe Gabe could help me find a way to better store the information from his journals so I could search them later. The over one hundred volumes were an intimidating number since I'd only gotten through so few. "Did my dad know about you? Did you know him? Dorien Merth?"

The angry racing of the creature's wings paused. He seemed to wilt, the fight going out of him. He went so still I reached to pick him up to be sure I hadn't accidentally hurt him with the spell.

He bit me.

"Ow! Fuck. What did you do that for?" Blood welled up on my thumb where he'd bitten me.

He smacked his lips, eyes filling with a sapphire fire. He bowed. *Child of Dorien, scion of the earth, forgive my insolence.*

"Um, okay. Just don't bite me again."

He flickered for a moment, brightening then fading, and I felt the binding spell snap. He fluttered upward, hovering in front of my face. My mind still spun. Faeries were real! And powerful. He shouldn't have been able to break my binding spell like that. Hadn't Gabe said he'd met some before? This tiny thing completely bent all laws of science. Was he created completely from magic? Would the Dominion have to change their curriculum? I supposed this proved that not everything could be learned from books.

He bowed again in midair. *As thy father before thee, I vow to serve thee.* At least his voice no longer rang through my head like a gong. Now it was quiet and subtle, a breeze moving through the trees.

"I don't need you to serve me, but it'd be nice if you'd stop turning on lights all the time. I imagine the power bill here is enormous as it is."

His wings seemed to falter for a moment. *But I have to serve thee.*

"You don't have to do anything. Did my father make you serve him?"

I served your sire with honor as commanded by his sire.

"Right. Okay. Did my father command you to serve me?"

He seemed to ponder that for a few moments. *No.*

"Great. 'Cause I don't need a servant. You're free to do whatever you want. I release you from whatever you may have been bound to."

He seemed to pause, wings stopping completely. I caught him before he could plummet to the bed and really hurt himself. He just lay in my grasp, gasping for breath, looking like a flower cut from the stalk too soon. Was it wrong to release him? I figured my uncle must have done something to him, but maybe faeries needed a bond to survive?

"Are you okay?"

You truly release me?

"Yep. Any buddies you have too. I don't need servants of any kind." I could have asked him about the ring, but he looked so shocked I didn't want to chance him having some sort of breakdown. "Do you need me to take you out to the garden or something? Faeries like flowers and living things, right? I can take you outside if you need to be near them."

Still he blinked at me, wide eyes blue glowing balls of confusion. His overly expressive face said he still hadn't grasped what I was telling him. *I'm free?*

I nodded. "Yep."

He suddenly flew upward, racing around the room like an overactive fly who couldn't find his way out. He smashed into the door and vanished in a flash of lights. I hoped he hadn't hurt himself. Maybe he'd gone right through it?

I shrugged to myself since there wasn't anything I could do to help him now, then pulled up the blankets and another journal. I bet my dad had something written somewhere about faeries. I just had to find it.

Browsing the next journal, I came up with much the same. Half spells, recounting of normal, everyday life, but nothing on faeries or the Ascendance. I put the book aside in frustration and slumped back on the bed. Maybe my dad had hidden that information. The Dominion had to know faeries were real. They couldn't just completely ignore an entire species made of magic, could they? I didn't think so. But then that meant the Dominion was hiding that information from the general population. Why? Were there more faerie rings to worry about? Maybe some that hadn't been corrupted?

My dad must have known more. That's why his spells were only partially complete, to keep others from using them. And his journals, while having a lot of insight into his emotions and the relationships in his life, dealt very little with magic. He didn't write about learning it or even what the half spells did. They came across almost as poetry. If I hadn't been studying spells and magic my whole life, I might not have known what they were.

I flipped through a few more journals. Not reading, more browsing for spells. It was the same sort of rhythm. Personal stuff, no magic, just half spells. I shoved the last book on the shelf and glared at it. I needed someone to work through ideas with. Usually that person was Gabe.

I glared at the clock. Where *was* Gabe? What was taking him so long? The night had half passed already.

I stared at the wooden ceiling, letting it go out of focus for a bit while sorting through my thoughts. It was then I saw the scratches on the beam above the bed. On the side facing the window, away from the room, small letters had been scored into the wood. I replayed the words a few times in my head. It really just sounded like a haiku.

"Imagine in your head, let it play once and again, imprint to recall." When I repeated the words out loud, a rush of power poured through me, racing around the house. I shivered, and then the door opened, yet it didn't. The man who strode inside could only be my father. His brandy-colored hair fell into his eyes, sapphire blue, like mine. He was tall and lanky but moved with the grace of a man who had control. He crossed the room with purpose, opened the bottom drawer of the dresser, pulled everything out of it, and then opened a false bottom.

Again the door opened. Only this time it was my mother who walked through it. Her hair was long, somewhat hippie-styled, straight and free of any binding. She wore jeans and a T-shirt that fit tightly over her small chest. I'd never seen her look so ordinary, so common.

"I can't let this happen, Dorien." She put her hands to her midsection. I saw the tiny bump. Was that me? "*We* can't let this happen."

"Tanaka, please." Dorien stood up and wrapped his arms around her. He pressed his face to her hair. "The baby is more important."

"I can't do this on my own."

"I'm not asking you to. Lily will help. You know she will love that baby like her own."

My mother pushed him away. "This is your responsibility, not your sister's."

Dorien closed his eyes and swallowed deeply. "We already talked about this. I have to do this."

"Die to save your brother? Just because he's done wrong? These are his crimes."

"He wants to atone. I need to give him that time." Dorien went back to the drawer and pulled out a journal and some other items. "I'm leaving my power to Jamie. He'll need it."

"What about our baby?"

"Our baby has plenty of power without needing mine. I can already feel him in my head. So strong and smart. Already in tune with the earth." He set the items aside and hugged her again.

"You know my parents will demand I abort when they find out it's a boy."

"I do. I also know that you'll protect him and give him life."

"I hate you."

He sighed and looked at the floor instead of at her. "If you need to."

Her eyes shone with tears. "Please don't do this."

A ghostly sound of the doorbell rang from below. They both turned. My mother gripped his shirt like she was trying to keep from falling to the floor. He gently pried her hands loose and kissed her on the forehead. He brushed the tiny bump of her belly and smiled sadly. "It's hard for me too. I want to see him grow up. Help him control his power. Teach him how to be strong and soft all at once."

"Then let's run away. Leave Charles to sleep in the bed he's made," she pleaded with him.

"This isn't just for Charles, Tanaka. I have to undo what my father began. Please don't watch. Go to Lily; she'll protect you." He left then as the ringing from the door became more persistent.

My mother collapsed to her knees, sobbing into the floor and holding her stomach. The image faded and I shook myself, feeling a little overwhelmed with emotion. My mother had really loved my father. I wondered why over the years she began to treat me worse and worse. It made sense that she would grow to hate Dorien for leaving her with child, with a male child even, in the Dominion-ruled world.

I went to the bathroom and stood in front of the mirror, glaring at myself. With my hair long again, I looked more like my father, despite the almond edge to my eyes and the pitch-black color of my hair. Did she see the man who left her each time she looked at me? Why did it make me feel so awful that my existence tortured her? Would I feel the same if I lost Gabe and was left with a child who looked like him?

No. I didn't think I would, but love was a powerful thing. It hurt like nothing else could and made the world seem both brighter and darker all at once. Would Gabe hate my children if something happened to me? I hoped, instead, that he would show them how much I would have loved them.

I sat down on the bed, and before I even knew it, I'd punched a number into my phone, not realizing how late it was. My mother picked up on the fourth ring. She sounded tired, but not as though she'd just woken up.

"Hi, Mom," I whispered.

"Seiran, how are you?" She didn't even ask about the time or why I'd call her just after 3:00 a.m. her time.

"I'm good. You?"

"I'm well." The tone of her voice changed to something lighter than I'd heard most of my life. "I have framed pictures of the babies. Just the ultrasound, but I can make copies. Would you like me to send you some for Solstice?"

She was offering to send me a gift? "That would be great. I'd love pictures of them."

"I found a lovely double frame to display them side-by-side. Do you need one for your apartment and for Gabe's?"

I was more than a little surprised. She'd never approved of Gabe. I think it was mostly because he couldn't bear my children. "Both would be good." Maybe it was time for Gabe and me to find someplace where we could stay together. The house here in California was nice, but I really loved Minnesota, harsh winters and all. Out of the blue, I said, "I'm going to apply for the Magic Investigations job." I really hadn't made the decision before that moment.

"You'll do very well. The head of the department is Lily Castage. She's very forward-thinking and will train you to do field work."

Lily? The same Lily who was my father's sister, my aunt? Why had I never heard of her before? "She won't treat me like the other witches treat me, will she?"

"She'll expect you to work hard, but she won't look down on you for being male."

I wanted to ask the question but couldn't get the words to come out. I supposed if I got the job, I could ask Lily myself if she was my aunt. Obviously my mother never did go to her for help after I was born since I didn't remember anyone named Lily. "I'll send her my résumé in the morning. Thanks, Mom."

"You're welcome, Seiran. Get some sleep." She hung up the phone before I could ask why she hadn't been sleeping herself. I'd always been a night owl; dating a vampire sort of did that to a person. She, on the other hand, had often disappeared after 8:00 p.m., not to be heard from until the next morning.

I sighed and put the phone away, the spell/haiku on my mind. What else could it show me? In school I'd read briefly about imprint magic, memories that could be replayed from the energy left in objects. However, the topic was something all my professors glossed over. Most of what they taught was law and Dominion Code. Perhaps they didn't see the value of learning from the past. Looking around now, I could almost see the glimmer of the lingering memories waiting to be replayed. This house was so full of imprint magic, I didn't know where to begin.

My father had given up his life to save Charles, but it appeared as though my uncle continued his evil works. Would there be some sort of imprint that would tell me how to stop the pulse of death magic the faerie ring produced? All I could do was begin searching for the answers.

Chapter 14

I MADE my way slowly through the house, watching small replays of my dad. I skipped the study simply because I could feel multiple imprints and didn't know where to begin. My father's normal room held little of him. He used the room only when people visited and expected to see him.

The kitchen was home to several memories of him and my mother together. He had made her breakfast while she studied, occasionally glancing up to watch her. She had smiled secretly, probably feeling his eyes on her, and returned his gaze when she thought he wasn't watching.

The tree in the foyer pulsed with a faded bit of imprinting. I sat down on the last step, chanted my dad's spell, and touched the trunk. A young man threw open the main door, slammed it shut, and stomped toward the tree. His long hair hung in his face, but he appeared to be in his early teens, lanky, and not quite developed completely. He grabbed a limb and swung himself up into the tree. Through semitransparent leaves, I could see him huddling against a large Y of the inside branches.

"Leave me alone." He scrambled up higher. I expected to see someone following him, maybe open the door again, but everything remained still. Then the sound of twigs snapping broke the silence. Leaves fluttered to the floor.

I had to climb the stairs to keep up with the imprint. The boy had to be my father, much younger. He swatted at something a few times, and then a blur of color raced around him. I grinned. The same annoying faerie flew at him, just as it had at me. So he had seen them, knew about them. I just had to find the information.

Finally, Dorien paused, looking up, almost staring right at me. His eyes flashed with anger. "Lyden?"

The door opened, startling me out of the vision, and had me nearly jumping off the stairs and into the tree.

"You okay?" Gabe stood at the bottom of the stairs, glancing from me to the tree and back. Sam leaned against the wall beside the door, looking tired but mostly human. He must have fed. Gabe should have looked better rested and fed too, but he didn't. At least his eyes were no longer red.

I sucked in a few deep breaths and willed my heart to beat normally. "You scared the crap out of me."

"It looked like you were in some sort of trance. I didn't know if that was a good or a bad thing."

The memories of all that had happened in the past few hours rushed back through my head. "Holy crap! There are faeries. Faeries are real. I saw one. Wait... what happened to you earlier? You got all scary and undead-like."

"Yes, there are faeries. They've been turning on your lights." He handed me a small potted plant that smelled strongly of mint. The bushy greenery flowed from the bucket, more like ivy than any mint I'd ever seen. "This should attract and relax any faeries we have in the area. We can probably get some information from them about the ring. They're more likely to talk to you than me. Faeries have never had much use for vampires."

I took the plant and wondered how he knew so much about faeries, but before I could ask, he was bounding up the stairs and answering my other question.

"The ring brought on bloodlust." He tugged me up the stairs. Sam followed several steps behind. "Overwhelming bloodlust. That ring needs to be destroyed. I filed a report with the Tri-Mega. You should let the Dominion know. They may have to null-bomb the area."

Sam shivered, probably thinking of Matthew, who had been a psychopath and a null, just as I did at that moment. He shrugged past us and disappeared into the bathroom instead of coming with us to the secret room. The scent of musk and man caught my nose. Had Sam gotten some play? And why did that smell so familiar? Like tree and motor oil.

I let Gabe lead me through the hall and up to our private room. Once I set the plant down and began stripping out of my clothes in the dark, it hit me. "Sam fed on Caleb?"

"We ran into him at the club. I don't know if he fed or just satisfied other needs. Leave it to you to find the hottest gay gardener in the city. Which reminds me. You may want to call him back. Your faeries have made a jungle out of your yard again."

"What? No way!" I kicked out of the rest of my things, leaving just my bright-purple euro-briefs, and climbed across the bed to peel back the heavy coating over the window. Far down below, I could see the mass of weeds and wild grass twisting across the side of the yard that only a few hours ago had been perfectly trimmed. "That's so unfair."

Gabe pushed the window covering back, grabbed me around the waist, and pulled me down beside him for a snuggle. He even wrapped the blanket around us. "They are probably thinking the same thing about you. Cutting down their hiding places. I bet that's why there were so many gardens. You'll need to replant those right away if you want to keep the paths clear."

I sighed. "How do you know so much about them, anyway?"

"They were all over Europe. Couldn't go anywhere without tangling with a mass of them. Sadly, a lot of them were wiped out during the industrial revolution. Occasionally you'll find patches of them now in protected areas, parks, forests, that sort of thing."

"Are they good or bad?"

He shrugged, his body hair tickling me, legs scratching against mine before settling, one between my knees and the other on top. Gabe always liked to sleep tangled up, his limbs curled around mine. He slept a bit like a shield, wrapping me up in warmth and protection I couldn't get from any ward. "They are a lot like humans, I suppose. Some good, some bad."

"Hmm," I said to him, feeling sleep weigh me down. I'd used a lot of magic, and apparently it was taking its toll on me.

"I'll order some plants to be delivered tomorrow that should help keep the faeries from messing with the house too much," Gabe told me.

"Thanks. Sorry. Dunno why I'm so tired."

But he was already running through my thoughts and all my little replays of my father. "You've had a busy day. Sleep. I'm here. We'll talk more about it in the morning."

Before I could ask more, dreams overtook me. In Gabe's arms, all I hoped to dream of was his happy smile.

The bright illumination of the overgrown flowers startled me out of a dead sleep. A flurry of activity filled the place, bugs moving back and forth. Roots and vines wove through the ground. I tried to keep out of the way while I watched them all work. My red-haired friend helped guide a thick stalk of green into the ground. Others rose up out of the dirt like some crazy, thorny spider legs ready to spear the ground. One pointy end headed right for Red's back. I darted around the masses, touched the dangerous growth, and directed it away. The vine pierced the ground, making an eruption of dirt and the sound of a sonic boom. My ears rang, and I had to blink back tears of pain.

Everything suddenly stopped. Not frozen in place, just halting, everyone turned toward me. Red's eyes widened. His eyes seemed to be swollen. Had he been crying?

He sucked in heavy breaths but kept his hands on the thorny vine. Blood stained his pants, chest, and hands. I crossed the distance to him without remembering moving and yanked him away from the harmful plant. He deflated in my arms, letting himself fall into my embrace, and sobbed. His tears smelled like a spring rain, blood like new soil. I let my instincts take over and pressed my luminescent skin to his and willed him to heal. The very core of me nearly screamed a possessive "mine" while holding him.

All remained still around us. The dangerous plant made more sense from this angle. It was a briar bush, nature's protection and punishment all wrapped in one. Only this shoot of prickly branches rose from the base of a stone that towered into the darkness.

"You gave us up," he whispered. "*They* demanded obedience."

Who was *they*? Gave up control how? I thought I'd retaken control of the house.

"And we die." Flashes of people speared on that bush trembled through my head. Not people, faeries, but still wickedly slaughtered. The vines glistened with blood, dripping the fluid from the highest tips like a cut jugular to fuel the ground, and rippled with magic. I dragged Red with me away from the stone. The sticky dirt clung to my pants and bare feet, bloody mud. Tears blurred my vision. Gone was the perfection I'd felt here before. Red pushed me away and turned back to the nasty plant that surely meant his death.

"It calls me."

"No!" I screamed to him. "Stop."

He stopped, twitching like his body fought the pause in movement.

"Tell me how to stop this," I demanded. The green glow of my skin brightened blindingly. His flaming hair faded under the light's assault. "No, don't go! I want to protect you. Please! You were mine first." But the early rise of the sun drove me out of the dream and into the morning.

Chapter 15

THE NIGHTMARES drove me out of bed early. By a quarter after eight, I'd done more than most people probably do all day. I'd called Caleb about the lawn and found a nursery that specialized in the slew of plants faeries liked, according to Gabe. They would deliver just after nine, and Caleb had already arrived to trim back the side yard and stir up the dirt, and outline the area with rocks in preparation for the new plants. I also read through the paperwork for the house, called Jamie with questions, and signed it. Hanna had taken my report about the ring over the phone and would be poring over Dominion texts with Allie most of the day. And Timothy would cross the yard at any time, since we would be going to the will reading today.

The journal my father had kept in the hidden drawer beneath his dresser was gone. In fact, nothing was left in the drawer but some photographs of him and my mother together. I decided to scan them and put together a scrapbook for her for Solstice, choosing one of the bunch to enlarge and frame—a picture of my father, his arms wrapped around my mother, who looked very young, with them both smiling. I planned on keeping a copy for myself for those times when my mom did something mean, so I could remember she hadn't always been that way.

A replay I'd somehow missed yesterday beckoned from the dresser. My father's hairbrush glistened with a faint pulse of power. I picked it up and quietly chanted the spell.

"Seiran," my father's voice called, deep, warm, and strong. I turned to see the ghostly image of him sitting on the edge of the bed. He appeared to stare right at me, smiling, eyes bright. "I hoped you'd find the spell. I hope that you have forgiven me."

Forgiven him for what? Dying?

"I never wanted to leave you. I suspect if you're viewing this, it's because I'm dead. Please forgive me for not being there, and take care of your mother. She's more fragile than she seems."

Tears flowed in the corners of my eyes and a lump formed in my throat.

My father seemed to be fighting tears too. "I bet you're strong and smart, handsome and good. Your momma wouldn't let you be any other way. I hope the world isn't so hard on you. Maybe there have been changes since I died. Perhaps the Dominion is more forgiving, or have even merged with the Ascendance to create an equal governing body." He laughed lightly. "Yeah, that sounds like a crazy dream, right? Maybe not to you."

He sighed heavily and stared off into the distance. "I've left you the house. I know you will bond with it just as I did. Even when you were in your mother's womb, I could feel your power and how the earth wanted to claim you." He shook his head and threw me another soft smile. "Don't be afraid."

Easy for him to say.

"It's never easy letting go of control. We as human beings are inherently bad at that. But the real truth lies within ourselves. Only when we truly let go of everything can we really experience all we are." He waved his hand at me. "And no, I'm not going to my execution with the idea that I will obtain some higher being. My power is going to Jamie so he can be strong enough to protect himself and you. My death will set back the Ascendance, perhaps push them in the right direction. My father's creation has also been the downfall of many male witches. We could have had equality by now; instead, we have fear and pain. My spirit will return to the earth. Here, in fact—" He looked around the room. "—the tree in particular, which is really just another kind of control. Apex of power and all that, or so my father claimed. He tried to right his wrong in the end, and they killed him for it."

He looked skeptical. I wished he were really here so I could ask him questions.

"In truth, Seiran, the only one you need to believe in is yourself. Everyone else of worth will prove themselves. Trust your instincts. Love with your whole being. And find peace in the earth." His image faded and I crumpled to my knees, overwhelmed with grief over losing a man I'd never met. My father had loved me. I took his advice and let go of all control, releasing all the tears.

I had cleaned up after my breakdown and was pulling the breakfast casserole from the oven when someone knocked on the backdoor. Timothy. He looked refreshed, like he'd slept, eaten, and could finally be normal and happy again. I searched his face for any sign of drugs but found none. Maybe being welcomed back on the property helped. Having a place to belong had always helped me.

"Morning," he said, plopping down on one of the breakfast barstools. "Still going to the meeting today?"

"Yes. I'm ready for it. Are you?" What would his father have left him? The Charles I'd been hearing about the past few days cared for no one but himself. My mother could have won Parent of the Year in comparison to him, which was saying a lot.

"As ready as ever. I don't suspect he'll have left me anything. I hadn't spoken to him in years." He stared at the countertop.

I didn't point out he wouldn't have been asked to come if he hadn't been left something. He looked up at me.

"What?" I finally asked, wondering if my eyes were still puffy. Gabe had held me for a while and kissed away the tears before I finally crawled out of his arms to face the rest of the day and let him sleep.

"The hair. Wow."

Heat flooded my cheeks. "Not quite sure how that happened, but I like it long. Gabe likes it long. It was long until a month or so ago..." I had spent some time trying to mimic the style I'd seen Red wear many times. To take the attention off me, I motioned to the casserole. "Hungry?"

His eyes widened as I scooped up a large chunk of French toast cinnamon egg casserole. The bottom was lined with thick slices of cinnamon-soaked toast, eggs, apple slices, and sausage crumbles. It smelled so wonderful I couldn't wait to dig in. This recipe was actually Jamie's, heavy on protein, but with a mix of fruit and starch to balance it out. No syrup needed, since I couldn't stand the stuff.

"Wow" was all he said when he dug into the large piece I set in front of him.

I cut myself a smaller piece. We ate in silence. Timothy devoured his so fast I pointed my fork at the dish. "Feel free to have more. There's plenty." I was used to cooking for more people.

He jumped up from his seat and rushed over to spoon up some more.

"Does the garden grow like crazy all the time?" I asked when he sat back down. The dream about killer briar bushes bothered me a lot.

"Yeah. It wasn't so bad when I was handling the house. We kept up the side gardens, and the lawn remained clear. When my dad kicked me out, it turned into a jungle and has been like that ever since."

So if I kept the actual gardens planted and growing, maybe the faeries would leave the rest of the yard alone. Poor Timothy must have waded through two feet of grass to get to the back door. "How much do you know about faeries?"

He paused, eyes darting around the room. Could he see them? He looked frightened at the mere mention of them. "Not much, other than what that ring can do."

"So you've never seen one?"

"No. Aunt Lily says that's why the yard is so crazy." He glanced back toward the main part of the house. "She'll be here soon. We're all driving to the meeting together."

My aunt was coming here? Was it the same Lily who was the head of the Magic Investigations department? "What's Lily's last name?" Girls always took their mother's last names in the Dominion; boys took them too if their mothers were from aristocratic families. Which meant that Timothy had not been born to a Dominion girl, since he had his father's last name.

"Castage. She's an earth witch too, level four, I believe. The only female child to be borne to John Ruffman. He fought for her. Wanted her to carry on his name. It's part of what earned him an execution. We both know how that worked out." He sighed and pushed his food around his plate. "She won't talk about him at all. I know she's been approached by a lot of people wanting to write books about him.

Research him. But she shuts them all down fast. Has to. She's big in the Dominion now. Important."

My brain went into panic mode. Lily Castage. Head of MI. Did that mean if I got the job, it would be considered some kind of favor to the family? I groaned. It didn't matter, did it? If I got the position, people would always say it was because of favors owed to my mother. Why did I have to be part of such a high-ranking family of the Dominion? I'd have to prove otherwise. Show them I was the best witch for the job. If I got the job.

I shook off the self-doubt, focusing on the window that looked out into the backyard. Start with what I could change and leave the other shit behind. Wasn't that what Kelly was always telling me? I wished I could be as easygoing as he was. "The house needs curtains or blinds. Something to make it safe for vampires to move around during the day."

"There's a supply store that has magnetic curtains not far from here. Magnets go around the window to keep the curtain from blowing open from a breeze. I can go get some and we can start putting them up. I don't think there's much we can do for the foyer and living room. The ceiling is bulletproof glass, but open so the tree can grow. I think it broke once from an earthquake, twenty or so years ago." He ran his hand through his hair. "Right around when your dad died, I think. My dad replaced it with something stronger. Paid a fortune for it. I remember the workmen being here for a couple weeks. My dad watched them the whole time like they were going to steal the silverware or something." He shrugged. "His paranoia was already starting way back then. I guess as a kid I didn't really notice it."

"We think a lot of things are normal when we're kids, only to grow up and learn it's something bad or wrong. Sometimes we think it's our fault." I thought of my mom and Matthew. What they did to me wasn't my fault. I wasn't bad. I didn't beg to be abused, neglected, or raped. I thought briefly of Brock, who hadn't much crossed my mind in the last few weeks. So many horrors in the past. And this house was filled with more ready to be awakened. I shivered, needing Gabe, wishing he could go to this meeting with me. "Maybe after the meeting, we can get blinds for the windows we can cover?"

"Sure. I don't think the reading will take long, so I'll pick up supplies afterward. If I recall correctly, there are something like fifty-seven windows in the house. That's including the ones in the front of the house around the tree. Do you want those covered for privacy?"

Did I? In front of the house, the fence was iron slats only a few inches apart. Most of the yard was surrounded by the same style, but in the back there was also a tall wooden privacy fence behind the iron one. If I put blinds up inside the house, it would be harder for people to look in from the street. Not like they could without binoculars anyway, but I liked the idea of privacy.

The question really was, how long was I going to stay here? If it were just Timothy staying in back, looking over the house while I was gone, he wouldn't care, right? Except that something about the tree kept nagging me. Like its existence wasn't meant to be public knowledge.

"Let's cover them for now. We can always change it later." I was pretty sure the garden had more eyes than it let on. How many faeries actually lived here? More questions for Gabe since he was the only one I knew who had any experience with faeries.

The doorbell rang. I got up slowly—breakfast sat like a lump of coal in my stomach—and went to the door, expecting to meet my aunt and possible future boss. Timothy followed closely behind, not worried at all. Maybe he had no aspirations to be anything other than a construction worker. He'd also grown up knowing Lily as just Aunt Lily, not Lily Castage, head of MI.

I swung the door open and stared at one of the most beautiful women I had ever seen. This was my aunt? She didn't look old enough. Her dark hair was a mass of curls that fell to her waist, eyes bright sapphire like mine, complexion pale and perfect like a model might be. She was dressed in a white button-up and a gray pencil skirt that accentuated her curves, her long legs in encased in black tights and ending in sparkly blue heels.

Everything she wore was probably top designer brands, but instead of smelling like money and confidence, her scent was of lilac, clover, and earth. I blinked at her a few times, taking in the sight over again. At first glance she could have been in her early thirties, or an older woman who took very good care of herself. The fact that she was probably closer to sixty floored me. I hoped I looked so good when I was her age.

Her smile grew to a hundred watts while she waited for me to respond. Odd how much that gesture mirrored mine. Finally, I cleared the fog and said, "Hello, you must be Lily." I held my hand out to her.

She took it, but instead of shaking it, she pulled me to her and hugged me fiercely. Unlike the rare hug my mother often bestowed on me, nothing about this one was awkward, just strong and warm. Her whole body moved with the hug, rocking back and forth, head bowed to press her cheek to mine. Even without the heels, she was probably three or four inches taller than me, but nothing about her towered.

"You're so handsome, Seiran. I've seen you in pictures but was beginning to think I'd never get to meet you in person." Her grip tightened almost painfully for a moment before she let go and stepped back to look me over. "Filled with earth too. Some Pillars never gain the acceptance from the earth that you have." She shivered, but smiled while doing so. "Touching you is like being at total peace with my magic." She suddenly looked a little sad. "And like looking at my little brother again. I can see his strength and fire in your eyes. He would have been so proud of you."

I didn't know what to say. My eyes blurred a little; stupid tears. I'd never even met my dad, so why could the thought of him make me cry at the drop of a hat? I blinked them away, stepped back inside the house, and said, "Lily, would you like to come in?"

"Love to, sweetheart." She stepped inside, welcomed by the house.

"I have breakfast if you're hungry." I headed back toward the kitchen, allowing myself the time to get back in control. Lily and Timothy followed. I heard her ruffle his hair and teasingly comment on the moppy mess it was. His reply was a warning not to touch, but his tone was happy.

In the kitchen, I pulled another plate down and dished up some of the casserole for my aunt. Funny how odd that term felt in my head. I'd never really had family other than my mom. Now I had a brother, an aunt, a cousin, and memories of a father who made me want to know more and more.

Why hadn't she come around? Why was I only finding out about them now? But I already knew, didn't I? My mother had raised me to believe that she was my only family. She hadn't told me about Jamie or Lily or how my dad really died, or that he had siblings. She wanted me all to herself, until she realized that I would never gain her what she really wanted—self-acceptance.

I stared at the plate for a minute, fighting back anger. She'd been young, angry and self-absorbed. How was I any different now? I had babies on the way. Would they look back when they were grown up and think I was a horrible father? No, I wouldn't deny them their family. If anything, I'd give them the biggest family anyone could hope for. Jamie and Hanna's family. Allie's family, my father's family. Hell, even Kelly and his slew of siblings could be uncles and aunts to my babies. They'd never be alone. Not like I was.

Someone touched my arm, startling me out of my thoughts and making me jump. "Sorry, sweetie. You okay?" Lily asked me.

"Sure, yeah. Great," I lied to her.

Lily stared at me a minute. Her eyes seemed to see right through me. And I was sure she'd say something about my lie, but she sat at the counter and made no girly fuss about not eating or having already eaten. She dug in, taking large bites like Timothy had, even talking with her mouth full. "Amazing. Your dad used to love to cook too. This is so good. If I cooked at all, I'd ask for the recipe. Maybe I can get it from you and give it to my personal chef." She plowed through the whole piece and was up piling on more while I sat in stunned silence, wondering how she stayed so fit eating so much. My mother ate like a bird most days and claimed the food I made would only make her fat. I bit back the pain. I wasn't a kid anymore. My mother couldn't control me anymore. She shouldn't have the power to control my emotions either. That was all on me.

I gave Lily a tight smile. "I didn't know my dad liked to cook." I didn't know anything about my dad. "Maybe you'll tell me more about him sometime."

"Of course, love. I have pictures and stories. We'll sit down sometime." She patted the back of my hand. "I'll give you lots of funny tales to share with your babies."

That made me really smile.

When Lily was finished, she set the plate aside, composed herself, and suddenly looked very much like a Dominion witch with power. "Now, Seiran, I received your résumé for the position in MI. I have to tell you that I can't favor you over the other candidates just because you're family. I will, however, ensure that you will get the same chance any other witch will. The position is entry level. It's hard work, lots of research, reports, and analysis. The data from the field is substantial, and it will be your job to sort it, report on it, and file it for future use. Most witches do the job for several years before moving into the field. Some don't last a month because the amount of information coming in is too great for them to handle. It's not as exciting as an episode of *CSI* or *Criminal Minds*, but it's necessary work. Is this still something you're interested in?"

"Yes," I replied without hesitation.

"Good. I'll be setting up interviews next week. My base is here in California, so if you're still here next week, we'll do it then, if not, let me know and I'll schedule yours early. No reason for either of us to fly elsewhere when we're already in one place. Your mother assures me that you'll be a good fit for the job; however, I'd like to see examples of your research and analysis." She looked over me like somehow my skills were apparent in the way I dressed. "You just finished school. Do you have any recent reports?"

"I have a copy of the final analysis of the class I taught on Counter Hexes, Curses, and Magic Nullification. It includes a copy of all the lesson plans, students' final papers, my grading of them, and the report of the class results." I didn't tell her I'd been asked to offer the Curses class as a regular seminar at least once a semester. Being paid for it was the only reason I'd accepted. Since the class would be held every other Saturday for four hours, it wouldn't interfere with any other job I had. At least, I hoped it wouldn't. Kelly had already signed up for the spring semester, which would be much more detailed than the original class had been.

"How soon can you get me a copy of that?"

There was a copy on Gabe's laptop, which was up in our room. "As soon as you want."

She pulled a card out of her purse. "E-mail it to me as soon as possible, then. Also, if you have any recommendation letters from your professors, that will help. I'm disregarding the ones from your mother and Hanna Browan, as they may have biased views of you." Her eyes scrunched up in a happy smile. "Can't wait to see those babies, though."

I didn't know Hanna had written me a recommendation letter. The idea made me smile. More and more she began to feel like family rather than just the mother of my children. Maybe she and Allie would spend Solstice with us. Of course, that meant I'd have to go home and actually be there for the holiday. With Jamie's help, I could make a pretty mean spread. Kelly joked about presents, but I found the idea of buying everyone gifts intimidating. Food I could do.

"I will ask a few of my professors." Professor Wrig would for sure; she'd already offered. I knew of a few I wouldn't ask, but had at least two or three who would probably write a decent letter for me.

"There is a little travel involved with the job. Probably once or twice a year. Most of your work will be from the Minneapolis office since the archives are there. Lots of computer work. You're good with computers, right?"

Not as good as Gabe, but I did okay. "I can't write programs, but I can work spreadsheets just fine."

"Good. Now"—she went back to Aunt Lily mode—"are we ready for the will reading?"

"As ready as ever." Timothy sighed.

Lily smacked him on the back of the head. "Be happy with whatever you get, child. And if your father left anything to that awful Ascendance, we'll be disputing that in court. That murderous organization needs to be put to an end."

"But your dad began it," I pointed out, fearing that her views really were so Dominion-tainted that she couldn't see the value of male witches.

"My father created an organization to give young male witches a voice. His goal was to have them incorporated seamlessly into the Dominion. Full equality. The Ascendance of today has lost that focus. They are building an army. They want to slaughter the Dominion and all its supporters so they can take control with the unnatural power they have stolen from others." She patted Timothy's wrist. "And they abuse children by forcing power on them they will never be able to control." She shook her head, lips drawn tight in rage. "How many young men have taken their own lives because of what was done to them? How many others became monsters or are tormented?"

"But the ring is still functioning," I muttered, wondering if she even knew about it.

"Yes. Well, my department is researching that. We did get the report from Hanna, but we have been working on it for years. I've had seven field workers disappear while investigating the ring on this property. All are assumed dead. I will send no more to their doom." She looked me over. "It's best if you stay away from it also."

"Gabe suggested a null-bomb." Did she know who Gabe was? "My boyfriend," I quickly said, just in case. "He's a vampire."

"Tried it." Lily shook her head. "We've tried everything. Even physically destroying it.

Nothing works. Machinery stops working around it. So we can't even tear up the stones."

Well, crap. That was not good news. "Water is a natural purifier," I pointed out while I put the dishes in the washer and wrapped up the casserole.

"Yes, but to get enough water to cleanse that would also end the drought in California. I've already had calls into my office requesting we bring your friend Kelly out here to see if he can end the drought, but the last Pillar of water tried, and it did little good. We'd disrupt too much of the earth to do it, maybe cause a major earthquake."

Unless, of course, the Pillar of earth—me—could direct that energy and disperse it. But the calculation and sheer force of it exhausted me just to think about. There had to be an easier way. I just had to brainstorm it out.

"Ready to go?" Lily asked as I stared out the window again at the backyard and the green growing beyond.

"Sure." I followed them to the door. Outside, the lawn was somewhat manageable again. Caleb was planting masses of flowers, ivy, and herbs in the garden that ran along the side of the house. The scent of fresh dirt and new greens made me giddy. Good thing I was leaving for a bit, or I'd be tempted to shift and roll in the dirt.

I sat in back, texting Jamie on my phone as we headed for the law office. He replied that he'd gotten a letter too, but would be attending the meeting by phone. It made me feel better to know he'd be there in some form.

The office was located in a nondescript one-level strip mall. Inside it actually looked very lawyerish: brown carpets, tan walls, expensive molding. Mr. Odagiri showed us into his office, which had a large, flat desk and several official-looking documents hanging on the wall.

A young man rose from one of the chairs, his brown hair and eyes vaguely familiar. He, like Timothy, could have been a model. What was it that made these California people so beautiful? The sunshine?

"This is Luca Depacio. He's sitting in for Maxwell Hart," Odagiri stated.

Lily looked him over somewhat harshly. "We've already stated that we will dispute anything going to the Ascendance."

"Mr. Hart is in agreement with you, Ms. Castage. His own funding and support to the Ascendance hinges on the results of this meeting. He is hoping for positive changes to the organization." Luca actually sounded like he was from Europe or something, his accent a soft edge that made him seem older than he looked.

"Everyone sit, please. I'd like to keep this as informal as possible. Mr. Rou, Mr. Browan said you could call him and put him on speakerphone when we were ready." Jonathon moved behind his desk and sat down, sorting through a stack of paperwork.

I dialed Jamie, said hello, put him on speaker, then set the phone on the edge of the desk.

"Whenever you're ready," I told everyone. I felt a bit like an outsider sitting in on something private. The house had never even been Charles's, yet he was giving it to me? How did that make sense?

Mr. Odagiri began, "I'm just going to read through the distributions. Please save any questions until the end."

"Okay," we all replied.

"To Lily Castage goes the estate in Europe and with it the business in Italy. This includes all stocks, revenue, and property outside the US."

Lily just nodded like she had expected that.

"To Jamie Browan, a lump sum of four-point-eight million dollars and all the American stocks."

Jamie didn't say a word, but my jaw dropped. He'd just been given nearly five million dollars!

"To Timothy Merth, the beach house in Washington and a lump sum of two million dollars, which shall remain his as long as he maintains the home. Should he lose the beach house to foreclosure, all monies shall then be donated to designated charities."

Timothy blinked and seemed to be in shock. He'd expected nothing but had been awarded more than I could imagine owning in my life.

"To Seiran Rou, as awarded in his father's will, the Los Angeles house, property, and all monies involved with maintaining the estate. Also to Seiran Rou goes the title and partial ownership of the corporation called Ascendance, including the twenty million dollars put in trust to further equality for male witches. Any and all spending of said monies must be approved by Mr. Rou from this day forth. As a requirement, Mr. Rou must take up a seat on the council of the Ascendance else all monies are forfeit, returned to the general fund within the group for council use."

My jaw dropped in disbelief as my brain tried to make sense of the words. Lily gripped my hand. My world spun. Twenty million dollars? A role in the Ascendance? And if I turned it down, all the money would go to continue messing up young witches and killing people? How was that fair?

"To Maxwell Hart, I leave the properties of the Ascendance, including the offices in California, Minnesota, New York, and Florida. The businesses within shall also go to Mr. Hart for full management and direction." Mr. Odagiri put the pages down. "Questions?"

"What does it mean?" Jamie spoke up. "That Seiran has to take a seat on the council?" I was glad he was asking the questions because I was pretty sure anything I tried to say at that moment would come out sounding like gibberish.

Luca spoke up. "The council of the Ascendance is much like the Dominion. They vote on policies and procedures, discuss changes, and make major decisions for the group. By taking Charles's seat, you'll actually have two votes, since he had his own vote and Dorien's. You could appoint someone to take Charles's place and remain on the council in Dorien's place. There are twelve total seats."

"This would be your chance to change the organization for the better," Lily pointed out.

"Or be corrupted by it, like my father was," Timothy said. He glared at the window behind the desk, staring at nothing.

"Seiran is stronger than that," Jamie said.

My heart pounded. I thought I was just getting the house that had been my father's. Now I had to be part of an organization that produced monsters like Brock Southerton and Andrew Roman. How could I change the entire scope of a group that believed in killing people just to spread the power out to others? Were they really creating an army? Did they truly plan to slaughter the Dominion? How would that create equality for anyone?

"Does anyone reject the terms set forth for them in this will?" Mr. Odagiri asked.

Everyone said, "I accept," but me.

I wanted to reject it. Everyone looked at me. I could feel them waiting, expecting. Everyone in the room wanted the Ascendance to change, and they were willing to dump the responsibility on my shoulders. My own thoughts ran around in a rush of panic. I opened the bond between Gabe and me and suddenly felt him awake and comforting. He knew instantly my hesitation, my fear, and reassured me that no matter what happened, he would not let me be corrupted by the mistakes of others in the past. He suggested I knew another very smart and powerful male witch who might help me make decisions for the Ascendance. Gabe pointed out this was the opportunity to make my grandfather's vision a reality, to correct the errors made in the past and create equality among witches.

Wow, that was a lot of responsibility.

You can do it, he told me. *If anyone can, you can. You know I'm with you. Jamie's with you, Kelly's with you. You're not alone.*

Finally, I said, "I accept."

"Great. Everyone please sign the bottom of this form."

Once the paperwork was signed, we headed back to the car. I kept Jamie on the phone, his voice saying soothing things in my ear, while Gabe mumbled comforting things in my head. Lily talked for a while about this being a wonderful opportunity, but I tuned her out. She hadn't just been placed as the head of an organization that killed people. Timothy stopped her chatter by placing a hand on her arm. I ignored her concerned expression all the way back to the house.

Chapter 16

Once inside the house, I finally let Jamie go and headed up to find Gabe. Even if he'd gone back to sleep, I still needed his arms around me. Maybe his touch could wash away this floating terror that devoured me. I could give up the money, as it meant little to me, but giving it up to the Ascendance I couldn't do. Damn Charles Merth for doing this to me. I didn't even know the man, but I hated him.

Luca had promised to arrange a phone meeting later in the day for all the members of the council. He would call me when he had everyone together. Whatever decision I began with would set the tone for anything I did with the Ascendance. I didn't have the power to disband them, but I did hold the purse strings. I called Kelly because he was always the voice of reason that never came across as coddling.

"The other council members are probably rich. So just having the power of the money won't necessarily stop them. At least not permanently."

"Max Hart said as much," I told him. "It sounds like he's got a lot of control over them."

"So is he friend or foe?"

"He's a vampire. Aren't they always a little of both?" I had to ask.

"Says the guy who's dating one."

"Gabe's different," I defended my boyfriend.

"Is he? Or is he just different to you? I've seen him do business. He can be ruthless. He's smart and also really old. Sounds like Max is old too. They don't live as long as they do by always being the nice guy."

"What are you saying?" I demanded of my best friend. "Are you saying Gabe is like Max? Or maybe even Roman?" The thought sickened me and made me angry all at once.

"No. Stop overthinking everything. I'm saying that he's crazy in love with you and is careful to not vamp out around you, but that he is first and foremost a vampire. This Max guy is a vamp too and you said he was crazy powerful. You thought maybe more powerful than Gabe."

"Yeah, maybe."

"Or maybe Gabe hasn't let you see his power 'cause he doesn't want to scare you."

I frowned into the phone.

"All I'm saying is that you can make this guy Max whatever you want him to be. Friend or foe, as you pointed out. Gabe loves you, will do a lot to keep you around. You can get another super vampire to like you, right?"

Now I really frowned at the phone. "Like seduce him?"

Kelly made an exasperated sound. "Like be nice to him. You're nice to Mike. He's a vampire."

"Not a very powerful one."

"Not true," Kelly said. "I've seen him break up bar fights. I've also seen him on the hunt. He's a baby compared to Gabe. But all vamps are powerful. He likes you. You're likable. Mostly."

"Hey!"

"Be nice to the new super vampire, but keep Gabe close. He's your ace in the hole. If Max turns out to be nuts, you turn him inside out. The Ascendance doesn't need money. I've been on the inside, remember? They need power. You are power. You just need to lead. Lead by example. You're good at that."

"Huh."

"Yeah?"

"Sometimes you're so smart," I told him.

"Sometimes? Remind me to kick your ass next time we spar when you get back. I'm so going to throw your ass on the mat until you're too sore to be fucked by your pretty vampire."

I gaped at the phone. "Evil."

He laughed and hung up. I put the phone beside the bed, set it to loud in case it rang, and watched Gabe for a few minutes. He granted me a sleepy smile. Instead of the lamp, he'd left the bathroom light on and mostly closed the door. Since I'd left him in total darkness that morning, I knew he'd done it just for me. His consideration made me love him even more.

"You're hot," I told him, liking how he looked all sleepy and mussed.

He lifted the blanket and motioned for me to curl up with him. I didn't bother stripping this time, just kicked off my shoes and plunged into the warm cocoon he created for me with his body and a couple of worn blankets. It wasn't until I was drifting off to sleep that I realized I hadn't had a panic attack when I should have.

Gabe's power. Was Kelly right? Was he hiding most of it from me? He seemed to control my power with ease. At least the calming part. Maybe he didn't know enough about magic to actually take over a spell. I sighed and pressed my nose into the crook of his neck, breathing in his scent.

Gabe was so deeply embedded in my head that I could almost feel him massaging my thoughts, lacing his own with mine to remind me how much he cared. If I'd known years ago how he could calm and comfort me like this, I might have become his focus sooner. I liked that he could help me sort through the swirl of emotion and stave off the worst of my anxiety.

His smile against my cheek was the last thing I remembered before dreams took me away to more peaceful things.

The chirp of a text woke me out of a light sleep a little while later. I blinked at the phone, trying to adjust to its brightness. Only an hour had passed. I really needed to get more than three hours of sleep at a time. Gabe was still wrapped around me like a vise, though now he was very still, in a deep sleep. His thoughts were calm. I wondered what he dreamt of, or if vampires dreamt at all.

Shopping for window coverings. Back in an hour, Timothy's message said.

I sighed and stretched. Maybe a little sunshine would wake me up. After kissing Gabe on the cheek and tucking the blankets around him, I made my way downstairs and out the back door. Caleb had cleared a path again, and fresh dirt lined the cobblestone pavers that led to the cottage house. He'd even removed the weeds from a marble bench that sat between two giant maples. I sat for a moment, soaking in the fresh air and warmth.

A breeze rustled the overgrown grass, causing an eerie whistling sound. The brown edge of a thorny branch made me shudder, the nightmare still fresh in my head, though it had been hours ago. I slid to the end of the bench and peered down into the growth of a small briar bush. *Shit.*

Without even thinking, I reached down and ripped the nasty thing from the soil. It fought me for a few seconds, tearing the hell out of my hands with its thorns, but then it came up roots and all. I almost expected to see the little bodies of faeries strewn in the dirt around the plant. There was nothing but dirt, dry and somewhat cracked, but only around where the plant had been. I felt triumphant for all of a minute and a half when I noticed another one by the fence.

I stomped around the side of the house to where Caleb slammed a shovel in the ground to clear another hole for some leafy green plant that appeared more native to California than Minnesota. "Help me!" I demanded of him.

He paused, glancing up, then blinked and stood up straight. "You're bleeding." He tried to reach for my hands, but I held the briar bush out instead.

"Don't worry about the blood. Help me get rid of these."

Caleb grabbed the weed from me and tossed it in the trashcan he had for the used planters. "Briars are pretty common in this area. They don't need a lot of water to grow. I can get some chemicals to kill them off if you'd like."

What about the faeries? Deadly chemicals couldn't be good for them. "Can I just borrow a shovel and a garbage bag?" I'd dig every last one of the damn things up if I had to.

"Knock yourself out." He pointed to a wheelbarrow that had shovels, rakes, and other supplies in it.

Grabbing a small hand shovel, trowel, a pair of gloves, and a trash bag, I surveyed the front yard. They really were everywhere, ugly brown patches of harmful thorns. These things kept critters out of the yard and stole sunlight from other plants. The vision of speared faeries kept flashing through my mind. I'd dug up a half dozen before making my way to the overgrown backyard. At the base of each plant, I searched for any little lives that might need rescue or had been lost, but found none. Had it really been only a dream? Shouldn't there be more faeries if the grounds were growing so wildly? Where were they?

I found another dozen more briars in the backyard, some incredibly large, and had to return to the front for a new bag. Caleb assured me he would haul the offensive plants off the property.

The wrought-iron fence had a pretty large gate on the opposite end from where the cottage stood. I left the gate open as I progressed into the wilder lands of the Merth family. Vaguely I recalled the path I'd followed as a lynx and how it wove through the forest, past a tiny stream, and around to the ring. This time, as I wound my way toward that awful place, I dug up thorny bushes and pressed each spot with earth and power. In school they called the ritual a blessing; to me it was more like a subtle spike of power to remind the ground it belonged to a greater whole.

The stream whistled by, untouched by briars, flowers blooming on the edge in bright colors instead, yet so close to that awful ring I could feel it. The ground snaked out in lines of cracked parchment, brown and dying, briars crawling across the barren path.

These, too, found a quick death and a new home in my trash bag, but my power couldn't touch the tainted ground. Each little shove of earth would bring a spike of unpleasant electricity coursing back through me.

Eventually, I stopped trying and continued to pull up plants. The effort had the effect of killing off wasps one at a time while trying to hurt the queen of a hive. It would never work, but it made me feel marginally better.

One giant brush glistened menacingly just a few feet outside the ring. The waist-high stones seemed glossed in brown, inviting the crawl of thorns up the side. This was the plant I remembered chasing a ladybug into several days ago. Cinnamon and red—had that been the faerie? I moved carefully around the base, prying up smaller plants and tossing them, then yanking out large branches to get to the root of the problem. The dirt was richer here, almost moist, and filled with nutrients. How was that possible when the rest of the ground appeared sucked dry of life?

I kept digging, praying I'd finally get the plant loose. It wobbled a little; progress. Breaking up the dirt and tugging worked it free enough that I stood up, put both hands around it, and yanked with everything I had. The briar roots popped out of the ground, sending me sprawling backward. The giant bulb that made up the roots lay beside me. I shook the dirt out of my hair and sat up to glare at the stubborn plant.

The numerous roots wove outward like little white shoots, all connecting to a dirty light-brown ball. I poked it with my shovel, having never seen anything like it before. It rolled slightly, settled again, a clump of mud falling off the side. Two empty eye sockets stared back at me.

I screamed like a girl.

Chapter 17

When the police arrived in my yard for the second time in a week, they weren't quite so friendly. The head detective looked hard at me, like he expected me to crack and admit I'd somehow killed these people. When I led him through the backyard to the ring and the skull I'd unearthed, he stood openmouthed for a few minutes before stepping away from me and making a call I couldn't hear.

Lily arrived—since I'd called her second—just as the rest of the police trickled in, brandishing shovels and body bags. Were they expecting more dead? I shivered at the idea that the entire yard could be covered in bodies. Maybe the entire two acres of land that made up the property. I really didn't want to know. My gloves were stained with what I thought was mud at first, but the drying brown wasn't mud. It was blood. Old blood, but not as old as the skull I'd found. Someone had died here recently. I stared at my hands and could almost feel the pulse of the ring, hypnotic, alluring, a siren call for the powerful. Except the closer I got to the ring, the more my skin burned and itched and my lungs tightened.

Whatever Lily said to the officers must have appeased them to her presence and mine, since they didn't ask us to leave. She sat with me, thumbs rubbing my injured hands while we sat in the grass. I don't know if she was oblivious to the blood or if it didn't really bother her. I wanted a shower something fierce, but I didn't think the police would like me just walking away to go clean up while they dug up the body I'd found.

"Do you think that is one of your missing people?" I asked her.

"Maybe." She seemed worlds away, eyes focused on the digging. They even brought a small backhoe out, but each time it got close to the ring, it stopped dead and had to be reversed.

The body they unearthed had likely been there a while, as it was just bones and bugs. More than a dozen other cops dug around the circle, looking for anything else. No one, not even the cadaver dogs they brought in, would go inside the ring. The rocks went down into the earth as far as they dug. A group exclaimed when they found another body.

Two hours, twelve bodies, one for each stone, all in shallow graves. One facing the house was still fairly fresh. He still had flesh and hair. The mass of bugs eating him and the smell had me throwing up and hiding behind a tree. Lily turned ghostly white when they pulled him up and zipped him in a bag.

"That one was Charles," she whispered to no one in particular. The lead detective turned her way as she began to topple. I caught her and helped cradle her to the ground, where I held her as she sobbed. My uncle, her baby brother, Timothy's dad, had been stuffed into a hole to fuel the death magic of the ring. That sounded a little worse than a heart attack to me.

Lily clung to me, even though she was bigger than me, as we headed back to the house. We left the cops to do their thing, and I made sure they knew where to find us. Timothy was pacing just inside the gate by the cottage house. "Bring her up to my place."

Did he know his father had been buried back there? My heart pounded with unease, but I followed him up the stairs, guiding Lily with me. Inside, the place was clean, neat, and very institutional. He invited us past some fairly strong wards on the threshold, then Timothy put together tea without being asked and brought Lily a blanket as I settled her on his large couch.

"Do I want to know?" he asked me almost too quietly to hear. "Not much rattles Lily."

"I don't think your father died of a heart attack," I told him, though I really didn't know. Maybe he had, but somehow I was pretty sure Charles Merth had been alive when he was brought to that circle.

He looked down at my stained hands and swallowed hard. At least this blood was mine. There was still dirt under my nails from before I'd retrieved the gloves from Caleb, but the worst of the gunk I left with the police in an evidence bag. I got up and used his sink to scrub away the blood. He took an industrial-sized bottle of orange cleaner out from under the sink and put it beside me. The small scrub brush helped more. I focused on cleaning the gunk out from under my nails, trying not to think too hard about what it was and giving Timothy a minute to cry unseen.

He looked away, his lips scrunching into a tight line. "I don't want to know."

I nodded. Probably for the best. Finally clean, I dried off my hands and returned to check on Lily. She was really pale and a little shocky. I touched my hands to her cheeks. My hands had been warmed by the water and the fierce scrubbing. She blinked at me like I'd woken her from a bad dream.

"You look so much like Dorien," she told me. "He would have loved you. I wanted to love you. Tanaka wanted no one." She sighed. "I should have insisted."

I frowned at her. "I'm doing okay."

She shook her head. "You're on the edge. One wrong move and you could turn out like Charles." Only she wasn't really looking at me when she spoke. She was looking at Timothy. He was pacing the room, wringing his hands and glancing at the back of the house in the direction of the ring.

Finally, he said, "I have magnetic curtains. I left them just inside the foyer." Again with the fast pacing and hands moving. "I should work on that. It will keep my mind off things." I got it then. His addiction—addictions—were screaming with need and tempting him with temporary solace. He needed a distraction. He looked at Lily, but she wasn't seeing either of us.

"Can you maybe reinforce the wards so if we leave her here, she's safe?"

"Sure." I stepped up to the door and poured my strength into the wards, adding a strong push so that any who did enter, human or otherwise, would lose all sense of violence they might have entered with. I tucked the blanket around Lily and made my way toward the big house with Timothy close behind.

Was I headed for darkness? I'd used my magic to kill once, but it'd been to save my life. Or had she been talking about Timothy?

"I'm not evil," I heard myself saying before really thinking it.

Timothy glanced at me. And Caleb stopped what he was doing to look my way as well.

"I'm not," I assured them both. "Just because I'm powerful, doesn't mean I'm evil."

"No one ever said you were," Timothy reassured me. "My dad was never that powerful, even after he took other people's power with the ring."

Caleb tilted his head our way. He wasn't a witch. We probably made no sense to him. "You okay?" he asked me.

I shrugged. I'd survive. "No one's killed me yet."

"Sounds like someone's tried before?" he said in his southern drawl.

I nodded. "And failed miserably." I met his gaze, wondering at the interest I was suddenly seeing there. Maybe he had a kink for guys with power? Didn't matter. If he was into Sam, I wasn't going to get involved. I looked him over. He was human. Sam could rip him apart with little trouble, but sometimes it wasn't about the physical strength. Sam was like a baby, just learning to crawl as a vampire. "You should know I take care of my friends," I told him. "Sam is a friend." He wasn't really. But we were trying.

Caleb nodded and gave me a good-old-boy smile, tipping his hat before returning to his digging. Timothy tugged me inside to see his haul of coverings. Apparently he'd cleaned out four stores of their entire stock. We didn't have enough to cover all the windows, but he had more on order.

"We could start with the back of the house. Make it safe for your boyfriend," Timothy said.

Gabe probably hated being confined to a room half the size of his bedroom. If I could get the windows covered, Gabe could actually spend time with me in the kitchen. I missed him watching me while I cooked or swinging me into a little dance while I cleaned. For a vampire, Gabe was almost always moving. I loved that about him.

Timothy waited for me in the foyer while I bandaged my hands, then brushed my teeth. He had apparently made several trips from the car, because the stack of curtain rods and giant bags of packages would never have made it in one.

"I got a bunch of different ones so we can try to match rooms. They are pretty easy to install. I did them in the cottage yesterday since I'm kind of a night owl." He grabbed one of the bags and strong-armed several boxes of rods and headed for the stairs. "How about we start upstairs and work our way down? You're staying in your dad's old room, right?"

I nodded, though technically it was a lie. But the bed was still made and it looked like I was staying there.

"Okay." I was pretty clueless when it came to fixing things, but I could pick out tools and hold things up. He wore a tool belt, and I grabbed the box with the drill in it he'd left by the stairs.

We actually got through four rooms fairly quickly. Once the first set had been installed, I knew how to put the magnets around the window to secure the fabric and snap the rod into place once the curtain was on it. They were pretty secure and very little light got through. There was even a cap that went over the top of the window, though since that light would never directly hit one of the vampires unless they were floating at the top of the room, it seemed sort of overkill.

My phone rang when we were halfway through the upstairs. I'd already borrowed Gabe's earpiece so if someone called, I could still talk hands-free. It was Luca.

"I've got the council meeting set for four o'clock. Do you have a pen handy to write the number down to call in?"

Timothy took the rod I was working on from me, and I whipped out my phone. "Go ahead." I typed in the number he gave me and saved it.

"Max will be at the meeting, and I will be mediating. We are making it mandatory for the entire council."

Apparently Max and maybe even Luca had a lot of power over the Ascendance. I wondered if they were really on my side or not. "Okay. I'm going to have Kelly Harding and Jamie Browan attend as well," I told him, wondering if I were breaking some sort of meeting etiquette.

"They will just have to announce who they are. Likely most of the council won't say much to any of you until you make your statements."

That was fine. I had a lot to say. "They aren't going to like me much."

"Probably not. No," Luca agreed. "They don't like change. And they like to be in charge. They've been fighting Max for years. Charles's madness slowed them down quite a bit."

"Did the ring make him crazy?" Did Luca know about the ring? He didn't talk as though he were actually a part of the Ascendance. Maybe he was just Max's assistant.

"Charles was always crazy. He just got worse with age. Heard the house you've been left is a little spooky too. He used to tell Max that he was hearing voices and people were watching him."

Which didn't necessarily mean Charles was mad. After all, it could have been the faeries. "I'll keep an eye out for anything suspicious," I told Luca, not planning to share with him that actual faeries existed on the property. He might think *I* was crazy. We said good-bye.

I sent texts to Jamie and Kelly. They would make themselves available. Both assured me we could do this. Change was within our grasp. We just had to reach for it.

Timothy and I continued with the window dressings. He surprised me with a covering for the kitchen entryway too. We completed most of the windows before I had to call in for the meeting.

"Do you want me to go?" he asked. He was a ridiculously efficient handyman. The curtains had been easy for him, and he knew the house well.

"Nah, keep working. I'm going to start on dinner while I do this; it will help keep me calm." I began pulling out ingredients for dinner, then dialed into the meeting. Timothy vanished into the giant dining room. There were four windows in there to be covered. The phone beeped.

"Hello, who joined?" Luca asked.

"This is Seiran Rou," I replied.

Two more beeps followed mine: Jamie and Kelly. Then another beep: Max.

"Everyone is here. I'm going to introduce everyone and then we can begin." Luca rattled off a bunch of names I wrote down and planned to research later. No one else spoke. "Now that the introductions are complete, I'm going to hand the meeting over to Seiran, who is currently in place for Charles and Dorien Merth, and is 40 percent shareholder. Seiran?"

Wow, talk about pressure. "Thanks, Luca. I asked for this meeting for several reasons. The first of which was to introduce myself and designate the extra chair. Secondly, I would like to review my agenda and some general changes that Charles Merth's will makes to the organization.

"I will be taking my father's seat on the council, and I would like to ask Kelly Harding to take Charles Merth's seat, so we have a full twelve members."

"Kelly, do you accept the position?" Luca asked.

"I do," Kelly replied. I wondered if he was as nervous as I was.

"In his will, Charles Merth left the bulk of the finances to me, and to help with management of those monies, I would like to appoint Jamie Browan as Financial Advisor," I told the group.

Luca spoke again. "Jamie, do you accept?"

"I do." Everyone was so quiet, I wondered what they were thinking.

"This is Max," Max spoke up. "I am designating Seiran Rou the 20 percent I own of Ascendance and providing him with full control and disclosure of all properties and monies. I will remain as a silent council member only. My vote is now Seiran's."

My jaw dropped again. What was he doing to me?

"This means Seiran Rou is 60 percent shareholder and therefore head of the council. All actions must be approved by the head before they can be taken," Luca stated to the group. "Any events forthwith that occur without the consent of the acting chairman can be punished with excommunication from the organization and blacklisting."

It seemed harsh, even to me, but changes had to start somewhere.

"This is ridiculous. They are children," one man spoke up.

"Pillar or not, this is a business, not a playhouse," another stated.

My mind reeled. It was like being placed as head of the Dominion by default. My heart pounded. The link to Gabe, still thrown wide, provided me with a bit of calm. I could do this, he assured me. In fact, this could benefit everyone. I ran through the ideas I'd been working on most of my life for equality among witches. How much could I propose? And now that I was the head of the group, how much power did I really have? I sucked in a deep breath and prepared for battle.

"Like it or not, I'm in charge," I pointed out. "I have appointed Jamie and Kelly because they both are well-prepared to help run this as the nonprofit business it should be. They are both male witches who have a strong wish for equality, just as I do, and that is the vision of this group, is it not?"

There was a grumbled reply of assent.

"Good. Since we are agreed, the first step I would like to take is to communicate with colleges and universities who offer magic studies programs. I would like for them to begin testing and accepting any and all natural witches, male or female." I specified natural because those who were stealing power by killing others had no right to the training they could get in school. If I could find a way to remove that inflated power from them, all the better.

"We've asked for that for decades and have always been denied."

"I just graduated from the magic studies program at the U of M. Kelly is enrolled, along with two other males. There will be almost two hundred males testing in the spring for the fall semester. I think many more schools are going to begin opening options to male students. Since two of the five Pillars are now male, they can no longer ignore us."

"Luca can begin contacting other schools. He's good at public relations," Max stated. I wondered for the first time if Luca was his focus, since he seemed to rely on him so much. I'd never met another vampire with a focus. Or at least not one they'd been open about.

"Equality needs to extend further than education," someone on the phone stated.

"I agree," I told them. "However, we can't expect the Dominion to offer jobs to uneducated male witches. I believe the road to equality must begin somewhere. Just like any other group facing discrimination, we must take one step at a time and not expect everything to change overnight. Gaining education and recognition is a big step."

"Agreed," Jamie, Kelly, Luca, and Max all said.

Time to drop the bomb. The ring and all its evil would end with me if at all possible. "I am also stating from this day forth, no witch, male or otherwise, shall be subjected to any sort of power enhancement spells. No rituals, curses, death magic, or anything to give one witch's power to another. Any use of the Inheritance ceremony must be filled and approved by the Dominion before the spell is cast."

The gasp from the group was audible. Was it not something they talked about in the council meetings? Did they not understand how bad it was to have power that was hard to control? None of them seemed ready to make a statement on the phone that they supported the murder of other witches to inflate their own power.

"Anyone found practicing these evils will be released from the group, reported to the authorities, and likely punished publicly for their crimes. Let it be known here and now, I will not tolerate murder."

"How can you say that when you have committed murder yourself?" someone demanded.

"I killed Brock Southerton in self-defense. He was trying to kill me to increase his own power. I did not take his power in return. I sent all that stolen power back to the earth. Had there been another way, I would not have killed him." How long had I beaten myself up over that very bit of truth? After the fact, I thought of a million ways to protect myself, to stop the rape, to stop Brock from hurting me. Sometimes in the heat of the moment, common sense gave way to fear and adrenaline. I would likely regret that night for the rest of my life, but survival had been more important. Which of us deserved more to live? That was not my decision, but I certainly wasn't going to let myself be killed for someone else's selfish goals.

"The Dominion would have killed him when they caught him anyway," one of the council members said. "He was being far too casual with magic."

Casual with magic? Killing people was casual magic? "He had killed others and murder is against the law, human and magic. Why is this even a debate?" I demanded. "The ends do *not* justify the means."

"Brock's death is what made you Pillar, and becoming Pillar is what sparked the change within the Dominion. They only accept you because the earth accepts you," another of them said. I wished I could see them so I'd know who was saying what and could put faces to names. Many of them were still silent. But maybe the few outspoken ones conveyed everyone's thoughts.

Jamie replied this time, "That is only partially true. The changes were happening even before Brock came into Seiran's life. Seiran was already in the magic studies program. He was already considered for several positions within the Dominion, and it was his persistence that got the university to begin accepting more male students. That was all before he became Pillar."

"Again, this is not up for debate," I told them, cutting them all off. Just how far would they let me push them? "Murder is unacceptable. Magic murder is unacceptable. Have you forgotten the very core of our laws? The threefold law? How many of you would like the awful things you've done to come back to you threefold? For good or ill shall be returned to us threefold. All witches know this."

"This statement will be written into the Ascendance Code," Luca stated. There was a bluster of voices all talking over each other. Comments about how the Dominion law shouldn't rule over Ascendance law. But I couldn't understand them all and didn't try.

I figured I'd probably stirred up a hornet's nest and should give them some time to digest it. "I have no further changes at this time."

No one said anything.

"All statements have been documented and will be used as a record for changes applied immediately. We will schedule the next meeting in a few weeks." Luca took control of shutting down the meeting. "Any complaints or questions can be filed through the proper channels for review." He closed out the call and let everyone go. I took the phone out of my ear, feeling a little dizzy and nauseous all at once. Timothy had stopped working on the curtains and just stared at me like he'd never seen me before.

"You totally just ripped apart the Ascendance. They live for power. They claim it's just to give more male witches power, but it's all about the control for them." He shook his head. "You just stripped them of control."

"I tried to do the right thing."

"Not all of them will see it that way. They will probably come after you."

I shrugged. So be it. Having people trying to hurt me wasn't new. Bring it on.

Chapter 18

Gabe wandered carefully out of the upstairs room. I could feel him asking questions and told him most of the house should be safe for him to travel through as long as he took the back stairs down. He appeared in the kitchen a few minutes later looking amazing as always.

He smiled at Timothy but crossed the room to kiss me like he meant it. I wallowed in his lips, loving his taste and his wonderful kissing skills. No one locked lips like Gabe could. He almost seemed to drink my soul through his lips, gaining life and love from me and strengthening our bond. I sighed and wrapped my arms around his waist.

Timothy's eyes were wide. Did he not know I was gay or was it being this close to vampires that made him nervous? He cleared his throat and got up from the counter. "I should go finish those windows." Then he was gone before I could protest.

Gabe chuckled but hugged me back. "You are amazing. Beautiful. Incredibly intelligent and amazing."

I pointed at him and gave him a funny look. "Be nice."

"What did I say that wasn't nice?"

"You tease me." I tried to pull away.

He yanked me back against him and kissed me again, then said, "Never."

"Stop. Or we'll get distracted. I should eat. You should probably eat too. There's QuickLife in the fridge."

He held me a minute longer, breathing in the scent of my hair it seemed, before letting go. I returned to making dinner.

"You're still amazing."

"How so?" I asked.

"Taking over the world, one crazy at a time." Obviously he was referring the meeting.

"Whatever." I rolled my eyes at him. "I don't know if they are all crazy or just power hungry."

"There's a difference?" Gabe inquired.

He had a point, but I frowned at him. "Do you have your lawyer on speed dial?" Whomever Gabe used was good, and I needed to make some changes fast.

"Yes. Of course. Why?"

"I should probably make sure that if something does happen to me, the Ascendance gets nothing."

Gabe's expression was suddenly unreadable, like he'd become a statue, lifeless and emotionless, standing there in the kitchen. But I could feel the pain the idea of losing me brought.

"It's just a precaution."

He blinked. It was long and slow, but it brought a little life back. And a flash of red in his eyes. Was something more wrong? I tried to probe our bond for more answers, but while he wasn't closed to me, he wasn't wide open either. He seemed careful. Like a mesh gate that let me glimpse beyond but never past, he held me at bay. What wasn't he sharing with me?

"Gabe?"

A tapping at the window interrupted us. We both turned, but the new curtains covered the glass. Again with the tapping. Gabe moved to the other side of the room, and I carefully peeled the edge of the fabric back. The little faerie tapped at the window, expression fierce. Was he going to dive-bomb me again if I let him in? Couldn't he just go through the window like he had my bedroom door? I pushed the window open a crack and he flew inside. I shut the drapes, locking them down with the magnets.

Gabe returned to the counter, watching the faerie fly around the room like a bee on steroids. "This your new friend?"

"Heh," I said. Friend. Sure. "Lyden, right?" I asked the bug.

He landed on the counter. *How do you know my name, child of Dorien?*

"'Cause I watched you attack my dad in the tree in the foyer. What's with that, anyway? Didn't I free you? Why are you back?"

You planted things for us.

I glanced at Gabe, who shrugged. "Yeah, I thought you'd like that and maybe leave the rest of the yard alone. I'd really like to not have to mow it every day just to walk to the gate."

He flew up and landed on my shoulder, big eyes blinking at me in confusion. They were so big and dark and shining that I could see my own reflection in them.

You want us to stay? But you released me.

"Just because you don't have to serve me doesn't mean you can't stay. The yard is plenty big for a couple of faeries."

Now if they could only tell me how to get rid of that damn cursed faerie ring, things would be even better.

How many?

"How many what? How many of you can stay? As many as you want. How many are there? Do I need to expand the gardens? Because I can. I just don't want to cut down any trees."

He flew up again, rushing around, darting across the room and back. I feared several times that he'd run into the wall and hurt himself. This time, he couldn't seem to leave unless I opened a door or window for him.

Let me out, child of Dorien.

"You got out just fine last time." I sighed and went to the window. Gabe shrugged. The sun was setting. As long as it didn't hit him full-on, he'd be fine.

"Maybe if you invite him in, he can come and go as he was," Gabe suggested. "He is a thing of magic and the new wards are pretty strong, renewed every time the earth spins. I can feel the vibration of the earth in my spine. It's pretty intense."

"Fine. Lyden, I welcome you and all your kind to come and go in peace within these walls and my home."

Lyden suddenly vanished. I blinked a few times and wondered if I'd just missed seeing him move, but no, he was really gone, no open window or anything.

I shook my head and went back to my work, stuffing the chicken with cheese and peppers, then popping it into the oven. "This has been a really odd trip."

Gabe pulled out his phone and dialed his lawyer. "Let's get this legal thing done. Sam will be down soon." Gabe's lawyer would draft up the paperwork and send it to my e-mail.

Timothy came back into the kitchen after finishing all the windows in the dining area. I invited him to dinner. He said he'd go clean up and come back. No reason for me to eat alone. Gabe and Sam couldn't touch the stuff. Gabe was at the counter on his computer, reading through some sort of history on faeries. I suspected Timothy wanted to check on Lily too.

"I'm going to take a peek at the new garden," I told him. I sort of just wanted to see if Lyden had really invited his friends that fast. So far he was the only faerie I'd seen up close.

Would the rest have to show themselves to me, or would anyone be able to see them?

Gabe nodded, quiet like he rarely was. I think the will thing had bothered him a lot. But I wasn't going to pry it out of him. He had to make an effort to talk to me too. And he could join me outside if he needed to.

The side yard bloomed with ivy and flowers. I didn't remember all those things showing up that morning. Caleb must have been working fast to get it all planted. A red blur buzzed around me several times on my way toward the back to where I heard digging and movement. A faerie, probably, but he didn't seem all that interested in talking to me. Or maybe it was a she. Hadn't Gabe said females were more common?

Caleb's blond hair was darkened with sweat, tank top stained with dirt and perspiration rings, but he dug and planted like a machine. He paused and glanced up at me with a wide smile.

"Your garden is growing like a possessed thing." He gestured to the blooming flowers he'd planted earlier in the day. "The second I put them in the ground, they take, grow, and blossom. I've never seen anything like it. Is this a Pillar thing? Timothy said you were super powerful."

I was pretty sure the growing garden had little to do with me and wondered if he saw the whirring dashes of color flying around and thought they were bugs. "The earth magic here is pretty strong," I told him.

He'd carved out ground all the way to the fence on both sides of the path and around the yard, like edging.

"You work fast."

"Planting is easy. Churning up the ground was pretty easy, too, since I have a machine that does it and I'm not going that deep. I'll come back tomorrow with mulch to keep the weeds out." He shrugged at the yard. "You'll probably want to hire someone to maintain all of this."

I smiled to myself. Wasn't that what the faeries were for?

"Unless you plan to sell the house. Heard you weren't from here."

"I inherited the house from my father. I don't think I'm ready to let it go yet. The house needs a little more work." Like getting rid of a certain faerie ring.

He looked me over, a frown on his face. "Your boyfriend staying?"

"Yes." Not sure why it mattered.

"Would be safer for you to go. People have been asking questions. Looking at the house."

Now I was frowning. "Thanks for the warning, Caleb. Let me know if you need anything else. Have a good evening."

He tipped his missing hat to me and went back to work. Was he talking about Max or someone else?

I headed back inside through the kitchen door. The smell of the spicy chicken made my mouth water. Sam sat beside Gabe at the counter now. The timer went off on the oven. I checked the temperature of the chicken and pulled it out since it was exactly 160 degrees.

Timothy came back in and paused, seeing the two vampires in the kitchen. Maybe he wasn't used to being this close to them. Finally, he moved and took the seat at the end of the counter, several feet away from the vampires.

"Need any help with anything?" he asked me.

I shook my head, mashed up the cauliflower and potatoes, and mixed the cheesy broccoli topping before dishing up a plate for each of us. The look on Timothy's face when I set the dish in front of him said he didn't get to eat well very often. I set my own dinner down and began cutting the chicken into small bites. The colors of the cheese and peppers made it bright, and when I tasted it, the flavor came through rich and spicy.

"Sorry," I said when he didn't touch his food. "I should have asked if there was something you didn't like."

"No, it's fine. I've just never had anyone cook for me like this. It looks great." Timothy dug into the chicken, then covered a broccoli floret in potato before stuffing it into his mouth.

Gabe threw me an amused smile. Sam seemed to be dozing in his chair. I glanced back to my plate and had to pause. Had I eaten all that already? Over half my chicken was gone. Maybe I was hungrier than I thought since I didn't remember eating more than a piece of it, and I was still far from satisfied.

A red blur passed the edge of my sight again. I looked up, searching the room for more movement. If faeries were going to be hanging around, I'd have to get used to them. No one else seemed to notice anything, and after a few minutes, I went back to my food, only to find the rest of the chicken gone. No way had I eaten that without realizing it.

I pushed a cheese-covered broccoli floret to the chicken side of my plate and watched intently. Nothing. Dammit. At least I'd made more chicken. Dishing myself up another piece and cutting it in a hurry, I figured I'd keep an eye on it this time, no matter what kept flying around me.

The blur landed when I pretended to be looking away. He snatched up a piece of chicken and swallowed it whole. "Holy crap!" I cried.

Gabe, Sam, and Timothy all looked startled. "What?" Gabe asked.

"There's a faerie eating my chicken!" Why had I figured they'd be vegetarians? Just because they looked bug-like from a distance didn't mean they fed on plants. A lot of creatures were carnivorous.

Gabe didn't look surprised at all. A smile tugged the corners of his lips, but he went back to his research. Sam and Timothy still stared at me like I was crazy. I wondered why the creature wasn't attacking Timothy's food, but he was bent very protectively over his plate. Then I remembered the mint plant Gabe had given me. I had fresh mint in the fridge. Pulling out a sprig, I left it beside my plate and waited.

Finally, the rushing blur stopped. It landed in the mint, rolled around a bit, then lay there. The long cinnamon-colored hair and copper skin told me nothing about whether it was a boy or a girl, but it could be Red. I picked up a small piece of chicken and offered it to the creature, who eyed me warily with its over-accentuated expression.

It took the piece carefully and stuffed it into a mouth that became momentarily larger than its head. I blinked at it and brought my face closer to the faerie's level, wondering if it would talk to me. Instead of speaking, I thought, *Who are you?* hoping it would hear me. *Are you the red-haired man from my dreams?*

I held out another piece of meat for it. Again it vanished inside that impossibly small creature. Before I could move my hand, it bit me. I yelped in surprise. Sam's eyes turned dark, red, and hungry at the smell of blood. Gabe grabbed his arm to keep him from moving. Timothy sat frozen in his seat, eyes as wide as saucers, waiting for whatever disaster was to come.

Sam's struggle played on his face. I could almost see in his eyes that he wanted to leap across the counter and rip a hole in my throat. He shuddered, turned, and headed toward the front door. Gabe glanced at me but followed him slowly.

"Be safe," I told them. Once the door slammed shut in the distance, Timothy sucked in a deep breath. I patted his hand. "Sam's working on it, but he's only a couple weeks old, vampire-wise."

"I get it. I've just never been that close to a vampire before."

The little red chicken thief had vanished again. Did that mean my little red-haired friend was safe? The color was right, but maybe it was a common color for a faerie. "I think I'm going to call him Bryar," I told Timothy.

"Who?"

"The faerie I keep seeing in my dreams. I searched out all the briars in the yard because that's where I last saw him. He said they took the names humans give them. Plus, he keeps biting me, so it's almost like he has thorns."

"What do they look like? Are there any in here now?" His eyes darted around the room, looking large enough to pop out of his head. I wondered if he'd take my suggestion and get some therapy for what the Ascendance had done to him.

"Small, kind of bug-like at first. I think they can change how you perceive them." I grabbed Gabe's computer and turned it my way. He had a page open that talked about faerie glamour and illusions. He'd bookmarked a half-dozen pages for me to read, but I had a lot more than just faeries to learn about. "Do you have a copy of the Ascendance Code that Luca was talking about?"

"Yeah. They will e-mail out a new one with the changes in it within twenty-four hours. Things happen fast in the Ascendance." He still searched the room for any sign of faeries, though I was pretty sure no faerie had ever hurt him.

I nodded and took my plate to the sink to clean up. "Lily okay?"

"Yeah. It's hard seeing her so shaken up. I remember when I was little and Dorien was killed. I think I was six at the time. Lily came home and found me alone; Dad gone as always. But she wrapped her arms around me and just cried for hours. I didn't know what to do. The idea that Dorien had been put to death really didn't make sense to me, being that young and all."

A lump formed in my throat and tears blurred my vision. *Dammit.* "Jamie won't talk about it either. I think he watched."

Timothy shivered. "How awful. Lily wouldn't let me see. I had a nanny at the time and no TV was allowed. Dorien had been good to me. Whenever he got back from spending time with Jamie, he doted on me for days. Bought me gifts, took me places, read me bedtime stories.

He was more my dad in those years than Charles ever was."

I ground my palms into my eyes, trying to will away the tears. My life would have been so much different if my father hadn't died before I was born. My mother would have been kinder, more loving. I would have had someone who took me places and hugged me like I mattered. The years at military school probably wouldn't have happened.

Timothy touched my back lightly. I hadn't even heard him move. "I'm sorry, Seiran. I didn't mean to upset you."

"It's okay," I managed to say. "I just can't control it sometimes, the emotions."

He laughed. "I think that's normal. They call it being human." He put his dishes in the washer and helped put away the rest of the leftovers. "I'm going to keep working on the curtains. You look tired. Get some sleep."

I sighed. I'd been doing a lot of sleeping, only rest wasn't really forthcoming. I headed toward the stairs, feeling soul-weary again. Who knew learning about the past could hurt so much?

The bed was cold without Gabe in it, so I rolled myself up in all the blankets like a sausage, left the bathroom light on, and closed my eyes. Sometimes letting the real world go for a while could sort out the troubles in my head. I would talk to Lily tomorrow about doing my interview early. I missed Jamie, Kelly, Hanna, and even my mom. I longed to sleep in my own bed, cook in my kitchen, and run the indoor track when my head got too full of crap. It was time to go home. Sleep took me with that thought.

Chapter 19

Back in the glowing garden, the peace had returned. Something lingered just on the edge of the giant flowers, darkness rolling in with the weight of a nasty storm. A hand clasped mine, bringing not only warmth but worry and my red-haired friend.

"I'm so happy to see you, Bryar." I yanked him into a tight hug. He hesitated for a second before finally returning my embrace.

"Bryar?" he asked.

"You're kind of prickly sometimes." I held up the thumb he'd bitten twice now. "And you bite."

His eyes met mine with an intensity that made me want to turn away. "You really gave me a name?"

"Don't you want one?" I shuffled my feet and looked away from him, searching the clouds for answers I didn't yet have. "I want you to have the freedom you long for. If you don't like the name, you don't have to take it."

"And if I accept it?"

Was he asking for more? I feared I was still disappointing him. "I don't know what you want from me. I thought you wanted me to give you a name."

"Bryar is a good name."

"And we can call you Ry for short." The silence between us stretched a few awkward minutes. "Or not, I guess."

He laughed. "Bryar it is, and Ry is fine. I accept with honor."

"Why do I feel like I just did more than give you a name?"

Ry gave me one last quick hug. "Because you're smarter than you should be."

"What's that supposed to mean?" But the world faded into a dreamless sleep, which refreshed me though I slept only a few hours before Gabe settling in beside me woke me up. "What time is it?" I asked.

"Just after midnight."

"You're back early."

"I wanted to be with you, not wandering some club watching Sam feed."

"You have to watch?" Feeding for us was usually sexual.

"So he doesn't take too much, yes." He kissed my hair, fingers running through it. I'd forgotten how much of an obsession he'd had with the length before Sam cut it. "Timothy said he upset you. Are you okay?"

"Yeah. He just shared some memories of my dad. I guess I didn't realize he was that much older than me." Or that he'd known my father. "I miss home. I want to go back."

"To Minnesota, you mean."

"Yes. To Jamie and Kelly and Hanna and my mom and my condo. Everything."

"Even if it's cold and the earth is sleeping?"

"Yes. I just have to talk to Lily first and do my interview for the MI position, but then we can leave."

"What about the house? The ring?"

I sighed because I truly didn't know. Nothing was ever really that cut-and-dried. I didn't want to get rid of the house because of the memories. My father had a ton of spells mentioned in his journals that could be perfected just by moving from room to room. The partial spells were all easily finished by adding my own words. Dorien Merth had been a very smart man. Most witches feared creating their own spells. He enjoyed it, even used the house as a way to experiment with his creations.

Yet the evil of what had been done on the property wouldn't be easily erased, and that gave me pause in keeping the house. Letting it sit empty was a waste. "Maybe once we figure out the ring thing, we can make it into a school or something. There's lots of rooms. It could be a place to train Dominion boys."

"That is a fabulous idea." I studied his face. Something was wrong. Gabe looked away and said, "We need to talk."

"Okay. Is this where you tell me, 'It's not me, it's you'?"

"No. Never. Fuck, you're my everything, Sei. I need to stop being an overprotective idiot. You hate it. I know you do. I need to stop being a hypocrite and telling you to talk to me when I haven't shared everything with you. I was afraid when I found you gone, and angry. So angry thinking about what might happen with you so far away." He let me lay my head on his chest.

"Tell me," I insisted.

"One of the Tri-Mega has gone rogue. Tresler said he was last seen in California. That's why I was so furious when you came here alone. It's likely he is the one you invited in by accident. Jamie told me about the letter. Sent me a text. I thought it was a trap. I came back home with Sam to find you gone."

"I thought the vampire I invited in was Max."

Gabe shook his head. "Doesn't make sense. Why he would introduce himself if he were already in your house? I've never met Maxwell Hart, but I've heard of him. He's powerful, but not with illusions. Nicholas Galloway, however, is a master of illusion."

"He's the Tri-Mega guy?"

"Yes. Tresler called me directly when I filed the paperwork to establish a nest. He warned me of Galloway. Galloway has been killing vamps along the coast. Decimating entire nests."

I listened to Gabe's heartbeat and wondered what it all meant. The politics of vampires were still so far beyond me. They didn't have a set rule book other than a few basics, which seemed like a bad idea for the world's deadliest predators. "He didn't do anything to me, though, if it was Galloway in the house. He had plenty of opportunity to hurt me."

"But what better way to lure me in than to take control of you?"

I snorted. "Even you don't have control of me."

He kissed my forehead. "Galloway doesn't know that."

"Why kill the vampires anyway?"

"Rumor has it he can absorb their power. I thought it was a legend. Never seen it happen myself. But I don't know why else he'd kill the other vampires. And then there's having you as my focus. No vampire has ever been bound to a Pillar before. However, vampires are rarely direct. So maybe he's not after me at all. Maybe he's looking for something else. I don't know. Tresler probably does but isn't going to share because he likes to watch us all flounder around."

"Does he know that Max makes you look like a baby vampire when it comes to power?"

"Really?" Gabe quirked a brow.

"The guy radiates power like Tresler did. That scary sort of I'm-gonna-fuck-you-up power." I thought back to our first meeting and the second at the ring. "And it was like he was holding back. He said he's not a witch, but he felt as powerful as a high-level witch."

"Hmm." Gabe rubbed my shoulder and back for a little bit, lost in thought. He was still so much better at choosing what he shared through our bond than I was. Finally, he said, "I have never heard anything negative about him, but if he has that kind of power, I'm surprised he hasn't taken out Galloway already."

"Maybe he's not interested. You don't care for politics. Maybe he's the same way. Does creating rules and being a boogeyman for vampires sound appealing to you?"

"No. Sounds like a lot of unwanted work."

"So are you really going to start recruiting vampires? Making vampires?" Did that mean I'd see even less of him?

"Recruiting, yes. Making new ones, no. I've called a few I've made in the past. They'll be moving up to the Cities to help with establishing the nest." He kissed me on the cheek, then the tip of my nose and across to my other cheek. "I find I have more important things to do than look after new vampires." He ground his cock into my thigh and slipped his knee between my legs. "There's this guy I'm sort of hung up on and he's kind of high maintenance, but he's so fucking hot, I just want to pound him into the wall. Can't do that with baby vampires everywhere."

"Who might this guy be?" I licked the outline of his lips and nipped the lower one. "Someone I know?"

"A certain brunette. He has these soulful blue eyes, silky hair, and skin like moonlight.

Then there's this smile of his." He sighed deeply and kissed my forehead. "The world makes sense every time I see that smile, and nothing else matters. Wish I could see it more often."

I didn't bother fighting the smile that split my face. He always made me feel like the most important person in the universe. My heart ran up and down a crazy roller coaster of emotions when I was with Gabe. But all those swings around treacherous corners, races down impossible cliffs, and journeys to incredible heights were so much better than the years of self-destructive loneliness I had lived.

We kissed for a while, entwined together, not sexual, just sensual. Not that I wasn't turned on, but the closeness mattered more than sex could any day.

"So, home for Solstice?" he asked.

"Yes. You'll still have time to pick a tree."

"You really hate the idea of having a dying tree in the house, don't you?"

I hid my face in his shoulder and opened up the bond between us, showing him all the recent dreams, nightmares, and pain when something happened to the earth. The Christmas tree thing really didn't seem that big of a deal anymore.

"You know I'm terrified of you walking away from me, right?" Gabe asked.

I glanced at him, surprised. "Why would you be afraid of that?"

"I spent years waiting for you, praying you'd find your way through all the mess and see me at the end, as the light in your tunnel." He rubbed my arm in slow circles. "It's like I'm waiting to wake up from a dream."

My stupid insecurities had done this to him, made him cautious and fearful. "I love you, Gabe. I'm not going anywhere. Even when I'm stupid and jealous. You had to know my coming here was only temporary. And it was only partially about you."

"Maybe we need to plan a vacation to someplace warm each winter. Become snowbirds or something."

"Maybe. It wasn't so bad last year."

He nodded. "You weren't Pillar last year."

True. Everything was more intense since becoming Pillar, not just the power, but my emotions, my anxiety, and even my reaction to the seasons.

He stared into my eyes for a few intense moments, like he was peering into my soul. "You have no idea what would have happened to me if I hadn't met you. If I'd never gone to that party. If I'd never approached you that night or if you'd never called back to pursue me. God. Everything seems so destined. Like some cosmic thread pulling us together. And as much I'd like to believe in greater powers, I've been around a long time. The only power I know that isn't bullshit is you." He smiled and hugged me tight. "And me. This thing we have. I'm just a planet orbiting the sun. Without you, I'd be a useless ball of ice. You complete me, like in those romances you read. You are my other half. I really hope you understand that someday."

"I do," I told him. Really, I did. Most of the time. "Sometimes my head gets in the way."

He nodded. "That's the truth. You overthink things. Talk yourself into situations that will never happen and freak yourself out."

"It's not always a bad thing," I protested. Because it wasn't.

"No. But it does make your life more difficult. Maybe we can just work on talking through more of the stuff that's in your head so you don't have to linger on it by yourself."

I sighed against him, loving how right it was to be back in his arms. "Okay."

He kissed me one last time. "I'm going to jump in the shower downstairs. You should get some sleep. See if you can do the interview with Lily tomorrow, and we can head home tomorrow night. I should check on Sam too."

"Okay. I think it's probably safe to leave the house and the ring to Lily."

"She seems smart. Normal." He winked at me. He tapped his forehead, "Going by your opinions of course. She's the most normal person in your family so far."

"Hey!" I threw a pillow at him. He caught it and laughed, dropping it back to the bed.

"Nap. I'll be back in a bit."

I watched him leave the room. Lying there without him wasn't what I wanted. The pulse of the earth ran through me strong and unrelenting here, but without Gabe, I was just a buoy floating without guidance in the waves of its power. At home there was distance and it was more manageable. I felt less insignificant. Which was stupid, because in reality, compared to the earth, I *was* insignificant.

I got up and started to pack. Most everything had been haphazardly shoved into my suitcase when the first streak of pain slashed through me. A sharp, white-hot knife cut down my spine as though someone were cutting me in half. It was like when Caleb had trimmed the trees, only intensified by a million. I passed out.

Chapter 20

Someone shook me awake, but the pain kept coming. Was it Gabe? I opened the link between us, only to find his end closed like a concrete wall against me. Another pulse of agony ripped through my entire body, tightening muscles and spasming them all at once. My blood boiled in my veins, pounding in my ears and spreading pain through every inch of my body. I'd smeared the tree with my life's essence by accident. It held me to that bond. Demanded my help. But I couldn't get up.

"Seiran, you have to move." The voice sounded only vaguely familiar, but I couldn't see past the pain behind my eyes. Someone held me up and even helped me to the ladder and down the hallway. Only then did I hear the sound of a chainsaw, not outside, but inside the house.

My first fear was that someone was hurting Gabe. His mind was blank to me because he was hurt, maybe even dead. I growled and fought my way to my feet, mind rolling through a dozen spells that were forbidden, dangerous, and deadly.

Each roar of the chainsaw slashed through me, knocking the wind out of me, causing me to stumble. Strong arms helped me up. I blinked, clearing my vision, though for some reason I saw red, and it wasn't just his coloring this time. It was like something primal left in Gabe had taken hold of me.

The arms around me belonged to the most beautiful man I'd ever seen: Bryar. Holy shit, he was big! People-sized. I gaped at him, fighting through the pain for breath and trying to find the clarity in my head to ask questions.

"Questions later. Stop the tree from dying first." He practically carried me to the top of the stairs in the main hall, where Gabe lay. Blood pooled around him, dripping down the stairs, splattered on the walls. His head was nothing more than a pulpy mess.

The world darkened, turning red around me, not with blood, but with indescribable rage. Bryar vanished while I stumbled down the stairs, to see Caleb sawing away at the oak that had seen more generations than he would ever dream of. Sam's crumpled form lay beside the door, prongs from some Taser-like device hanging from him.

Caleb paused only long enough to pull out the Taser and pop off a round at me. I dodged to the left, falling down the last few steps, but missing the sting of the tines. He struggled to reload, but I flew at him, all the rage, pain, and earth in my punch. His head snapped back like something had broken. He staggered back a few feet, dropping the Taser and chainsaw. His head looked like it was on wrong, crooked, yet he still moved—staggering like a broken doll from some horror movie. He was alive. And it shouldn't have been possible. Not unless he was a vampire. I hadn't sensed him being a vampire. Could I have missed it? Would Gabe have missed it? No. Caleb had been outside in the sunlight, unbothered. Not a vampire. But maybe a vampire's focus.

His neck crunched with a sickening sound, popping his head back in place. He rolled his head from side to side, the bones popping and crackling like he was just stretching after a long day of work. His expression was cold compared to my white-hot rage. He crossed the space and hit me hard enough to send me sprawling to the floor. My head smashed into the tile. I felt the back of my skull split. Lights broke through my vision, dizziness spinning me in darkness for a minute. Then the stinging pain of the Taser hit me, pouring raw energy through me. I blacked out again, but probably only for a few seconds. When I awoke again, it was to the annoying buzzing of Bryar by my ear, back in his tiny faerie/bug form.

Get up, Seiran. Stop him!

Easier said than done. My limbs didn't want to work. My brain told them to move, but I couldn't feel anything. Had Caleb broken my back, my neck? Oddly, I felt detached from my physical body, like I was just a head, and though that hurt, the rest felt like dead weight.

"Who are you?" I demanded, though it came out more like "whoru." The better question was *what* was he, since I'd hit him hard enough to break his neck and he'd shaken it off only to turn around and wallop me. If he was truly a focus, did that mean I could take a hit like that and survive? Maybe I already had.

The sound of footsteps came from the kitchen. Timothy? Was he part of this too? He appeared in the doorway to the kitchen, eyes wide with shock. He stared at me, horror clear on his face.

I willed him silently to run away, call for help. Anything but be part of this awful conspiracy to destroy everything and everyone I cared about again. Instead, he raced across the room and jumped on Caleb's back, trying to wrench the chainsaw out of his hands. Timothy wrapped his arms around Caleb's throat, digging in and choking him while Caleb struggled.

"You killed them!" Timothy screamed at him.

Caleb dropped the chainsaw and yanked at Timothy's hair. Timothy must have had a great deal of strength because he fought Caleb for a few minutes. Finally, Caleb slammed him into the wall. The hit seemed to stun Timothy for a bit because he shook his head like he was seeing stars. Caleb threw him off and across the room like he weighed nothing.

"You are a waste of space, Merth. You should grow some balls like your old man. You could have been a leader. Now you're just fuel." Caleb kicked Timothy in the stomach, resulting in a sick crunch of bones and a cry of pain from Timothy.

Sam groaned and began to wake up. Caleb turned, slammed another cartridge into his Taser, and shot Sam again. Sam convulsed, eyes rolling back in his head. He still fought, baring his teeth and trying to move, but Caleb leaned forward and smashed his fist into the side of Sam's head. "Stay down, vampire. You've done your part by inviting me in, now you can wait to die like the rest."

Bryar buzzed at lightning speed from me to the tree and back, his panic almost visible in streaks of color. My limbs refused to respond. Blood trickled from my skull, a warm flow that made me think of Gabe. It was sad to waste all that blood. Gabe would have licked the wound closed, and together we could heal it by pulling power from the earth. We'd been working on control for a few weeks, but I couldn't feel anything from him other than the concrete wall between us. How long would it take him to heal? No matter what, I was pretty sure I couldn't count on him to rescue us.

The chainsaw kicked on again. The tree toppled with an awful thud, landing opposite the stairs. The power from the intersecting ley lines surged upward, a blast beyond that of a lightning bolt coming from the ground instead of the sky. Color and light erupted, cascading across the room and shattering the glass ceiling, which rained down on us. A red light hovered over me, and the glass slid to my sides instead of hitting me. The red returned to Bryar's tiny form, and he darted down to sit between my eyes.

This is bad, Seiran. You have to control the power.

I'd get right on that, as soon as I could feel my body again. A bright splash of light and power smashed into me, and the pain of my awakening limbs was akin to thousands of needles puncturing my skin. The scream it pulled from me rattled the walls, hurting my own ears. Agony beyond anything I'd ever experienced before ripped me apart from the inside out. The change poured over me, only to pause, reverse, and then flow back. I tried to scream again, but even that sound was lost in the horrific breaking and mending of bone and muscle.

How many nightmares had I had as a kid of being stuck mid-transformation, unable to hold a form? Trapped, helpless, a mass of writhing flesh and bones. The hot rush of blood poured from me so fast I feared I'd bleed out. I blacked out again, but the piercing sting didn't allow me to rest long. Obviously I'd lost more than a few minutes since Sam and Timothy were gone. Caleb stood over me, looking every bit like the crazy man he was, eyes wide, blood on his face, and chainsaw strapped to his back like some sort of apocalyptic warrior ready to find a legion of zombies.

"Time for you to be useful, Rou." He reached down and gripped me by the hair, dragging me out the door and down the stairs. "You are the freak of all freaks, you know that? A monster now, stuck between human and cat. Disgusting." He spit and then smacked something away from his eyes. A barrage of tiny colors swarmed him, forcing him to pause and release my hair for a moment. He swatted wildly at the bugs, probably not realizing they were faeries. Hundreds of them swarmed him, biting him. I could smell his blood.

The yard grew like the one in my dreams. Daisies, orchids, and ivy rose in glowing bunches larger than any giant sunflower I'd ever seen. The front gate was barred shut with a wall of green so thick I couldn't see beyond it to the street. The flashes of color still shot from the broken windows toward the garden, landing and making things grow in seconds to a hundred times the size they would ever have been normally. A few streams of wild power hit patches of faeries trying to dodge the madness, and my heart skipped a beat when I felt them die. Too much power. The earth gushed out like a geyser of water, hot and spraying damage into the distance. I could barely breathe through the weight of the energy.

The power of the earth coursed through me, healing as well as hurting, mending broken bones only to have them snap again when it insisted I change to my lynx form, then repeating the cycle. The ground shook like the slow building of a massive earthquake. Only I couldn't get enough of a grip on the power to actually control it. How many would die if this continued? I fought with the earth, trying to distribute the power evenly, slowly, but it ignored me as though I were powerless.

I had to stop this somehow. Bryar clung to me, hiding behind my ear, chanting, *Oh*

Goddess, oh Goddess, oh Goddess. It seemed an odd phrase for a faerie.

Caleb finally freed himself from the throng of faeries and continued to drag me through the yard and out to the ring. He lifted me and carefully stepped around the holes dug into the ground to throw me into the center of the circle. Sam, Timothy, and Gabe had been placed in the empty graves. Bodies of other men I didn't recognize filled the other holes. Death magic to fuel more death magic. My skin crawled.

The nightmares of the ring stung only slightly less than the continual shifting of my body. Was Caleb planning on taking all my power for himself? Why bother cutting down the tree? I closed my eyes as he brandished a knife and slit his hands to let the blood flow over me.

Help me, Bryar. I tried to speak mind to him mind to mind, not knowing if it would work. His panicked chanting stopped. I felt him move, brushing back my hair. My scalp burned from the constant changing and Caleb's pull on it. The tingling sensation in my limbs had returned, and I hurt in places I didn't know I could hurt. I tried to gather the strength of the earth around me to stop the change and get back some sense of stability.

Caleb chanted and walked around the circle. Did he think I planned to give up? Maybe he didn't know about the last two men who'd tried to kill me. No way would I die before knowing that Gabe, Sam, and Timothy were safe.

What do you want me to do? Bryar asked.

Anything! Distract him. Hit him with a truck. Whatever. Just do something!

A red blur flew upward, smashing into Caleb hard enough to send him sprawling. The man sputtered. Bryar wouldn't leave him alone. Bright flashes of light exploded in front of him, making Caleb rub his eyes and blink. My brain moved at snail speed while I tried to figure out what to do.

The water, Seiran! Bryar shouted to me, but it made no sense. I wasn't a water witch. That was Kelly. Sure, I could feel the stream not far away. The peace it gave the earth clearly proved its purification properties.

Purification, shit, that was it!

Caleb fought his tiny attacker for a few more seconds. And Bryar was fierce, unrelenting. He dodged Caleb's fists and smashed into him hard enough to knock him to the ground several times.

I knew I was running out of time. The earth was going wild, and without Gabe's control, this level of power was so far beyond my ability to rein it in, I didn't know where to begin. If I survived this, I would need much more practice.

The only thing I could think of was to bring the water to us. The power that bounced wildly around didn't care much for my guidance, but I pushed at it anyway, adding my own will to the strength coursing through my blood, and pressed it into the ground. Bryar added his strength to mine, and suddenly there were thousands of little blips of power pressing in the same direction, guiding the earth.

A vision of a peaceful stream winding through the forest filled my head, separating the stones and washing away the blood to sparkle with clear, pure water. Vegetation, nutrient-filled dirt, and the soft sound of water gliding over smooth rocks completed the scene.

The ground responded a little to the vision —shifting, cracking—and water glided forward, but it wasn't enough. I reached out mentally, forcing all my pain into the earth instead, putting the wild magic back into the ground and guiding it to the stream. The thousands adding to my power morphed into uncountable amounts. I fed small bits to Sam, Gabe, and Timothy, asking the earth to heal them.

The strain of multiplying influence built in the ground like a tsunami of earth trying to hold back the water. Letting it go made blood burst forth from my nose and pour down my face. The explosion of power shook the earth beneath us.

Caleb hopped up but had a hard time keeping his footing. I curled my hand outward, blood sticking my skin to itself and muscles tight, but willed the earth to protect my friends. Roots shot out of the ground, gripped Sam, Gabe, and Timothy, and lifted them up out of the ground. Caleb howled with rage and kicked me hard in the head.

Stars erupted in my sight, but I kept fueling the pain and power into the stream, which grew into a raging river as the land made way for it. I became nothing but a conduit, not really controlling the power, just guiding it, and it hurt. I bled and couldn't breathe, but I kept the flow going.

A gap in the ground formed, expanding and shoving up water tables to add to the flow. Bryar returned to his safe spot behind my ear just before the ground split beneath me and the water poured over my head. I sputtered, unable to do anything to keep myself afloat while still focusing on the power.

The water battered at the stones of the ring until they gave. I prayed that Sam, Timothy, and Gabe would escape. The roots that held them rose higher, stretching more branches up to help hold the others. I directed all I could of the power into the growing crevasse.

The break curved around and through the property, finally opening enough to take the water back. I kept pouring the wild earth back into the ground, not knowing what else to do with the power that had been released from the tree. The energy sizzled through me like fire, burning until I felt nothing physically anymore. All that I was became one with the earth.

Roots dug into my body, pulling me down beneath the waves, while my spirit wanted so badly to float free of it all. The earth needed fuel, and power alone couldn't do that. Sacrifice was required. I had to give it something.

The stump of the tree pulsed in the distance with pain and fading strength. I recalled the levels testing and how a tree had been reborn from the stump when I touched it. Perhaps that was why the tree existed to begin with, just to saddle the strength of the earth with its stability. There was no way I could actually touch the dying wood to rekindle its flame. But I could still feel it.

I bobbed beneath the water, still fighting the grip of the earth. My eyes were heavy, corporeal consciousness leaving me, and water filled my lungs. Finally, I released my physical form, giving the earth my blessing to use the shell however it needed. The mass of ever-changing flesh was useless to me anyway.

For a few seconds there was a dizzying sense of separation, floating, sinking, pain, peace, and then finally a snap. My soul flew above the ground. The water formed a stream that flowed up and out of the middle of the circle. It trickled down like a fountain. Mud swirled around in a whirlpool pattern that sucked the extra water away, along with all the filth of past wrongs.

Caleb climbed free of the water, looking exhausted from fighting its pull. A dark form stepped before him. The moonlight and spatters of colored lights flashing like fireworks overhead revealed Lily, Taser in hand. She shot him with it, slapped in another cartridge, and shot him again. He writhed and screamed, but he was going nowhere.

Sam struggled to release himself from the grip of the roots that held him, finally got free, and splashed into the water. When he reached for Gabe, who began to wake and move, I continued forward beyond the overgrown yard. I felt every part of myself ingrained into the earth now. Everything glowed with life and strength, even the house. Had the simple gesture of giving up my body done this?

A small stream wove through the yard, and I watched tiny fish jump over one another to get their own space as I floated above them.

Finally, I glided through the wall of the house with little resistance and passed from room to room, renewing the vitality of the vines and branches as I went. The tree stump raged with sparkling lights, uncontrolled power, and threats of tipping the balance of the earth into a deadly spiral. I drifted to the shorn stump and knelt. This tree had capped centuries of energy, balanced it and renewed it. Placing my spectral hands to the base, I directed the power back into the tree, willing it to bloom and blossom again. The millions of little flickers of power had vanished, leaving me unsure and alone to tame the beast.

The fireworks fizzled but didn't die. Only a tiny little stalk curled up through the stump. I put one hand on my mostly invisible knee and glared at the new bud. No way was that little thing going to be able to contain all that power. It had to grow. Maybe not be as big as the old one—there would be time for that sort of solidity to form—but something at least as thick around as I was would be necessary.

I put both hands beside the sprout and willed the little thing to develop. Only a few more inches appeared. Never in my life had I had to try so hard to make something grow. I took a deep breath and wondered what it would take. Another sacrifice, perhaps. But what to give? There wasn't much left to me.

My father had died to stop the Ascendance from succeeding. He'd given his spirit back to the earth to rebalance the elements. Perhaps if I put that last bit forward, it would be enough. I concentrated my effort and poured everything I was into the seedling. The peace expanded outward, flowing through me in a soft warmth as if I were sitting in the grass on a sunny day. I prayed that everyone would be safe and that the earth would correct itself once my spirit had infused it.

Darkness dragged me down, but the tree was growing.

That was all that mattered as I faded into nothing.

Chapter 21

Whatever I expected death to be, it wasn't the glowing garden of my dreams. However, that's exactly what where I was. Only this garden had no night—it shone bright and clear, flowers blooming everywhere, soft grass beneath my feet, and peace surrounding my soul. Was this heaven? I'd never really believed in life after death, but if this was it, I was all for it.

A ladybug big enough to be a golden retriever walked beside me, then shifted, changing from bug to man. Bryar. Was he dead too? I would feel awful if I'd killed him with the water somehow.

He put his hand in mine again, long fingers warm and solid in my grasp, and walked with me to a little area filled with plants growing to look like furniture. "You can stay here, you know," he said to me.

"I don't even understand what this place is."

"It's where you feel most at home."

"The earth," I said without question.

"Of course. This is how Gaea welcomes you, what she offers."

"It's very peaceful." I sat down on the soft petal of a chair and leaned back to put my feet up. My hair fell over my chest, even longer than before. It was now a bright mossy green, the glow of my skin a blinding pale green. I looked up at Bryar. He didn't sit or even look at me. The disquiet in him worried me. "What's wrong? Did I hurt you? I didn't mean to."

He dropped to his knees, head bowed like I was some sort of king. "You could never hurt me. Your heart is too pure. But I'm selfish and not ready to share you yet. I sought for so long to find your weakness so I could send you running. I'm stupid. You truly are the GreenMan, Father Earth, master to all of mine. I have no right to keep you when others need you so much more."

"What do you mean?"

An image of Gabe flashed through my head. He looked tired and sad. Then another flash, this one of Jamie sobbing while Kelly held him and tried not to cry himself. My heart ached, and I sucked in a deep breath.

"I should go back. Everyone's worried. Can you wake me up from this dream?" Too often I hurt them.

Bryar wrapped his arms around my legs and held me tightly. "I am your servant, so I must do as you ask, but I beg you, all that awaits you out there is pain. Stay here. Let them go. Gaea is not always kind, but she's protective of what's hers."

I wanted to say that he wasn't my servant, to release him from any demands, but he put his fingers to my lips. "I am happy serving you. You gave me a name and I give you my loyalty. You saved my life, and I will save yours."

"Why do you talk in riddles? Can you take me back? I need to be sure that Gabe is okay." Distantly I felt him in my head, but for some reason, I couldn't open the bond to him. The absence ached more than when he normally had himself closed to me. "The earth is no place for me without Gabe. Do you understand? I need him."

"If I say that others will continue to try to hurt you, will you stay?"

Another vision flashed by my inner sight, this one of a little red-haired boy with bright sapphire eyes. He turned his head toward me and revealed a little girl with dark curls and a similar blue gaze who clung to his hand. My soul soared with a happiness I'd never felt before, realizing these had to be my babies. I agonized every day about never having had a father. Leaving them was not an option. Sweet Gaea, I had to go back. "I have babies who need me. Did you see them, Bryar? Did you see how beautiful they will be?"

"Blessed Father Earth, will you at least let me stay with you?" Bryar begged.

"Don't call me that. But, sure, you can stay with me. I'm kind of good at collecting orphans." I thought of the tree that Kelly had gifted me. It sat in the living room next to my favorite reading spot. "There's a tree you can live in. Let's go back. I'll show you my babies."

Bryar's laugh sounded pained. "If you insist."

"I do."

The world brightened, almost blinding me as the tiny sitting area disappeared into the light. The sun's warmth had me stretching out my paws and rolling to get up. I shook out my fur. The smell of clean earth filled me with joy and peace. Strolling toward where I sensed Gabe's presence, I played in the water a bit, danced in the grass, and even flipped over a few small rocks to bat at the bugs that scrambled for cover.

A red ladybug landed in my path, and we played awhile until we got to the door of a human dwelling. It landed on the white frame, crawling up slowly. Were we done? I still had so much energy to play. He floated down and landed on my head, right by my ear.

Scratch on the door. They will let you in.

Why do I want in? I asked back, happy my little friend could speak to me. *I want to play.*

They have food. Yummy chicken.

My tummy rumbled, making me snort. Well, if they were going to share chicken with me, being inside couldn't hurt. I was sure there would be plenty for my bug friend and me. When I ran my claws down the door, little white ribbons curled around me.

How fun!

I jumped on them, breaking them to bits, then scratched a little more, freeing more streamers from the door. The door opened while I was happily grunting at the white flakes. I bit the painted wood frame and chewed on its blunt edge.

Shouting came from inside, then grabby hands. I backed away. None of the words made sense. Everyone soon disappeared back inside. They left the door open a crack, and my little bug friend and I cautiously made our way inside. The smell of chicken hit me as soon as I poked my head through the door. I raced to the plate set across the room, devouring the juicy chicken left out for me. The scent of cucumber and mint traveled to my side, and a moment later a man sat down.

A gentle hand ran through my fur, rubbing my spine so sweetly I couldn't help but purr and arch into the touch.

Footsteps approaching made me pause and look up. I growled. The crowd of man-things made me want to run for the door, which was still open. The one touching me was my earthman. He often gave me chicken and a warm space to sleep, but he didn't have claws to protect himself and me. I prepared myself to defend him if I needed to.

No one came closer. Everyone in the room stood frozen, all staring at me. When they didn't move or speak, I continued eating, and the hand returned to stroking my back. My earthman offered his lap for me, but I wasn't ready for a cuddle yet.

He was a good man-thing, opening cans of chicken and scratching behind my ears in that spot I could never reach. When the chicken was gone, I licked the plate clean and let him coax me into his lap, where I curled up with a full belly. His touch warmed me. I snoozed lightly while he rubbed my back in slow circles. My little bug friend nestled by my chin. Hushed words floated over me. Gradually they began to make sense, but I brushed them all aside. My eyes suddenly felt so heavy. Sleep took me down into dreamless darkness, and all I felt was safe.

Chapter 22

The sound of little voices whispered through the nothingness of my exhaustion. Two small voices chattered about things I couldn't understand, but they were close. I blinked my eyes open. I was in the attic room again and the giant bed surrounded me. Gabe's scent lingered on the pillow beneath my head, but when I turned my head, it was Hanna who sat in a chair reading. A new lamp hung over her from a bended pole.

She glanced up, and our eyes met. Her smile was so sweet. She rested one hand on her belly and put the book aside with the other. Did she hear them too? Could she understand them? Did she know the babies were in there talking to each other already? Could she fathom how beautiful they would be?

"I'm glad you're awake and human. I was a little worried I'd have to explain to the children that their daddy was a cat." A blush stained her cheeks. "I think that would have been more awkward as they got older."

I snorted and tried to sit up, expecting pain, but nothing hurt. My hands looked normal, skin unbroken, bones all in place. Had it all been a dream? Even the lingering ache from the back injury months ago had vanished.

"What happened?" My voice sounded rough, somewhat like I was still a cat trying to speak.

The door opened, and Gabe stepped inside. "I've got it, Hanna. Do you need help getting down?"

She rose from her chair, straightened her long skirt, gathered up her books, and headed toward the door. "No. I'm not that big yet. Where is everyone else?"

"Kitchen. Jamie said dinner would be in a couple hours. You probably have enough time for a nap." Gabe held her hand as she climbed down the ladder.

"I may just do that."

The door closed. When Gabe crossed the room to the bed, the floodgate opened in our bond and everything came through in a rush: his pain, fear, self-doubt, and self-loathing. He'd failed to save me again and hated himself for it. He'd frantically searched the yard for hours, only relenting when the sun rose, to be back at it the second it set. I'd vanished. But that made sense, since I'd given my body to the earth. Yet here I was. Alive, but somehow different.

"I don't need saving," I reminded him.

He disappeared into the bathroom for a moment, then returned with a glass of water. I gulped down the whole thing before he said anything else. He shared his memories with me. How he'd freed himself from the root and plunged into the water to try to save me. No matter how it battered at him, he fought and dug into the earth, trying to get me back. "I thought I'd lost you. But I could still feel you." He frowned. "Like you were in my head, only there was some sort of wall between us. Then you were just gone. Even from my head. I thought you'd died."

"Says the guy who had his brains bashed in." I rubbed my eyes. "I'm fine. Alive and feel pretty good. How about you? Any lingering side effects? Headache? Memory loss?" He shook his head, eyes bright with unshed laughter. "Guess it pays to be a big bad vampire, eh?"

He brushed a hank of hair out of my face. "Big bad Pillar too." He wrapped his arms around me and inhaled the scent of my hair. "You don't smell the same. You smell more like the earth—green."

The GreenMan. Hadn't Bryar called me that? "Yeah, superhero is I," I joked. "Seriously, how is everyone? Sam okay? Timothy? What about that bastard Caleb?"

"Everyone is fine. Caleb, well he's under Dominion lock and key. He probably will be executed."

"He's a witch? But I broke his neck, and he just kept going."

"He's someone's focus," Gabe said quietly.

"Galloway?" I had to ask, hating the idea of having a new boogeyman. Wasn't three in a lifetime enough for anyone?

"Don't know. Galloway didn't have one registered, and Caleb isn't registered to anyone. Timothy said the guy did occasional yard work in the neighborhood before his dad died, but never anything that made him suspect he was a witch or a vampire focus. He's not really Caleb anyway. The real Caleb Bentley was found dead in your carriage house less than a week ago."

"So it's an illusion?"

Gabe nodded. "One he seems unwilling to let go of."

I sighed. Fire would be a sure way to destroy whatever he was, though I really didn't like the idea of anyone dying by fire, deserved or not. There was always someone around to cause trouble so the old rules survived. Speaking of someones, where was Bryar?

A warm pulse by my ear reminded me he was still with me. He roused with a sleepiness I could feel. "Hey now," I said. "You can be big. I saw you."

The little red pulse of light left my side and flashed in front of the bed, turning into a human-sized version of Bryar. "You have need of me, Master?" He wouldn't look Gabe or me in the eye.

"Not master. Seiran. And hey, I want you to do whatever you want." I turned to Gabe. "This is Bryar. He helped out a lot." Understatement of the year.

"Nice to meet you, Bryar." Funny how Gabe wasn't surprised at all that Bryar could be human sized. I really needed to get down to some serious interrogation of my boyfriend's knowledge of faeries.

When Bryar didn't respond, I nudged him with my foot. "Hey, do you want me to release you?"

He flew across the bed and put his hands over my mouth. "No! Please."

"The can only do this when they are bound," Gabe told me. He motioned to Bryar. "The human-size thing. But he's better at illusion in the other form. Faerie glamour, they call it. Why some see him as a bug and others see the faeries."

I pushed Bryar's hands away. "Okay, so then be normal. Do what you want. Live your life and be happy."

"I will be happy as long as I can remain by your side." It sounded a lot like a pledge.

I sighed. "Kinda creepy and stalkerish, but I think that's normal for faeries, right?" I glanced at Gabe, who shrugged. "You can stick with me as long as you're not spying on private moments like sex. I really just want you to be who you are, whatever that means. So tell me what you'd like to do. Have a garden? Become a chef? Be a beach bum?"

Bryar's face scrunched up in thought before he finally said, "A firefighter."

I blinked at him. "Like a guy who runs in burning buildings to save people?"

"Yes." He smiled wide enough to make my face hurt. It was almost not a human smile. I had a feeling we'd have to work on him blending in in this form.

"Okay, sure. Once we get home, we'll see if we can find a department that is looking for help and offers training." Who would have thought, a firefighting faerie?

Gabe got up from the bed and pulled some clothes out of my suitcase for me. He handed me a pair of soft trousers in gray and a beige cashmere sweater. Dressy for a normal evening.

"It's Solstice," Gabe said quietly while I pulled on the clothes.

I stopped. "But we were going to go home. I was going to invite everyone to a big meal that I made and give everyone Solstice wishes."

Gabe helped me button my pants and tugged on my sweater. "You might want to comb that mossy mess of yours before we go down and meet everyone for dinner. I think there may just be enough time for you to make a Yule cake."

Bryar looked away, popped into his tiny form, and flew back to curl up in the oversized collar of my sweater. "Mossy mess?" I asked, narrowing my gaze at him, then stomped to the bathroom. Flicking the light on, I had to rub away the brightness before finally seeing it.

My scream echoed off the walls.

Chapter 23

By the time I descended the steps and found my way to the kitchen, Bryar had styled my dark green—yes, dark green—hair on top of my head and made it look fairly nice despite the color. I really hoped it wasn't permanent. The other hair on my body was still black, so there was good reason to believe the odd color would fade. If not, there was always hair dye.

Jamie and Kelly were in the kitchen, both mixing and checking on things that would make up Solstice dinner. They held hands when they could, but both turned when I entered the room. In seconds, I was engulfed in their embrace. Jamie stifled a sob and Kelly squeezed tighter than he normally did and petted my hair. "Green's a good color for you."

"Argh! I hope it fades."

Jamie laughed. "Truly the GreenMan, fertility, earth, and life. If you really don't like it, I know a good colorist."

I growled at him. He shook his head at me, not intimidated at all. Kelly separated us and took me to a corner of the counter that had been cleared. "We need a Yule cake, Sei. I was beginning to think I'd have to make one. You know what a disaster that would be."

Somehow I didn't think he'd do wrong with it at all. I checked all the ingredients and threw together a red velvet cake, cream cheese frosting, and a chocolate ganache layer for the top. Gabe found me there and wrapped his arms around me from behind, moving to a tune I couldn't hear. We danced together slowly while the Yule cake baked. Hanna, Allie, Sam, and Timothy appeared in the kitchen just as Jamie was taking the turkey and honey-glazed ham from the ovens. Both smelled amazing.

"Everything is almost done. Maybe we should share Solstice wishes?" Kelly suggested.

A murmured assent rumbled through the room. Kelly spoke first. "My wish is for you all to have peace and strength of heart for the new season and beyond."

"I wish for you all to find and hold on to love for the new season and beyond," Jamie told us. He hugged Kelly to his chest.

"I wish for you all to feel hope for the new season and beyond," Timothy stated.

"I wish for health for everyone for the new season and beyond," Allie whispered, holding on to Hanna tight.

"I wish for family to be drawn closer for the new season and beyond," Hanna said, smiling at me.

"I wish for vitality to everyone for the new season and beyond," Gabe said.

Sam frowned. "So I just wish for something? This is so not like Christmas."

Gabe nudged him. "You share a wish for everyone."

"Okay." He sighed heavily and thought for a moment. "I wish for good friends for everyone for the new season and beyond?" He looked at Gabe, who nodded his approval.

I wish for lots of chicken for everyone! Bryar told me, making me laugh. I shared the joke with them.

"For myself, I have no wishes, because I am forever grateful for the amazing family and friends I have. For all of you, however, I wish for the protection of the earth to guide you each day for the new season and beyond," I told them all.

Now can we eat?

I laughed.

Everyone began talking: Kelly and Jamie discussing ideas on how to make the house a retreat for young witches; Timothy about how Lily would be arriving for dinner and probably grilling me for the interview afterward; Hanna and Allie rambling about the babies and their new house. Sam had broken away, pushing himself into a corner of the room, where it seemed like he was part of the group, but not. We couldn't have that now, could we?

I tugged him to me, and he reluctantly followed me back to the counter, where I was working on the cake. "Help me get the frosting in so I can roll it, okay?"

He frowned at the cake. "I don't want to ruin it."

"Wouldn't matter if you did, we'd all still eat it, but it's pretty easy. Just spread the frosting across here." I dumped all the white mix out in a big glob onto the cake and handed him the spatula. He took on the task with laser-focused concentration.

Gabe snagged my hand and pulled me into his embrace. "I was going to wait until Christmas, but I can't wait another moment."

"For what?" We were in a room full of people. Did he think we could just run away and do the funky monkey without anyone noticing?

He kissed me, his tongue plunging inside my mouth with the skill of a deep-sea diver. His body pressed to mine, waves of power naturally flowing through us, and my heartbeat against his couldn't have been more perfect. He finally let me go and stepped away to hold a small box out to me. I blinked at it a few times, knowing it was a jewelry box, but it was the wrong size for earrings, which were the only jewelry I wore. It was even too small for nipple rings. I'd left the only pair I had of those at home in my rush to escape my personal demons.

Gabe released me and dropped to his knee as he opened the box. The room fell deathly silent, but he didn't hesitate. "Seiran Rou, will you marry me?"

I gulped. The room spun for a second or two. I actually felt Bryar shift into his other form to hold me up. My vision narrowed down to Gabe's face and the ring, which was white gold with an onyx stone set in the middle and a crescent moon made out of tiny diamonds. It was like looking at the midnight sky just days before the new moon.

When I found my voice, it came out as a croak at first, and I had to say it three times before it came out understandable.

"Yes."

The smile that lit up Gabe's face reminded me so much of that first smile that drew me to him that I threw myself into his arms and covered his faces with kisses. We were already as bonded as two people could ever be. This, however, would display our love to the world. He really wanted to keep me, forever keep me.

"Did someone say something about a wedding?" Lily appeared in the doorway to the kitchen from the foyer. "I would love to plan a wedding."

"Now can we eat?" Bryar demanded. We all laughed.

Epilogue

No one's first day at work should be walking into the bowels of a Dominion prison. My actual job description as a Magic Investigations Research Analyst mentioned nothing about interviewing prisoners, but Caleb Bentley, or whoever was impersonating the dead man, vowed to speak only to me.

The witches who acted as guards barely spared me a glance while they opened doors for me. Gray brick walls settled deep within the earth enhanced the gloomy atmosphere. The titanium bars with nullification artifacts embedded within dampened even my power. If Caleb tried something, most witches would be powerless to stop him.

However, in the past three weeks, Kelly had intensified my defensive training. He praised me for how easily I picked up all the moves and flowed with them. I would never mention to him that I spent hours practicing with Bryar or Gabe just to keep my mind and body in fluid motion. The new control infiltrated every aspect of my life, my magic, my anxiety, and even my cooking.

Gabe and I set aside time each night just to talk about whatever we were feeling or worried us. At first it was awkward; now I looked forward to getting all that crap off my chest and hearing about my lover's insecurities. Knowing his troubles actually helped me sort through mine faster. Unfortunately, he couldn't come with me today since vampires were not allowed inside the prison.

The final door loomed before me to a small, secure conference room where Caleb would be waiting. The guard at the door gave me a ghost of a smile. "We'll be watching, so if he tries anything, we'll be in there in seconds. Don't worry."

The room looked like a hospital and a TV cop-show interrogation room had a baby: sterile, barren, with black glass surrounding all sides except the door. Caleb sat chained to the wall on a bench made of steel. His jumpsuit was a calming but ugly shade of seafoam green. The dark bags surrounding his eyes and gaunt slant to his cheeks made him look starved.

I sat down in the chair behind a table across the room, both also steel and bolted to the floor. The room felt like a dead zone, strong with nullification power.

"Hello, Caleb," I whispered, not really sure what to say. "Don't suppose you'll tell me your real name?"

"Doesn't matter," he replied.

The Dominion had given me a list of questions to ask. I glanced at it and then back up to him. "Who's your master?"

The corner of his lips turned up slightly. "God."

"Whose god?" I waited for a few seconds, but he didn't reply. "I want to help you. Do you know the Dominion has sentenced you to death?

By fire?" The mere idea of it made me shudder. I'd been asked to attend and refused. "Don't you have family you want to speak to? Someone who will miss you? I can get a message to them. Bring them before..."

He laughed. "I've been around for seven centuries, Rou. Family is all dead. You'll understand soon enough since you're bound to Santini. That burly brother of yours, those babies on the way, they'll all be dead before you realize it. It will hurt less if you let them go now."

I swallowed back a reply. Gabe and I had spoken about what the bond truly meant, why Caleb hadn't died, and how long I would likely live. The decision we'd come up with was that we would love our family as long and as much as we could until they were gone. Beyond that, we would only learn with time. "Is that why you attacked me? Destroyed the tree? Why would you need all that power?"

He wouldn't look at me, but his grief was tangible. We both sat in silence for a minute or two. I drew a breath in, channeling the earth. Despite the nullification, it came so easily. The power rolled to the surface, making my skin glow and hair curl in bright green waves. I crossed the room, caressing his pain away with gentle noncorporeal fingers.

"Tell me your real name," I whispered.

He resisted, but his soul echoed a reply without any such indecision. *Jonahs McLaurien.*

"Hello, Jonahs." I paced the room slowly. Flowers and grass bloomed around my feet as I moved, leaving a trail of green wherever I walked. Since the other question had caused him pain, I decided to rephrase what the Dominion wanted me to ask. "Who is your lover?"

He sighed and shook his head, unwilling to give him up.

I ran my fingers down his cheek, adding to the subtle magic touch that revived him a little. After all, earth was life and death in one beautiful package. "Companion? Best friend? What is he to you now? Simply a master?"

"No." His grief intensified, and tears filled his eyes.

I felt awful but wanted him to have some closure before he was put to death. How would I feel sitting there? Would I die protecting Gabe? The answer was an instant yes. "Will you tell me why?"

"He doesn't know."

I didn't try to ask who again. "What do you want me to tell him?"

"I'm sorry I failed. I wanted to give him all he wanted." Jonahs glared at the wall. "I thought I could get him back if I gave him the power he craved. Even if it was the last thing I did."

"You were going to give all the power to him? From the tree and from those who died at the ring?" Sacrifice his own life to direct the power to someone else, his master who obviously craved it.

"Yes. It's all that matters to him anymore. He doesn't see me. I wanted him to see me again." He finally looked back at me, his eyes meeting mine, and a flood of knowledge poured into me. I saw Jonahs, the man he called master, and others, many I didn't recognize, and a few I did, like Max and Tresler. Jonahs had been impersonating a member of the Ascendance Council to learn how to use the ring, only to find out they hesitated to use it after Andrew Roman died. I'd have to notify Luca that someone was missing.

Jonahs's master was a fond memory for him. Friends first, then lovers, he treasured the times they spent together. As time progressed, though, his master began to pull away, which confused and angered Jonahs. I watched the memories replay and ached for all the times they had together in sweet romance, only to lose it over passing years.

The vampire had beautiful blond hair and pale green eyes, a lot like Gabe, but the recollections of him were nothing like my man. Jonahs's vampire had lost the light in his eyes, choosing instead to fade into the darkness, a skeleton of fear, pain, and loneliness. The image of him deteriorating from lack of will had me anxious to get this terrible interview over and back to Gabe. Was this what Gabe would have become if he hadn't met me? Sweet Gaea!

"It's better that I go before him. Prepare for him," Jonahs said quietly.

"The earth will make a home for both of you," I promised.

He looked up at me, the image of Caleb fading away to reveal a young man who wasn't all that different from myself. His history had been just as jaded, life tainted by people who only sought to hurt him. He'd survived clinging to his master, and now that his master had lost his will to live, so had Jonahs.

"Destroy him," he whispered, "so he can follow me. Please?"

"When we find him. Do you know where he is?" He shook his head. There was no doubt the vampire would have to die. He was one step away from the madness that would end in thousands, if not hundreds of thousands of people dying.

Jonahs closed his eyes and relaxed against the wall. "Thanks, Rou. Blessed be to you and all of yours."

I nodded at his words and reined my power back in, restoring the room to what it was meant to be. Reeling in the power was so much easier now that I had control of it. Would the Dominion fear the power I had? Likely if they had just watched the display I'd offered them, but they could only dream of coming against me and mine.

I left Jonahs with a final breezy touch and whispered a spell to release his spirit back to the earth from which it came. He could let go of his body whenever he was ready, before or after they killed him. He didn't have to wait for the fire. I needed to go home and spend time with my family.

The guards walked me out, keeping a more-than-polite distance between themselves and me, likely out of fear of what they'd seen in the interview room. What they thought of me mattered little. Sometimes it was easier to scare people.

In the parking lot, Gabe's black sedan idled in the no-parking zone. I opened the door and then slid into the passenger seat. He leaned over and kissed me lightly, likely tasting the tears I finally set free to drip down my cheeks. I didn't want Jonahs McLaurien's memories, even if they might hold future truths. I just wanted to discover what Gabe and I had together one day at a time.

"Nicholas Galloway isn't dead yet," I told the love of my life.

Gabe gripped my hand, sharing the memories with me. He sorted through them methodically, not as affected by the emotions as I was. Or if he was, he hid it well.

"He won't survive the death of his focus. He should have held on with everything he had."

I couldn't have agreed more.

About the Author

Lissa Kasey lives in St. Paul, MN, has a Bachelor's Degree in Creative Writing, and collects Asian Ball Joint Dolls who look like her characters. She has three cats who enjoy waking her up an hour before her alarm every morning and sitting on her lap to help her write. She can often be found at Anime Conventions masquerading as random characters when she's not writing about boy romance.

OTHER BOOKS BY LISSA KASEY

Hidden Gem
Cardinal Sins
Candy Land (Coming Spring of 2016)

Model Citizen

Evolution
Evolution: Genesis

Other Dominion books:
Inheritance
Reclamation
Conviction
Ascendance

Free Shorts:
Friction
Resolute
Decadence
Consequences
Devotion
Samhain

Printed in Great Britain
by Amazon